A TOUCH OF MOONLIGHT

Also by Yaffa S. Santos

A Taste of Sage

A TOUCH OF MOONLIGHT

a novel

YAFFA S. SANTOS

HARPER

NEW YORK • LONDON • TORONTO • SYDNEY

HARPER

A TOUCH OF MOONLIGHT. Copyright © 2022 by Yaffa Seraph-Santos. All rights reserved. Printed in the United States of America. No part of this book may be used or reproduced in any manner whatsoever without written permission except in the case of brief quotations embodied in critical articles and reviews. For information, address HarperCollins Publishers, 195 Broadway, New York, NY 10007.

HarperCollins books may be purchased for educational, business, or sales promotional use. For information, please email the Special Markets Department at SPsales@harpercollins.com.

FIRST EDITION

Designed by Jen Overstreet

Library of Congress Cataloging-in-Publication Data has been applied for.

ISBN 978-0-06-315903-7 (pbk.)

22 23 24 25 26   LSC   10 9 8 7 6 5 4 3 2 1

For Rose

A Touch of Moonlight

1

The first rays of morning light scattered across Larimar's pillow, illuminating her two-toned hair. Her stomach rumbled as she rolled out of bed and trudged, eyes half open, to the coffee maker. She stretched her aching legs, yawned, and surveyed the messages on her phone.

Her eyes shot open as she came to one from thirty minutes earlier from her father:

Come downstairs. Your mother made mangú with the 3 golpes.

The three "golpes" were salami, fried cheese, and fried egg. Just the kind of breakfast her parents needed while watching their cholesterol and her father's diabetes. She would reprimand them after she was safely back in her apartment with a plate of mangú in front of her. Her eyes flashed to her black studded wristwatch. She was going to need to hurry to grab breakfast from her parents' apartment one floor down and still make the 7:56 train into Manhattan.

Larimar threw on her fluffy navy-blue bathrobe and matching velvet slippers, grabbed her keys, and locked her apartment.

She punched the elevator button and hummed to herself as she waited. The gears creaked as the rusty elevator rose to meet her one centimeter at a time.

She stepped inside. Taking the elevator was not her favorite in the morning, as it sometimes dropped with a sickening lurch. If anyone wondered whether she loved her parents or not, they only had to look at the building she lived in for confirmation. From the once-white floral wallpaper that had long been morphing toward yellow to the elevator whose jolts put amusement park rides to shame, it was a real winner.

She shuffled out on the third floor and grasped the doorknob to apartment 3A. It would be unlocked, of course. Her parents knew she couldn't say no to mangú. Sure enough, when she entered the apartment, there they were, sitting on stools at the breakfast bar and sipping their morning coffee in plain beige mugs.

"'Cion Mami, 'cion Papi," she greeted them as they exchanged air kisses. "You two are on your second coffee already?" Mami and Papi had hand-painted earthenware mugs from Santo Domingo that they used for the first coffee of the day. After that, they used any old mug.

Doña Berenice leaned in and sniffed her hair, smoothing back the white curl that framed Larimar's face and tucking it behind her ear. "You're one to talk." Her father smiled and motioned to a plate covered in aluminum foil as her mother reached around him for a mug of coffee and handed it to Larimar.

"Here, take this for after you eat. So you don't have to make the trip again so soon," Berenice said. The trip clearly meaning the guilt trip.

Larimar would roll her eyes if she didn't know Mami was not beyond giving her a chancletazo even though she was thirty-four. "We live in the same friggin' building, Doña. I can come back here anytime."

"Oh, sí? If that's so, why don't you visit more?" her mother said, her voice rising an octave.

"More than I already do?"

Mami ignored Larimar's question and nudged her shoulder. "Ven, the mangú is getting cold," she said.

Larimar picked up the foil-wrapped plate and headed for the door. She felt like being alone for a bit before starting the work-day, as grateful as she was for her parents' attentions.

"I have a report for Ms. Beacon to double-check before I leave," she said. "Gracias, and I'll see you tomorrow."

Mami heaved a long sigh, shaking her short salt-and-pepper curls and adjusting her horn-rimmed cat's-eye glasses over the bridge of her nose. "Ay, this girl, always working." She glanced at Papi, who shrugged and kept chewing his fried cheese.

With her breakfast plate safely secured in one hand, Larimar let herself back into her apartment and pulled up a chair at her wooden kitchen table. Beams of light filtered through the silver linen curtains and warmed her face as she ate and enjoyed the smooth, buttery flavor of the mashed plantains. When she finished, she stretched out on her couch. It was too early to go into a food coma, so she dialed her best friend, Brynne, on video chat.

Brynne answered on the third ring, and as the picture

popped up on her end, Larimar saw her friend standing next to a huge vase of tangerine-colored tiger lilies. Brynne had short coiled curls and two armfuls of jingly bangles. She wore round John Lennon glasses, a white button-down blouse, and a green Fair Isle vest. Since ninth grade, Larimar had been affectionately describing Brynne's dress style as "librarian on an acid trip."

Larimar checked her watch in disbelief. It was early for Brynne to be at her flower shop. "Hey, honey!" she said, waving at Brynne. "You're at the shop already?"

Brynne waved back and nodded. "Hey, love. Yes, I'm doing a wedding today."

"Nice. Whereabouts?"

"Perth Amboy. Close to where the band and I had our last gig."

"Oh, okay. I wish I could help but . . . you know. Friday," she said, shrugging in view of the camera.

Brynne shook her head. "I'm good, hun, I hired staff. Drop by the house when you have a chance, though."

"I will," Larimar said. She blew Brynne a kiss, waved goodbye, and set the phone down on her coffee table. Brynne and Larimar checked in most mornings, even if just to say a quick hello.

She would've loved to stay lounging on her couch, but that life would have to wait for when she won the lottery. Instead, she forced herself to trudge into her bedroom, where she threw on an eggplant-colored short-sleeved sweater and black slacks. She checked her reflection in the mirror and gave herself a cheeky wink. She looked totally average. That was what she liked to see.

Car keys and black tufted satchel in hand, she eased herself out of her apartment for the second time that morning and rode the rickety elevator down to the lobby. The lobby was lined with mirrors and let out directly onto the parking lot of Covington Arms. Her noble steed was a silver 2000 Beetle she'd had since high school. She climbed in and put the keys in the ignition. The engine sputtered and then roared to life.

She drove to the Roselle Park New Jersey Transit train station and squeezed her car into the last remaining parking spot in the shade. It was the last Friday in September, so the sun would still be strong while she was gone, and if she could avoid her car baking all day, she would.

The train pulled up to the platform, brakes squeaking, and Larimar hopped on. This was her daily routine, which she navigated on autopilot. The train and subsequent subway ride passed by in a blur until she stood before 798 Fifth Avenue, home of the number-one bakery-café corporation in the tri-state area, Beacon Foods. Larimar worked for Beacon as a brand manager, supervising the implementation of the Beacon brand in all the new locations.

798 Fifth was a streamlined building outfitted in chrome and glass from the first floor to the twenty-first. *Just like Covington Arms*, Larimar liked to joke. The staff was away for an American Bakery Association conference she had managed to get out of citing the need to tie up loose ends on her latest project.

At her desk, she opened the file for her latest project, the installation of a Beacon Café location in the Pelham Bay area of the Bronx. She smiled in satisfaction as she looked over the photos pinned to the top of the file. Glossy bakery cases displayed delectable-looking muffins and scones alongside a steaming coffee machine; to her credit, everything from the napkins to the welcome mat was on brand. She felt a little tug in her chest when she closed the file. She didn't know what her next project would be, but seeing how well she'd pulled this one off, it had to be good.

The morning breezed by, and before she knew, it was five o'clock. She packed up her papers, ready to begin her weekend.

2

The exit signs of the New Jersey Turnpike whizzed by as Larimar sped down the highway. She alternated between keeping both hands trained on the steering wheel and raising one flat white in a travel cup to her lips. She had jumped in her car as soon as she got off the train and began heading south toward Philly.

Reel Big Fish was blaring on the Beetle's tin-can stereo, emphasizing the staccato trumpet notes. She felt a thrill in her chest as she went over the Ben Franklin bridge, and then a slight chill. It was getting close to dusk.

The Beetle sped along until she reached the twisty streets of Manayunk, the charming Philadelphia neighborhood where her brother, Moisés Oliver Cintrón Luna, lived. Parking was hell on Oliver's tiny street, and these were the times she thanked her lucky stars for her Beetle.

She squeezed into a spot with almost no sweat, and skipped up the steps of Oliver's brownstone. The sun was beginning to set, spreading rosy fingers across the sky. She knocked on Oliver's door, and then rang the bell for good measure. A few moments passed. She knocked again. She raised her fist to bang with all her might, then restrained the urge.

Coño. Why did Oliver have to be so damn irresponsible? He knew she would be coming for dinner, and he knew that at this hour on the full moon, she could not afford to stand outside. She raised her fist to the door and fell in as the door gave way and was replaced with hardwood flooring and the scent of lemongrass.

"Whoa!" she called as she stretched her arms out in front of her to break the fall.

Her palms hit the cold wood floor of the foyer, but they stopped the rest of her from doing the same. She cringed as she noticed two feet next to her. The feet were wearing pink Sperry boots. The feet were not Oliver's. She looked up one degree at a time to see who had witnessed her embarrassment. A kind face beamed back at her.

The woman held out her hand, and Larimar took it, chagrined as ever, but admitting her back was not what it was in her twenties. She dusted herself off and regarded the person standing in front of her. She was an inch or two taller than Larimar, with glossy black hair, and equally luminescent skin. She was way more beautiful than she had a right to be.

They stared at each other awkwardly before Larimar thought to stick a hand out.

"Hi, I'm Larimar. Sister of the ruffian who abides in these premises."

The woman chuckled. "I'm Melissa, girlfriend of the—" She paused and bit her lip.

"It's okay. You don't have to call him a ruffian. If you did, you wouldn't be wrong, though."

Melissa smiled. "Come in. I'm just about done cooking."

Larimar blew out a dramatic exhale. "Oh, my God. I'm so relieved that it's not Oliver who's cooking. I almost packed a bag dinner. You have no idea."

"Hey! I can hear you." A booming voice echoed from upstairs.

"Good. Nothing I wouldn't say to your face, Oli-nerd."

Oliver bounded down the stairs two at a time. He had gelled his curls and was wearing a tight black muscle shirt.

"I can see late-nineties merengue is still your fashion inspiration," Larimar said.

Oliver rolled his eyes. "Liss, this is my sister, Larimar."

"What happened in late-nineties merengue?" Melissa asked.

"A lot of tight clothing," Larimar said, turning to Melissa.

Melissa nodded, and Larimar could see the mirth in her eyes at watching her boyfriend in the role of brother.

"Come on, let's go upstairs," Oliver said, and three sets of feet creaked over the ancient stairway to the second floor. Oliver's townhouse had to be at least one hundred years old. They reached the open living room and dining room, and Larimar could see that Melissa had been adding her touch here and there. First of all, she could see the floor. Second of all, she could see the countertops.

"The place looks good, Oli-nerd," she said.

"Oli-nerd," Melissa repeated to herself with a small grin. "I like it."

"I don't," Oliver said, and they exchanged a look.

Melissa motioned to the sitting area, and Oliver rested his hand on the small of her back. He had told Larimar they'd been dating for five months, but to Larimar it looked like longer.

"Would you like to sit down, or are you hungry? We can eat."

Before Larimar did any of that, she had to put her skirt on before this pleasant night turned into an episode of paranormal mystery.

"That sounds great!" she said. "I just need to duck into the bathroom."

Melissa and Oliver made goo-goo eyes at each other as she stole into the bathroom and pulled her floor-length skirt out of her duffel bag. The telltale swiveling began in her ankle joints, but she ignored it and pulled on her skirt, then peeled off her pants and stuffed them in the bag.

When she came out of the bathroom, Melissa and Oliver were already seated at the dinner table. Oliver did not give her a second look. If Melissa did, she was very surreptitious about it.

She got close to the table and sat down as soon as she could. With her feet safely absconded under the table, the dinner could begin.

The centerpiece of the dinner Melissa had prepared was fried fish. Side plates held garlic noodles, rice, steamed dumplings, and a green papaya salad. Both Oliver and Melissa passed the plates to Larimar first, and she served herself demurely before passing them back.

"Sinvergüenza," Oliver said. "Don't be shy. You eat way more than that."

Larimar gave him a good-natured eye roll. "Can it, bro," she said.

Melissa watched them carry on with an amused glint in her eye.

Larimar chewed in utter bliss before said, "Melissa, this food is spectacular! Where did you learn to cook like this?"

Melissa beamed at her. "These are some of the Thai dishes I grew up with," she said simply.

Oliver patted Melissa's shoulder and then leveled his gaze at Larimar. "Melissa, you would never know it by looking at my sister, but she is a—" Had he actually lost his whole mind?

"Head of brand at Beacon Foods!" She cut him off as quickly as she could and shot daggers at him with her glance.

Oliver twisted his mouth at her as if to say, *you're no fun*.

Melissa cocked her head to the side, and Larimar could tell she was trying to figure out what Oliver had been about to say. Not that it was something she could guess in a million years. She tucked her feet a little farther under her chair.

"So, Oliver, how's real estate?" Larimar asked.

Melissa popped into the kitchen and returned with a glass plate bearing two desserts: a pumpkin pie and some cupcakes with gorgeous tufts of pale-yellow frosting.

"Pretty slow," Oliver said quickly, helping himself to a slice of the pie. Larimar bit down extra hard on her bite of cupcake. Even if it wasn't slow, he was bound to say it was lest she ask him to help out with their parents' expenses the way she did each month.

When the last bite of pie was safely tucked away in Oliver's belly, Melissa stood up to clear the table.

"I'll help," Larimar said, at the same time Oliver started piling the plates.

"It's okay, manita, I got it," he said. "You just sit and relax."

Larimar shook her head vigorously. "No, no, I got it!" she said, snatching the plates out of Oliver's hands with one hand and smoothing down her skirt with the other as she stood. Luckily, she had learned to stay steady on her feet.

When Melissa was out of earshot in the kitchen, Oliver leaned in. "I think you can tell Melissa. She's very open-minded, you know."

Larimar gritted her teeth at his soul-searching expression. "NO." She hurried away with the plates before he could add any more to his mini therapy session.

In the kitchen, Melissa ran warm water over each plate, scrubbing it with a scouring pad before placing it in the dishwasher.

"My mom would love this. She does the dishes the exact same way."

"Doesn't everybody?"

"Nope. I don't. What's the point of using the dishwasher if I still have to wash them by hand?"

Melissa laughed.

"I knew you would be cool, but you're a lot cooler in person."

Larimar's cheeks reddened.

"It's been great meeting you and getting to spend some time, Larimar. You know what? I would love to show you my salon! It's only three blocks away." She and Oliver exchanged glances, and Oliver gave her an encouraging nod. What a help he was.

"We can walk over, and I can give you a manicure! On the house."

Larimar froze. It pained her to receive Melissa's offer. On the one hand, Melissa was so great. She would be intrigued to see how Melissa had set up her business, and she loved getting manicures. On the other hand . . . what if once she was there, she also wanted to give Larimar a pedicure? Or what if she tripped and her feet were under her, and—what was she saying? Her feet were always under her and—oh God. She forced herself to take a deep breath.

What were her options? Her mind was drawing a blank.

"Uh . . . I gotta go," she said.

"You sure? We were just going to pop open a couple beers, and we could head to the salon right after!"

"I gotta go."

Oliver popped his head into the kitchen. "What the fuck, Lari? I thought you were sleeping over."

Larimar looked at him and hoped he didn't see the sadness in her eyes.

"I-I gotta go."

"Just don't go to the salon, okay? But you can still stay."

Larimar shook her head, staring straight down at the floor, where her feet would have been visible if it was earlier in the day.

"Okay, okay! You gotta go. Here," he said, passing her a wrapped bundle of food.

"Give these to Mamá and Papá."

Larimar took them and nodded. "It was great meeting you, Melissa," she said, avoiding Melissa's confused expression. She gave Oliver a quick hug and hastened out, not stopping until she was safely in her car, knowing Oliver was at the door watching her.

She exhaled heavily as she settled in the driver's seat. "Sorry, Liss."

CHAMOMILE LEMON CUPCAKES WITH HONEY BUTTERCREAM

Makes 14 cupcakes

FOR THE CUPCAKES

1 cup granulated sugar

Zest of one lemon

1 cup/2 sticks unsalted butter

½ cup chamomile tea leaves

3 eggs, separated

1½ cups all-purpose flour

½ cup whole milk

¼ cup white sugar

FOR THE FROSTING

1 cup/2 sticks unsalted butter, at room temperature

¼ cup confectioners' sugar

½ cup honey

Make the cupcakes: In a small bowl, whisk together ¾ cup of the sugar and the lemon zest and set aside for 30 minutes. In a saucepan, melt the butter, then stir in tea leaves and heat over low for 5 minutes. Remove from the heat and allow to cool completely.

Preheat the oven to 350 degrees Fahrenheit. Prepare cupcake pans with cupcake liners.

Whisk the tea-infused butter into the lemon sugar. Whisk in the egg yolks until completely mixed. Alternately add the flour and milk to create a smooth batter.

In a separate, clean bowl, whisk the egg whites until foamy. Add the remaining ¼ cup sugar and whisk until stiff peaks form. Gently fold the egg whites into the batter in three additions.

Fill the cupcake liners two-thirds full and bake for 20 minutes. Allow to cool completely on a wire rack.

Make the frosting: In a large bowl, beat together the butter and confectioners' sugar until smooth. Add the honey and beat until smooth. Pipe the frosting over the cooled cupcakes. Enjoy!

3

The wood of the Asbury Park boardwalk reverberated under Larimar's feet, the echo ringing hollow in the long, painted hallway of the convention center. After leaving Oliver's, she had gone east instead of north like she needed to in order to get home. The Beetle had brought her, almost of its own volition, to the beach of her childhood and her favorite place for collecting her thoughts and catching a quiet moment to herself.

One of her favorite things to do when she came to Asbury Park was to walk through the hallway and step on the hollow boards, skip from one board to the next, and look at the paintings. Her favorite was the mermaid octopus lady. In her mind she made up a story where they were sisters.

She was a ciguapa, and the mermaid octopus lady was . . . herself. They would get together next to the ocean and drink lemongrass tea. Larimar would let her brush her long hair. It would be a full moon night, so her hair would be straight down her back instead of her usual bouncy curls. The octopus lady would show Larimar her tentacles, and Larimar would show her her backward-facing feet. And maybe the octopus lady would let her borrow some of her jewelry. She had the sick twenties-era pieces. The kind you could hardly find anymore in thrift stores, but you might get lucky if you looked in South Jersey near the retirement homes.

A twinge in her heart pulled her away from the mural. The octopus lady would never be her sister, and no one would ever know what it was like to be a freak of nature. Except her mother. And her grandmother. And her great-grandmother. She drew in a deep breath.

Something sparkled on the beach, and she decided to check it out. The sand pulled her down as soon as she reached the dunes, and before she knew it, she was lying on a sand hill and growing sleepy. She would sleep the night on the beach, as she often did. If anyone bothered her, she would show them her feet.

She drifted off to sleep, and in her dream, she was walking down a steep riverbank. It was dotted with green tufts of grass alternating with muddy puddles. When she reached the river, she stood and looked into the water. As she stared, a folder floated up to the surface and the current carried it to the banks.

She descended the banks to get a closer look and noticed an eerie light pulsing around the folder. Something was glowing from within. She got closer to try to grab it, but it floated just out of her grasp. She was deciding whether to swim after it or keep her clothes dry when she was awoken by the cries of seagulls.

Larimar stood up and dusted the sand off her sleeves and skirt. The sun was rising, casting a persimmon glow over the entire beach, and as such, the transformation had been reversed. Luckily, it was Saturday, and her to-do list was short. She only had one thing on it: go home.

She stopped on the boardwalk for a latte and chocolate croissant, which she sipped and ate slowly as she walked to her car. Her mother had taught her it was bad manners to eat in public, but she was too hungry to give a rat's ass about social conventions.

The drive home to Roselle Park stretched on, until she remembered she had a Sirius station that was all classic rock. She didn't listen to classic rock all the time, but when she did, it reminded her of Papi. She made a mental note to stop by her parents' when she got home.

The first song on the radio was Steppenwolf's "Born to Be Wild." She caught herself rolling her eyes remembering how Papi would play this song over, and over, and over again when she and Oliver were kids. He would make them pancakes on Sunday mornings while their mother was in church, because if she was home she would declare the breakfast "vaina de gringo" and bemoan its lacking nutritional value.

It was when Doña Berenice was away on those mornings that he told his children about his time in the Army. Papi, a gangly teenager who had come from the Dominican Republic when he was fourteen. Papi, who listened to his mother's sobs over an ancient and hardly working phone line when he got drafted at eighteen. Papi, who months later found himself on a warplane to Vietnam.

When they were kids, Larimar and Oliver would roll their eyes when he started with his war tales. A lick of shame bit her as she realized she was about to roll her eyes again.

The blaring music helped the trip go faster, and before she knew it, she was pulling into her parking spot. Impatient, she skipped up the steps instead of waiting for the elevator, and let herself into her parents' apartment. Papi was sitting in his pumpkin-hued recliner, reading *Car and Driver* magazine while Mami flipped through the channels, looking for her novela.

She came across the Latin Grammys and rested on that, the sound of urban rhythms and Maluma filling the room.

"Berenice, apagame esa mierda," Papi said.

Mami shot him a dangerous look. "Who are you now, Hipólito?" The channel stayed where it was, Mami not making any moves to hide her ogling of the young, virile dancers.

Papi raised his hands heavenward and shook them, and Larimar used her linen scarf to stifle a giggle.

"Pretty different than what I was listening to in the car," she said to Papi.

His eyebrows perked up in curiosity. "Oh, yeah? What were you listening to?"

"Steppenwolf."

He smiled. "I taught you well," he said. "You and Oliver. I guess two out of three ain't bad," he said, giving a meaningful glance in Mami's direction.

"Papi, what was it like in the Army?"

Papi almost choked on his water. He would definitely not be expecting Larimar to ask him any questions about his time in the war.

"You really want to hear about this?"

She scooted her chair closer. "I do."

"I'm so surprised, I don't even know where to start." And Larimar believed him. Papi looked positively flummoxed. But pleased.

"Start with the day you got your draft card."

At this, his face lit up. "Ahhhh, sí. So I was eighteen years old, just graduated from George Washington High School," he said.

"Yes," Larimar said, leaning in a little closer.

"I was living with Tío Juan Pablo and Tía Nereida in the little apartment on Audubon Avenue," he said. Papá gazed off into the distance, transporting himself to his old apartment.

"Some said the draft cards would be coming. Others said those were just rumors. And then, one day, there was an envelope addressed to me sitting in our mailbox. Roberto Cintrón, the handwritten label read. I never got mail."

Larimar took a deep breath, imagining a younger version of her father opening this very heavy letter. "What did it say?"

"'This is to certify that Roberto Aurelio Cintrón Carvajal, Selective Service Number 97–24–23–587, is classified in Class 1A until . . .' The ending date was blank."

"Wow." She released a weighty exhale. "And then what? What did you think?"

Papi inhaled and reclined in his chair. "It was a mix of excitement and dread. All I knew for sure was that my life was going to change for good."

"And you were right."

"Yes, I was right. There's not really a way for one to go into war and come out unchanged. And we were just kids."

"Roberto, have you seen my glasses?" Berenice called from the other room.

"Let me see, Bere," he said, and turned to Larimar. "More on that another time. But Larimar?"

"Yes?"

"Thanks for asking, hija," he said.

Larimar leaned in and gave him a quick hug.

Papi rose and ambled into the kitchen, followed closely by Larimar, who was the second to notice Mami's bifocals perched right behind her hairline.

"They're on your head, mi amor," he said with a wry smile.

"Conchale! If they were a dog, they would've bit me," Mami said.

Larimar smiled to herself. It was good they had each other.

4

Larimar raised an amber ale bottle to her lips and took a long drink. "The day-drinking gods were smiling down on us when they decided this company lunch would be held at Cipriani on a Monday," she said to Emerson, her friend and coworker. She placed the beer down on a navy blue-and-white embossed napkin, which represented Beacon Foods' signature colors. Emerson smoothed the silk tablecloth with her perfect lacquered fingernails, smiled, and took a dainty sip from her champagne flute. "Sure were."

Emerson leaned back in her chair to appraise her friend. "Seriously, Lari, you are the only person who orders a beer at Cipriani."

Larimar frowned, but then shook her head and nodded toward the podium. "Looks like you are mistaken, m'lady. Check out Ms. Beacon. Oh! She's about to do her speech."

An audible wave of excitement fluttered through the room before the company's 110 employees fell silent out of respect for the CEO and founder, Ms. Regina Beacon. Ms. Beacon was the founder and CEO of Beacon Foods, and her outfit showed it. She wore tiny little gold-rimmed glasses, a burgundy stamped velvet vest, and pressed linen pants with walnut-brown spectator shoes. Larimar would never stop thinking she resembled Mrs. Claus in character for a Western role. When it came to her clothes, she was from another era, but in business, she was from the year 3100. Light-years ahead of everyone else around her. Ms. Beacon set her beer on the podium and cleared her throat, smoothing down the lapels of her vest before she spoke.

"Thank you all for being here today for our Fall luncheon. Before I get into the details, I would like to make a toast to Larimar Cintrón!"

Larimar's heart froze, and she smiled awkwardly, keeping her gaze laser-trained on the podium instead of looking around the room.

"Since becoming brand manager, she has helmed the opening of nine new locales and ensured flawless implementation of the Beacon Foods brand. She is just about to start a new project this week, so let's all raise a glass and wish her the best of luck!"

She was? This was the first Larimar had heard of a new project, but damn if she was going to let on. She smiled her biggest megawatt smile and thrust her beer bottle into the air to join the toast. She was getting another project. Nice. Work was the one area of life where things consistently worked out for Larimar. Perhaps because it was predictable: you put in the work, you got the results. And it was all done in the daytime. All the easier to keep separate from her ciguapa life.

Emerson patted her on the shoulder. "Good luck, champ," she said.

Larimar nodded to say thanks. This could be her big chance

to get promoted. And a promotion would mean she would be able to give her parents and abuela the down payment they needed to buy their house. Beacon's timing couldn't have been better.

The next day, Larimar stepped off the N train at 59th and 5th. The commute from Roselle Park was long and had only been lengthened by a trash fire on the train tracks. It was a miracle she was still on time for work.

The elevator ride up to the twelfth floor was a short one, and before she knew it she was sitting at her desk, coffee in hand, ready to look over her files. An hour whizzed by, and she barely noticed until her desk phone rang.

"Larimar Cintrón's desk," she answered.

"Is this Larimar's desk, or Larimar?" Ms. Beacon asked.

Her cue to fake a laugh. "Ha ha ha, of course it's me, Ms. Beacon. How may I help you today?"

"Stop by my office when you have a moment, please," she said.

This had to be the new assignment Ms. Beacon mentioned at the company lunch. She picked up a notepad and her favorite gold gel pen and ambled over to Ms. Beacon's office.

Her boasted a glossy mahogany desk and was decorated with sumptuous gold-toned accents. She motioned for Larimar to sit in the chair in front of her desk.

"So, the cat's out of the bag," she said.

Larimar didn't nod or shake her head.

Ms. Beacon chuckled. "I may have gotten a little ahead of myself yesterday. But the truth stands—Larimar, I have an exciting new assignment for you."

"Wonderful, Ms. Beacon. I'd love to hear what it is."

Ms. Beacon picked up a file and set it in front of her on the desk.

"This is the next property we are looking to acquire," she said.

Larimar opened the folder and took a look. A glossy photo showcasing a storefront was pinned to the top of the file.

"The establishment in question is a commercial space on Stuyvesant Avenue in Union, New Jersey. Right in your neck of the woods."

"Oh!" she said. She was yet to have an assignment close to home.

"I'd like you to go by there this week, please. Check the place out, gauge the area, and get a feel for it. And then . . . we begin."

"Yes, Ms. Beacon. I'm on it. I will head on over as soon as I can. It's in the bag," she said, giving her a conspiratorial smile she hoped was still professional.

"I know you got this," she affirmed. "Good luck." Larimar thanked her and picked up the file.

If she knows I've got this, why is she wishing me good luck? Larimar wondered as she walked back to her desk.

The silver Beetle pulled into the parking lot of the Iglesia Hispana right before nightfall. Larimar turned off the ignition and just sat in the car for a moment. She went over her usual self-talk before walking into a space filled with strangers: shoulders back, spine straight, and smiling, but not the whole time. Then she took hold of her purse, locked the car, and skipped up the steps straight to the church's meeting salon. She entered a darkened room where women were sitting in a circle on metal chairs. There was one empty chair next to the buffet table, and Larimar hurried over to it.

The buffet table was divided into an interesting mix of punch and cookies on one side and hair products on the other. Someone had made a multi-tiered "cake" composed of curl milks, leave-in conditioners, and shine sprays. Tiny candles ringed the table, their glow illuminating the offerings. When the last of the chairs was full, a woman with springy ringlets moved her chair into the center of the circle.

"Dearly beloveds, we are gathered here today with a singular mission: HAIR!"

A few in the crowd broke into giggles. "Nah, in all seriousness, welcome to the first meeting of the Rizos Curl Club. We are here to support each other on our curly hair journeys and affirm the joy it is to live and love in our natural hair."

Larimar nodded along. Sounded good to her. And with the current meeting schedule as outlined in the Facebook group file, she should never have a conflict with her full-moon nights.

"Okay, let's go around the circle and introduce ourselves," the speaker said. "Please tell us your name, where you're from, how you found us, and where you are on your natural hair journey."

Six pairs of eyes stared back at her without making a move to budge.

"Okay, I'll go first," the speaker said. "I'm Anairis, and I live here in Union. I started relaxing my hair—well, my mom started relaxing my hair—when I was seven years old."

Audible "mm-hmm"s echoed around the circle. "I kept on relaxing it until five years ago, when I got tired. I decided to let my hair grow out with no chemicals. It's been a ride, but today I am proud of my curls," she said, shaking her head for effect amid claps and whoops of appreciation.

"Who would like to go next?" she asked.

A stout woman with copper-colored braids down her back raised her hand. Anairis nodded in her direction.

"I'm Miguelina, and I live in Elizabeth. When I was growing up, my mother would always send me to 'fix' my hair. 'Peínate . . . you look like a wild woman,' she would say. I used to blow-dry and flat-iron my hair every morning. No more," she said, gesturing to her braids.

The other women smiled at her, and Miguelina, who was sitting on Larimar's left, looked expectantly at Larimar.

It was Larimar's cue to go next. She took a deep breath and began. "I'm Larimar, and I live in Roselle Park. I—" How was she supposed to explain that she had curly hair with brief intervals of straight that she couldn't do anything about? Her mind went blank, and six pairs of eyes rested on her face.

"Um . . ." Her hesitation was silly. All she had to do was stay away during the full moon. "Yeah! So, I wore my hair natural until middle school, when, like Miguelina, I started blow-drying it." Miguelina gave her an understanding smile. "I kept going until a year ago, when I felt my hair was more brittle than ever and decided I had to leave it alone, no matter what it took to get used to it." She let out a low exhale.

"Your curls will come in," Miguelina said with a nod of reassurance.

The remaining women introduced themselves, and cups of punch were ladled out and passed around the circle. The attention went back to Anairis, who had prepared a small card table with avocado, mayonnaise, olive oil, an egg, and a blender.

"Today we're going to go over how to make a moisturizing hair mask," she said. She cut the avocado and removed the pit, then spooned out the flesh. A glob of mayonnaise, stream of olive oil, and the egg were next to go into the blender. She then pressed the "power" button and they all watched as the distinct ingredients became one uniform green mixture.

Anairis appraised the color and texture with a glance of approval. "I'm not going to do it now, but next you distribute it through your hair and leave it on for twenty minutes."

The women nodded.

"Okay!" Anairis said. "Cafecito hour. I'll bring out the coffee, and feel free to help yourselves to more punch."

Larimar looked around the circle nervously. This was the part that got her.

When she had to be professional, it was easy for her to make conversation, because it wasn't about her. There was a predetermined list of approved subjects, and she didn't have to get into anything more personal, because the truth was nobody cared. And being in a circle with eyes on her had a way of making her feel like she had magically become transparent.

She glanced at Miguelina out of the corner of her eye, and saw that Miguelina was looking at her furtively too. Oh, this was silly.

"I can relate to what you said," Larimar said. It seemed a

good enough intro.

Miguelina relaxed into her chair. "Thank you," she said. "I think it was a common experience for a lot of us."

Larimar nodded emphatically. "Fix your hair, you look like a loca! I can hear my mother even now." Miguelina laughed.

"Did it take you long to get here?" she asked Larimar.

Larimar shook her head. "No, not at all. I live in Roselle Park, so about ten minutes from here. How about you?"

Miguelina shook her head as well, her braids flying over her back. "About fifteen minutes away. I live on Division Street, down by the port," she said.

"Oh! Do you ever go to La Mantilla tapas bar? I love their flamenco night," Larimar said.

"No. I know where La Mantilla is, but I didn't know they did live music. Thanks!"

Larimar smiled at her, and Miguelina smiled back. This was going better than she had expected.

The social time came to a close, and Anairis stood up in the center of the circle to get the women's attention. "Thank you all for coming out tonight. We had a wonderful time. We are skipping October due to scheduling conflicts, so our next meeting will be during the first week of November. We'll confirm the date in the FB group. Look forward to seeing you all then."

First week of November. The first week of November would not be a full moon, according to her calculations. This could work, this could really work. She could learn to hydrate her curls, and maybe make a friend or two at the same time. Brynne was the best friend she could ask for, but it would feel good to belong to a community, as well.

After the meeting, once she was back in her car, she eased into the seat and took a deep breath, resting her hands on the steering wheel. The meeting had gone better than she'd expected.

"That's because they don't know what you really are," she said aloud. The silence that followed echoed against the four walls of the Beetle. She shook her head as she exhaled, and gunned the ignition, as if she could drive away and leave the thought in the parking lot.

CHAMPAGNE CUPCAKES

(Recipe adapted from lifelovesugar.com)

Makes 12 to 14 cupcakes

FOR THE CHAMPAGNE REDUCTION

1½ cups champagne

FOR THE CUPCAKES

1¼ cups all-purpose flour

1½ teaspoons baking powder

¼ teaspoon salt

6 tablespoons unsalted butter, room temperature

¾ cup sugar

1½ tablespoons vegetable oil

2 large eggs

½ teaspoon vanilla extract

2 tablespoons whole milk

FOR THE CHAMPAGNE BUTTERCREAM

¾ cup unsalted butter, at room temperature

¼ cup shortening

4 cups confectioners' sugar

⅛ teaspoon salt

Sprinkles, for decorating (optional)

Make the champagne reduction: In a medium-sized saucepan over medium heat, cook the champagne until ¾ cup remains. Do not boil. To measure how much champagne remains, pour it into a glass liquid measuring cup. When done, refrigerate until cool.

Make the cupcakes: Preheat the oven to 350 degrees Fahrenheit. Prepare a cupcake pan with cupcake liners.

In a medium bowl, combine the flour, baking powder, and salt.

In the bowl of a stand mixer, combine the butter, sugar and oil and beat until light in color and fluffy, about 3 minutes. Do not skimp on the creaming time.

Add the eggs, one at a time, mixing until mostly combined after each. Add the vanilla extract with the second egg. Scrape down the sides of the bowl as needed to ensure all the ingredients are well incorporated.

Add half of the dry ingredients to the batter and stir until mostly combined.

Add the milk and ½ cup of the champagne reduction and stir until well combined. It's okay if the batter looks a little curdled.

Add the remaining dry ingredients and stir until well combined and smooth. Do not overmix the batter.

Fill the cupcake liners about three-quarters full and bake for 14–16 minutes or until a toothpick inserted into the center comes out clean. Allow to cool completely on a wire rack.

Make the buttercream: In the bowl of a stand mixer, combine the butter and shortening and beat until smooth. Add about half of the confectioners' sugar and mix until smooth and well combined.

Add 3 tablespoons of the champagne reduction and

the salt to the frosting and mix until well combined.

Add the remaining confectioners' sugar and mix until smooth. Add additional champagne reduction as needed to get the right consistency.

Pipe the frosting onto the cupcakes. Add sprinkles, if desired. Note that if you're going to serve the cupcakes more than a few hours after adding the sprinkles, you may want to use a sprinkle that doesn't bleed. Enjoy.

5

After the hair club meeting, Larimar drove home craving buttery mantecado cookies. When this craving hit, usually only her abuela's cinnamon-dusted version would do. She parked in the lot and took the old elevator to the second floor. Doña Bélgica lived in Covington Arms in her own one-bedroom apartment. She vowed that she wouldn't move in with her daughter and son-in-law until she was unable to be on her own. At eighty-four, that time still had not come.

Larimar let herself in with her key and called, "Mamá! Estoy aquí," so as not to startle the elder.

Although truth be told, it was hard to shake or startle Doña Bélgica with anything. The woman was steel incarnate.

"Dios te bendiga, my dear granddaughter," Doña Bélgica said. "How was your day?"

Larimar pulled up a chair at her grandmother's kitchen table, complete with the flowery white lace tablecloth she had embroidered by hand. Doña Bélgica's apartment had the same exact layout as hers, but the décor could not be more different.

"Mamá? Do you have any mantecaditos today?" Larimar asked.

The elder shook her head gently, displacing her pristine white curls. "No, but we can make some, m'ija," she said.

Larimar didn't have any plans for the evening, and it had been a while since she had made mantecaditos with her abuela. At her abuela's instruction, she preheated the oven, pulled out bags of flour and sugar from the pantry, and retrieved the glass butter dish from the refrigerator. Doña Bélgica broke two eggs into a blue earthenware bowl and began to mix them with the sugar.

They worked in silence side by side. By the time the oven dinged, they were ready to scoop small spoonfuls onto a cookie sheet to bake. Larimar spooned some coffee grounds into the percolator and left the espresso maker in place atop the stove.

They hugged on the couch as they waited for the mantecaditos to be ready. A mouthwatering aroma filled the air, and Larimar rested her head on her abuela's shoulder.

When the cookies were done, Larimar put on an oven mitt and retrieved the tray from the middle rack. She turned on the stove burner, and shortly after, the espresso bubbled up. Doña Bélgica moved the cookies onto a ceramic plate decorated with tiny red roses, and they sat down together at the kitchen table. Doña Bélgica served Larimar several cookies, and they ate and sipped their coffee in contented silence.

Full and happy, they settled back onto the couch. Larimar bumped her elbow on something on the end table. She pulled out the offending item, emitting a little sound of surprise when she saw what it was.

"Oh! Your old photo album," she said. "It's been a while since we looked at this, Mamá."

"Mm," Doña Bélgica nodded, taking the last sip of her coffee.

Larimar flipped the pages open and they crinkled as she passed them one by one.

The first page was just as she remembered—photos of the beaches of Barahona. Pebbly sand and pristine waves combined to produce a feeling of nostalgia in her. It was odd—nostalgia for a place she had never been, but nonetheless felt a connection to.

On the following page, there was a photo of Doña Bélgica. She looked to be about thirty, with long straight hair that flowed over her entire body, covering what appeared to be her nudity judging by her bare arms and legs. On the right side of her hair, she had a white streak just like Larimar's.

She had seen the photo before, but in a way it still surprised her. More than anything, it was the fact that her abuela would have felt comfortable back in the day to have someone take her picture in this state. As far as she knew, having one's picture taken in the 1960s in the Dominican Republic was a formal event with lots of preparation and fancy clothes. Not everyone had a camera like they did in the present age of cell phones.

"You were beautiful here," Larimar said. "I mean, you still are."

Doña Bélgica gave a wave of her hand, dissipating the notion.

"No, you were. There's a glow about you."

Doña Bélgica smiled, but it was a smile that didn't reach her eyes.

"Well, yes. I was young, and after all, it was daytime."

Larimar nodded in understanding. Of course. In the daytime, her abuela would have felt free. Judging by the position of the sun, she would still have had a few hours left before she could not be outside or in view of people.

Her grandmother reached over and patted her shoulder.

"It will all be okay, Pulguita," she said, using the nickname she had called Larimar since she was a toddler. "One way or another, it will be okay."

Larimar reached back and squeezed her abuela's hand. "Yes," she said with new confidence, "it will be okay."

She settled into the doily-covered couch cushions and her abuela did the same. Before she knew it, light snores were echoing next to her ear. Whether she had been planning to stay longer or not, now she definitely would be. No way she was waking her abuela up from a nap. Larimar fished in her pockets for her phone to keep busy while Doña Bélgica snoozed.

She skimmed her Instagram feed but nothing caught her eye. As she tried to search without moving her shoulder, she accidentally clicked on her saved photos. There were puppies getting baths, makeovers, muscle cars. There was a photo of her and Brynne in full makeup and vintage dress backstage at Brynne's first concert. And then there was that one of the punk guy from 1999. It was an obviously dated Polaroid of a teenager with black hair smiling from what appeared to be the middle of a mosh pit. The caption read, "#tbt 1999. #midtown concert, Union NJ. You haven't truly lived unless you've been kicked in the face at a ska show." She had almost commented the time she came across the photo while scrolling her feed, but that seemed a bit much.

There was always commenting. But no . . . she wasn't up to it. Instead, she clicked on the photo and sent it to Brynne in a private message.

Wow. Midtown concert in Union NJ, 1999. This brings back so many memories. Hope he didn't need a fake ID to get in like we did in those days.

Her abuela shifted next to her and settled her head, touching Larimar's shoulder. She wasn't going anywhere for a while.

As she stared at the phone, a notification appeared.

REPLY FROM: @BRYNNEBRINSON: We most certainly did. ☺

Larimar tapped the screen to begin typing.

REPLY FROM: @THELARIMARCINTRON: The good old days. Wish they still had ska punk shows.

She sent and waited a moment. Cars drove by and a few honks blared from the avenue. Nothing. Next to her, Doña Bélgica stirred in place.

"Ay, Dios mio. I went and dozed off, just like that! I must be getting old," she said, rubbing her eyes.

Larimar took her hand and squeezed it. "Did you have a good rest?"

Doña Bélgica nodded. "Yes, and even more so because you were here."

They leaned their heads together for a moment before Doña Bélgica held out her hand for Larimar to assist her in standing up.

"Will you be staying for dinner, m'ija?" she asked as she took hold of Larimar's hand.

Larimar considered it for a minute. On the one hand, she didn't have any plans. On the other hand, she still had some work to do, and she wanted to finish before it got too late.

"I think I'll go home, Mamá. I still have some work to do. Let's do dinner tomorrow."

"Okay," Doña Bélgica said. "If you pick up some ground beef on your way home, we can make pastelitos," she added with a smile.

They hugged good night, Doña Bélgica gave Larimar a kiss on her forehead, and Larimar headed upstairs to her apartment.

She sat down at her kitchen table and pulled her laptop out of her briefcase. It was covered with a case that imitated the appearance of marble, which she loved.

Her fingers tapped over the keys as she constructed an email to Ms. Beacon.

A little ping sounded on her phone.

REPLY FROM @BRYNNEBRINSON: Um, excuse me! What are you calling my shows then?

@THELARIMARCINTRON: Hey! You have some pretty awesome shows. But I'd say they're more on the punk side than the ska side.

@BRYNNEBRINSON: Whatever, dude. I can't do anything about my horn player quitting on me. By the way, the guy in that photo looks vaguely familiar.

@THELARIMARCINTRON: Really? From where?

@BRYNNEBRINSON: Not sure.

@THELARIMARCINTRON: Like you know him?
@BRYNNEBRINSON: I think so . . .

There was a pause in the conversation as Brynne typed and erased a message, then began again.

@BRYNNEBRINSON: You know what, I don't know. Never mind.
@THELARIMARCINTRON: Um, alrighty then. See you Thursday for BMW night?
@BRYNNEBRINSON: See you Thursday, hunny.

Larimar gave Brynne's message a like and set the phone down on her coffee table.

The night stretched on, and a weary Larimar finally shut her laptop. She paced over to her sink, where she filled her electric tea kettle with water and picked out a chamomile blend as she waited for the water to boil. Once the kettle whistled, she poured the water into a mug and settled into a chair at her dinette. She took a few deep breaths and allowed her mind to wander to the most recent full moon night.

The moon was glowing light and bright, and the scent of autumn leaves threaded through the breeze. The night was ripe for a run. Her muscles implored her to get outside and move. She needed to run to recharge the elemental in her. Larimar stretched her arms overhead and rocked back and forth on her feet to test her balance. She was ready.

It was fifty-two degrees, but she wore a cutoff white Sex Pistols T-shirt and black leggings, no socks or shoes. As soon as she started running, her body would heat up. Just as she did when she was a teenager, she took her knit bag and stuffed it under the wheel cap of the Beetle. Her skirt would be there for her to put on before she entered the building when she came back. She was usually too tired to climb the stairs after a run.

The chill of the night nipped at the soft flesh of her arms, making the little hairs stand on end. She took a step back to gain momentum and then she dashed off down the street, her feet barely touching the ground.

Her long, straight hair flowed behind her as she passed cars stopped in traffic, and knew that to their drivers, she resembled little more than a passing breeze.

Maybe it was an idea she'd come up with to indulge her inner masochist, but when she was transformed, she enjoyed running to places she loved visiting as a human. The best thing was there was no traffic. Just a zip through trees and over pavement to wherever she desired to go.

Her first stop was Gino's, her favorite pizza place in Montclair. If she had driven, it would've taken her thirty minutes to get there from home. But on her ciguapa run, she made it in ten minutes flat. When there was water nearby, it was that much easier for her to move quickly, and there was a brook that ran right behind Gino's.

She stopped next to the brook, grabbing a tree to break her momentum. The tree nearly snapped from the impact, but she was quick to let go before it did. Her footsteps led her to the narrow alleyway that went from the back of Gino's to Church Street, the bustling shopper's heaven it sat on.

Gino's had forest-green wire tables and benches out front, and with a look left and right, Larimar snuck up and took a seat at one of them, sitting cross-legged on the bench. Gino's closed at midnight, and her Casio showed it was 11:05. There were still a couple of patrons chatting and nursing espressos around the tables, since Gino's was known for their coffee in addition to their pizza.

She sat alone at a round green table, staring through the latticework of the metal whenever she felt anyone's gaze on her. She was the only one who was unaccompanied, but she knew she wasn't the only one who was alone. Her gaze jumped from couples staring into space instead of at each other to people talking while their friends checked their phones. There was comfort in being alone with other people.

Once or twice, she had brought some money with her in her leggings pocket to buy a slice of pizza when she got to Gino's, but this time she had nothing, and that was okay. It was enough just to inhale the aroma of the espresso and take a breather at the green latticework table.

Her next stop around the corner was the record shop where she had bought her first Sex Pistols record in 1998. Papi had taken her with him to Montclair to pick up some tailoring work, and she had wandered up and down Church Street while her father and his client shot the breeze.

The shop had smelled of old paper and skunky beer. She ran her fingers over every record before settling on *Never Mind the*

Bollocks and forking over the $5.99 she had left from her Christmas money. She had tucked the record under her arm, hiding the title from Papi's view when they reunited in front of the client's door.

It didn't matter. He saw it anyway. "What's this now?" he asked in the tone he used when he didn't want to sound alarming.

Larimar had been sullen and silent all the way home, and when they had entered the apartment, Papi reported to Mami right away.

"Berenice, you've got to see what your daughter bought at the store today," he'd said in a low voice.

Berenice took one look at the record and huffed, "Y esa mierda? The devil is a liar. I'm not letting that filth in this house. In fact, I'm calling Hermana Katherine right now. Ahora pero ahora mísmo."

Larimar had grabbed her record, made a run for it, and locked herself in her room until Oliver bribed her out with Cosmic Brownies. It was nice to go back as an adult. She didn't need to buy anything, but she could pass by, look through the windows, and feel how far she had come since those days. She missed them often, but the struggles with her parents, not so much.

Her next stop was two blocks up. She flitted up the pavement and stopped in front of Lulu's Thrift Shop, her favorite vintage store. She checked out the display to see what new arrivals they had. New to her, at least. This was how she, once a month, got the drop on the best finds. She checked the window display at night, and the next morning she would drive by and pick them up. It was genius.

Her laugh rang out, and it didn't matter who heard it. There was nobody around who would recognize her laugh. There was nobody around, period.

And in those moments, she was, as her college yoga instructor would say, in the world, but not of it. She made a left back into the alleyway and burst into the woods, running until she got back to Elizabeth. She glided over the hillsides, whipped up the leaves underfoot, and gloried in the solitude of the night. Her night runs were nothing, and they were everything. She went out without an agenda or map, and always came back with what she needed.

Her legs urged her to keep running even after she touched down on the banks of the Elizabeth River, but she rocked back on her heels and willed herself to turn toward home. After all, she had a business meeting in the morning.

DOÑA BÉLGICA'S MANTECADITO (BUTTER) COOKIES

Makes about 72 cookies

1 cup/2 sticks unsalted butter, at room temperature

1 cup granulated sugar

1 large egg

1 teaspoon vanilla extract

3 cups all-purpose flour

2 teaspoons baking powder

¼ teaspoon salt

In the bowl of a stand mixer, cream together the butter and sugar, then add the egg and vanilla. Mix well and then sift in the flour, baking powder, and salt. Do not overmix. Chill the dough in the refrigerator for 15 to 20 minutes.

Meanwhile, preheat the oven to 400 degrees Fahrenheit. Drop the chilled dough by tablespoonfuls onto greased cookie sheets about 1 inch apart. Bake for 8 to 12 minutes, or until the centers are firm and the edges start to brown.

6

DONA RELGICA'S MANTECADOS
BUTTER COOKIES

Makes about 22 cookies   1 large egg
1 cup (2 sticks) unsalted   1 tea-spoon vanilla extract
butter, at room   3 cups all-purpose flour
temperature   2 teaspoons baking powder
1 cup granulated sugar   ½ teaspoon salt

Two days later, Larimar let herself into the new Beacon location with the key Ms. Beacon had given her, and luckily it worked the first time. She was terrible with keys. They often didn't turn for her, and one time she even broke one in the lock trying to get into a new location and had to call a locksmith. Embarrassing times.

"Ms. Brand Manager?" a tall, thin man with an olive complexion, five o'clock shadow, and round glasses called from the doorway.

"Please, I'll blush. Just Larimar is fine. Come on in," she said, sticking out her hand for a handshake as he strode over.

"I'm Mr. Gerges," he said. "Nice to meet you." They shook hands, and he gestured to the space around him. "So, what're we looking at today?"

"A whole lotta work," she replied.

Mr. Gerges regarded her with a straight face and a curious expression.

"Um, just kidding," she said.

"Oh." He nodded.

It was okay. It wasn't the first time in her life her humor had gone unappreciated. She pulled her laptop out of her briefcase. There was nowhere to set it up since there were no tables, chairs, or anything except a beige refrigerator from 1998 that was most likely going to need to be replaced. The purpose of the meeting was for Mr. Gerges to explain the scope of work to install Beacon's trademark fixtures, and give Larimar a quote for his services.

She would be happy to wrap up this meeting quickly and make her way over to Brynne's. Her job was just her job. It didn't define her, and it was nowhere near as close to her heart as punk music. She just needed the money to live and help her parents.

A faint aroma wafting in from outside was enough to turn her head. It was one she would recognize anywhere, and would stop her in her tracks no matter what she was doing: BUTTER.

She tried to peer outside while simultaneously maintaining the appearance of paying attention to Mr. Gerges's review of the architectural plans. Her gaze traveled up and down the street until her eyes settled on a simple storefront on the other side of the main intersection of Union Center. From what she could make out at that distance, the sign read "Borrachitos."

Borrachitos? Little drunk ones? Little drunk whats? It piqued her curiosity, and her first instinct was to cross the street, walk down to the store, and check it out. She couldn't leave Mr. Gerges alone in the new storefront with a file of blueprints in his hands, though. She sighed inwardly and trained her attention on the files. With any luck, they would get squared away quickly and she could pop over to Brynne's flower shop down the street before continuing on to check out Borrachitos.

"What do you think, Lari? Hydrangeas with camellias, or tulips with calla lillies?" Brynne asked. Brynne's shop, Wildflowers, was the only florist in Union Center.

Larimar looked over the flowers. They were all . . . flowers? That answer wouldn't help Brynne, though.

"Um, I'm partial to the hydrangeas," Larimar said.

"Cool," said Brynne.

Brynne gathered the flowers into a tall glass vase and tied a ribbon right under the blooms. "It's so nice to have you around. How long is this project supposed to last?"

Larimar counted on her fingers. "Just as long as it takes to get this locale up and running," she said.

Brynne nodded. "Sweet."

"Got any plans for tonight?" Larimar asked.

"BMW . . . remember!?"

BMW stood for book, mask, and wine.

"Oh, yeah! And I could use a BMW night myself. I'll be at your house at six," Larimar said.

"Sounds good," Brynne replied. "Now, any chance you can help me load these camellias into the van. . .and deliver them to Roselle Park?" She bit her lip as she asked.

Oh. Larimar had been planning to walk down to that business, Borrachitos. She couldn't say no to Brynne needing help, though.

"Sure, let's go." It would have to wait.

Arms full of vases, they marched out to the parking lot.

"Do you have any aloe?" Larimar asked.

Brynne paused to think. "There should be a few full leaves on the plants in the sunroom," she said. Brynne's sunroom was one of the reasons she had fought so hard to keep her house in the divorce. It was a mini jungle. There were all stripes of plants growing in there, and Larimar didn't know if they were succulents or varietals, but they were beautiful.

"Did you bring your book?" she asked, and Larimar nodded. She pulled a glossy paperback out of her oversized bag and let it thump onto the kitchen table. Brynne had covered it in tiles with sunflowers printed on them.

While Brynne selected a bottle of wine from her wine rack, Larimar walked out to the sunroom. She inhaled deeply and exhaled as the cares of the day began to melt away. The aloe plants were sitting on a small rectangular table, where the sunlamp Brynne had hung over them illuminated their leaves. The sparkles of light were so radiant that she almost didn't want to cut one off. Almost. She sliced off the smallest leaf and brought it back to the kitchen with her.

"You know, we should be eating this, too. Aloe gel is great for detoxing."

Brynne looked at her askance. "I'll cheer you on. You know I've never been much for eating bitter or slimy things. Okra is a stretch for me."

Larimar cut off a thin square and slid the knife around the translucent chunk, peeling away the vibrant green skin. She downed the astringent aloe in one gulp, chasing it with a swig of beer from an open bottle on the kitchen table. Her throat tightened as the harsh flavor mixed with the bitter and bubbly beer.

"Ugh!" she cried out. "Next time I'll just pour lighter fluid on my tongue."

Brynne cracked a smile. "All right. Well, unless you want it for dinner, the rest of this is becoming our mask."

"Yes, please," Larimar said. "I'm done. I've fulfilled my aloe quotient for the day."

Brynne peeled the rest of the aloe and dropped it in the blender. She added a splash of water and pureed the aloe for several seconds. When it was done, they poured the mixture into an earthenware bowl, scooped up globs of it, and spread it across their faces.

"Now, for the wine," Larimar said, and Brynne proffered a bottle of merlot.

"Works for me," Larimar said.

Brynne poured the wine and they raised their glasses up high.

"To BMW night," they said in unison, and gave each other a salutatory click.

They settled into Brynne's cozy old olive-green corduroy couch with their books.

Larimar's was a thriller about a girl who is left searching for her best friend after she vanishes. She bent the title slightly away from Brynne's line of sight. A timer buzzed, notifying them that twenty minutes had passed. The women washed off their masks and returned to their couch lounging.

"Hey, Lari. Do you remember that man I told you about?"

Larimar drew a blank. "Which one?"

"The business owner from town."

Oh, yeah. Brynne had been telling her about someone she wanted to set Larimar up with for a while.

Larimar clucked her tongue and shook her head. "I don't

know, Brynne. I can't see it going anywhere."

"Where does it have to go? Just go on a date and see how you feel. It's not marriage, it's just one date."

Larimar considered this. "Even if it does go well. How would I keep him from knowing about . . . me?" she said, the corners of her lips turning down into a frown.

Brynne took a deep breath. "Larimar. You can't keep people away forever just because you're afraid of how they'll relate to one aspect of who you are. Because you are so much more than that."

Larimar shook her head. "Yes, I can," she said, and Brynne tossed a throw pillow at her.

"Come on, now."

Larimar grabbed the pillow and hugged it close to her. Brynne had a point. She was thirty-four and she had never had a relationship that had gone past the full moon. Not since William, at least.

"Fine," she said softly. "I'll give it a try."

Brynne bounced up and down on the sofa with glee. "And since you both like punk, you can both come to my show Saturday!"

Now, that could be fun. Larimar did love punk, and she loved supporting her friend even more.

"Wait, this someone you know likes punk? Are you sure he's single?" Larimar asked.

Brynne took a mock-exasperated breath. "Yessss, I'm sure. Now let me send him a text about Saturday."

Larimar's chest tightened. She hoped this was as good an idea as Brynne thought it was.

7

The Saturday of Brynne's concert, Larimar woke up at six and made oatmeal rich with evaporated milk for herself, Mami, and Papi. She filled a large square Tupperware container and hopped the elevator ride down to their apartment.

She let herself in and placed the hot container on the counter. As she scoured the countertop for a dish towel to place under it, a grumbly voice came from behind her, accompanied by loud and exaggerated air sniffing.

"Where's my oatmeal?"

Larimar whirled around to find Oliver sprawled out on the couch.

"Holy shit, you scared me, bro," she said.

"You look great in the morning, too," he said.

Larimar rolled her eyes. "I didn't see you there when I came in. Up for the weekend?"

Oliver nodded. "Melissa is in California visiting her sister."

"Mami and Papi still asleep? That's weird." Usually her parents were up at the crack of dawn.

Oliver shrugged. "We drank a bottle of Jameson last night and watched old merengue videos from the eighties and bachata videos from the nineties."

"Oh damn, I missed it," she said with a trace of sarcasm in her voice. "Well, tell them I left them this avena—don't fucking eat it all yourself—and that I'll be back sometime later. I have a little recon to do."

Oliver grinned. "You stalking someone again, Lari?"

"No, I am not stalking anyone and never have. It's for work."

"Oh, okay. Bring me any free samples if they give you some."

"I won't."

She turned on her heel, but then hung back for a minute.

"Hey, Oliver?"

"Mm-hmm?" he said.

"I'm working on putting a down payment together to help Mami, Papi, and Abuela buy a house, and we sure could get there sooner if you could kick in something, too."

Oliver ambled over to the Tupperware container holding the oatmeal, not meeting her gaze. "Would that I could, Lari . . . would that I could."

Larimar shot him a glare. "Would that I could? What kind of Shakespeare shit is that?"

"I don't have any closings this month," he said.

"And you don't have any savings, either?"

"I do, but I have plans," Oliver said.

"Right. I should never have asked you," Larimar said.

Oliver shrugged and settled back into the couch with his plate of oatmeal.

She let herself out, not looking back to avoid seeing her punkass brother. Back in her own apartment, she threw on a collared sweater and wool pants and stepped into some pumps. The parking lot of Covington Arms looked more like a shady glen, which she always thought was a waste. It would have been nice as a park, but instead it was ringed with beat-up pickups and crusty Camaros. She slid into the Beetle, the door creaking as she closed it at her side. She gunned the engine and it let out a cough as she peeled out of the parking lot and onto the main street.

She flipped on the car radio and synced up her favorite playlist, Skapulario and other punk bands from the Caribbean. Before she knew it, she was at the busy intersection of Stuyvesant Avenue. A split-second glance up and down the block revealed that parking was scarce. She drove by the front of Borrachitos, but with no available spaces in sight, she was forced to continue on. She would have to wait until another day to find out just what was drunk inside the mysterious shop.

"Damn, it's been years!" Larimar said to herself as she drove down the waterfront of Perth Amboy, New Jersey. Dominicans affectionately referred to it as the Malecón even though the only thing it had in common with the waterfront of Santo Domingo was the water.

The Malecón of Perth Amboy was a vestige of her childhood, dating back to when Papá would take them to his favorite restaurant, El Vesuvio, on weekends. It wasn't funny to her that the humdrum stretch of street was called the Malecón until she traveled to Santo Domingo and saw the difference.

Brynne's show was at a little music club tucked onto the base of a hill directly across from the Malecón. Parallel parking was not Larimar's strong suit, so she breathed a grateful sigh when she found a pull-in parking space at the bottom of the hill. The Beetle zipped right into the space and she turned off the engine and her headlights. Seven o'clock was dark in October.

A gentle breeze caressed her hair, and she felt the call of the water just as she knew she would. She considered crossing the street to sit by the ocean for a few minutes, but she was already late. For most other events, she would be okay with that, but she wanted to see Brynne before the start of the show. And she had agreed to meet her date, Ray, at seven.

She turned instead and crossed the street to the club. She flashed her ID and the VIP pass Brynne had given her to the bouncer and was ushered back to the dressing rooms.

"You made it!" Brynne exclaimed, wrapping her in a hug. Larimar hugged her back, and then clasped her hands together with a grimace on her face.

"Don't be nervous," Brynne said.

"Thanks," Larimar said. She wished it were that easy.

Brynne grabbed Larimar by the arm and spirited her out into the main hall. She tugged on her sleeve and pointed her in the direction of the disco ball. Under it stood a man in a leather jacket with soft-looking curls. When Brynne waved at him, their eyes met and for the first time in her life, Larimar felt her knees get weak and realized that was an actual thing and not a stupid cliché. She held on to Brynne to stop herself from dropping to the floor.

What was that about? Why did people's knees get weak? Was it a warning sign? As in, *danger, danger, your life will never be the same?* It felt that way to Larimar as Ray strode over to where she and Brynne were standing. He gave Brynne a cordial hug and then turned to Larimar. She panicked and stuck out her hand.

When she shook it, she suddenly felt stronger than she ever had. Weaker, stronger, this was an overload. They started shaking hands and kept shaking until it became clear to both of them they'd been shaking hands for longer than was socially acceptable.

"Um, Larimar, this is Ray; Ray, this is Larimar," Brynne said. Larimar heard her in the distance. What was in front of her was Ray, his kind brown eyes, and his tousled black curls.

He smiled, and she forgot what she was thinking. "Nice to meet you, Larimar," he said, his voice warm and clear.

She grinned back. Brynne clapped her hands together. "Well, then! I'll leave you two to it. Next time I see you will be from onstage."

A thread of terror pulled at Larimar's heart knowing Brynne was going to leave her alone with a stranger, albeit a cute and friendly stranger. Well, this was what blind dates were about, right? Larimar nodded at her dutifully and clapped her on the back.

"You'll do great, *querida*," she said. Onstage, Brynne's band was tuning up the guitars and completing their final sound tests. It was getting loud. She and Ray glanced at each other, then glanced away, then slowly brought their focus back.

Larimar tried to think of what to say, but came up blank. Her eyes darted around the room. "I don't think they could have gotten a bigger disco ball," she said finally, both of them observing the glittery globe spinning on its axis.

Ray was still smiling. That couldn't be a bad sign. "Well, as long as it stays attached, we're all good."

People were starting to drift onto the dance floor, beers in hand. She sneaked another glance at Ray. He looked a little nervous too. That made her feel a little better. He also looked like he could be Dominican. She decided to go out on a limb.

"So, did you get a chance to check out the Malecón before coming in here?" she asked.

Ray chuckled, and the corners of his eyes creased adorably. "Not today," he said. "But I've been to the famous Malecón of Perth Amboy before." He stuck his tongue out at the corner of his mouth and it was just the cutest thing ever.

"Ever been to El Vesuvio?" she asked.

He pushed a stray curl off his forehead and nodded. "That was my abuela's birthday restaurant, every year."

"'K, you're Dominican," she said matter-of-factly. He nodded slowly.

"Can I get you a beer?"

Was it the right time to reveal alcohol was like water to her?

"Sure. And if you don't mind, a shot of Henny on the side." That was her custom at bars, to drink beer with a shot on the side. She would have those two together and be set for the night. She had to drive home, after all.

At that he broke into a wide grin. "Okay! I see you." He disappeared in the direction of the bar, and she tried to bop in time to the band's guitar practice while she waited. So far it wasn't going so bad. Nobody had died. He returned with two beers, necks clasped between the fingers of one hand, and the requested shot in the other.

Larimar thanked him and downed the shot in one gulp. They clinked the beer bottles together and waited for the music to start. All of a sudden, theatrical fog began to spread and the lights facing the stage flashed in rapid succession, by turns magenta, neon yellow, and green. When they stopped and the smoke cleared, Brynne and her band, The Kitties, were poised onstage.

Brynne looked as psychedelic as ever with a fuchsia paisley bandanna tied around her head, a faded denim vest over a CBGB T-shirt, a kaleidoscopic floral miniskirt, and knee-high purple combat boots. The band consisted of herself as the singer; Arthur, the drummer; Ji Won, the guitarist; and Orhan, the bassist. It was a very New Jersey band.

"Hello, Perth Amboy!" Brynne said into the mic. "We are The Kitties. Not Kittie. The Kitties. We've got a set of our signature delicate love songs all lined up. So grab a beer at the fabulous bar, and here we go!" Larimar winced at the intro. She hoped Ray would be ready for this. If he had only seen her in a professional setting so far, he might not be expecting Brynne's stage persona.

The guitar and bass played their opening notes as Arthur began to drum. Brynne closed her eyes and stepped closer to the mic, wrapping her hands around it and letting her eyelids flutter. The audience fell silent, all eyes on her. When she opened her eyes, she began to sing in a low purr.

You promised you would love me
Forever and a day

But now it turns out forever is much shorter than you said
I saw you with that other girl, don't need that in my life
So please excuse me darling when I begin to twist the knife
Twist the knife, twist the knife
Don't it feel so good
Twist the knife, twist the knife
You're gonna pay just like you should
You left me with a heart-shaped hole that will not heal for life
So please excuse me darling when I begin to twist the knife

She punctuated the chorus with a guttural scream, and the crowd went wild cheering.

"Wow," Ray said. "Looking at Brynne, I would not know she had it in her."

Larimar nodded. "She surprises people all the time. I think it's the secret of the band's success."

Ray nodded as if to say that made sense. "The element of surprise," he said. "Does she write her songs herself?"

"Yes. I think that's her other secret."

"Cool."

"Brynne mentioned that you liked punk rock."

"I do," Ray agreed. "I listen to a lot of rock en español, too."

"Oh, me too!" she clapped. "Do you have a favorite band?"

"Los Amigos Invisibles," he said.

"Ah, they're pretty cool," Larimar said. "Saw them in concert once in Central Park."

"Nice!" He took another swig of his beer.

The clapping faded and The Kitties launched into another

heart-ripping song of despecho. By the time The Kitties finished their set, Larimar and Ray and the rest of the audience were riled up and ready to seek revenge on whoever may have done them wrong, even if it was the vending machine in the office break room. The Kitties took their bows and the audience began a rousing round of clapping.

"So . . . Brynne mentioned that you also dealt in flour!" Ray yelled over the clapping.

Did he say flour or flowers? She wasn't sure, but she nodded.

The Kitties ceded the stage to the next musical group. "Hair band?" Ray asked in slight confusion as five white dudes with long white hair shuffled onstage.

They took their posts and started some absolutely cacophonous drumming accompanied by arhythmic booms from a sound machine. At the first bang, Ray jumped. His gaze darted around the room, the first time and every time another boom followed. He did not seem to be enjoying himself at all. Larimar leaned in and placed her hand on his forearm lightly.

"Hey, do you want to go?"

"If that's okay with you," he said. His face had turned tight and stony; it was a huge change from when they had swayed through Brynne's set. Seeing him that way worried her, even though they had just met. She wasn't sure what was going on, but she could see he needed to get out.

"I'll text Brynne," she said, knowing Brynne saw them stay until the end of her set. "Let's go."

"Wow, that was something else," Ray said as they stepped out of the club.

"That's a good way to describe it," Larimar said. "God bless Brynne's heart . . . and her vocal cords."

When she arrived, Larimar had not seen that on the other side of the club, there was a Dominican bodega. Now, it was impossible not to notice. They were blasting perico ripiao at the highest possible volume, and the delicious aroma of coffee was drifting out. At 9 p.m. Of course it was.

Ray noticed the bodega around the same time she did, and she saw something change in his expression. It may just have been the relief at not having his ears assaulted by five angry instruments. Either way, she asked him, "Do you want to go in?"

His face was thoughtful. "Okay! I was just thinking I could use some . . . coconut candy."

"Were you?" she asked.

"Uh, sure," he said.

Inside the bodega, the music blasted to the point where they could barely hear each other. The smell of freshly percolated coffee pervaded her senses. They picked up a few coconut candies, Country Club red sodas, and some other wrapped snacks. They obviously had no reason to be in there besides for the fact that it felt homey, and the music was a palate cleanser from the band that had followed Brynne.

There were a few people in line in front of them, and Larimar bopped in place to the music. Ray did too, and the bodeguero called to them from the cash register, "You can dance if you want! Misu! Get out of the way." He shooed the cat dozing in the middle of the floor. The cat shot him a death stare but seemed to understand and lumbered off to a faraway corner where no one would bother him.

Ray glanced at Larimar, studying her expression. "Do you want to dance?" he asked.

Larimar shrugged. One dance on a first date was no big deal. There were ten people watching, but whatever. She had grown up dancing with her uncles and cousins at family parties. "Why not."

He grinned and placed their items down on a nearby stand to free both hands. One thing about being a ciguapa was that even in human form, she could spin in circles at a velocity that was not normal for humankind. She reminded herself to slow down so that she wouldn't scare him. Ray's hand was warm, and she felt her body relax as he got closer.

"This okay?" he asked as he raised a hand to her waist.

"Yeah, it's fine," she said. "Not my first rodeo."

He laughed as he laid his hand on her waist, and they began to sway in time to the music. She would guess that he had grown up dancing too. He danced like water—like it was no thing. Like they weren't in the middle of a bodega with ten people and a grumpy cat watching and cheering them on.

One of the watchers whooped as Ray spun her, and they laughed at the improbability of it all. Twenty minutes ago, they were in the middle of a punk-rock concert with people screaming their heads off, and here they were dancing in a bodega ten steps from where they had come from.

The song ended, and she felt obliged to take a little bow, still holding Ray's hand. She remembered the coconut candies and red sodas, and let go so Ray could pick them up again. The bodeguero shook his head to indicate they were on the house, but Ray paid him anyway and they took their goodies out to the bench outside.

They sat, and Ray passed her some coconut candies and a soda. "Thank you. That was fun," she said.

Ray smiled from ear to ear. "That was awesome," he said. "And you can dance."

Larimar shrugged. "You know how it is," she said. "I didn't really have a choice growing up. At our birthday parties the rule was: whoever doesn't dance is doing the dishes. I danced from the time the appetizers came out till the cake was finished."

Ray laughed out loud, and the joyful sound warmed her heart. He was so sweet.

"I gotta tell ya," she said. "This went a lot worse in my head."

He looked at her in surprise. "This . . . blind date, you mean?"

She nodded emphatically. "Um, yes."

He looked straight into her eyes, and his expression was warm. "I'm glad."

"What about you? Were you nervous to go on a blind date?"

He thought for a moment. "I mean, I think there's a certain nervousness that comes with the occasion, but other than that . . . I've known Brynne for a few years now, although not super well, and she is very kind and sincere. I didn't think she would suggest it unless she thought that we could, well, you know . . . get along."

This was true. She thought back to when they were attempting to have a conversation over the raucous roar of the guitars and beating drums. Had he asked her if she dealt in flour or flowers? She had said yes without being a hundred percent sure. She was about to ask him when another thought popped up. Did she remember to put on deodorant? Oh, shit. Something in the background vaguely smelled like water buffalo. She could not and would not smell herself in front of him.

She nodded politely and then said, "Um, Ray? I'm going to run to the bathroom real quick." She dashed into the bodega and headed straight for the back, which was where the bathroom usually was. Door closed, she sniffed her pits. Her deodorant was still there, but barely. She pulled a stick out from the bottom of her bag and slathered her armpits with it.

Comforted at having avoided a BO disaster, she returned and sat down calmly on the bench. It was getting colder, and she pulled her jacket closer to her body.

"So, what should we do now?" he asked, and her heart seized in terror. The date was winding down, and she assumed he would be thinking of a kiss. He seemed to intuit her anxiety and asked, "Do you want to walk the Malecón a bit?"

Larimar let out the breath she had been holding. "Yes," she said, and they pushed off the bench in unison. She felt the call of the water once more as they crossed the street, but she ignored it, focusing instead on the charming man at her side.

What had happened to him that loud noises bothered him so much? Her heart softened thinking of the panic on his face when Hair Band turned on the sound machine. It was a prying personal question for a first date, though, and a blind one at that. She filed it away for another occasion. She wasn't sure yet if there would be a second date, but she would like there to be.

They walked along, the wind whipping their faces. They didn't talk, and that was okay. Not having to make small talk was huge for her. When they reached the end of the drag where the more expansive end of the Malecón started to give way to seedy-looking junkyards and mechanic shops, they turned around and he walked her to her car.

She leaned against the Beetle, and Ray followed suit. As she was looking down, he reached up and brushed a stray curl off her forehead, sending shivers down her neck.

"Sure you're okay to drive home?" he asked, concern clouding his face.

Larimar laughed it off. "Yes, sir, I can still walk in a straight line and everything."

A ray of a smile broke through, and he took her hand and squeezed it.

"Can I give you a hug?" he asked.

Her eyes floated up to his. "Yes, that would be okay," she said. He reached out and gave her the warmest hug she'd had in a long time. When he let her go, she was almost dizzy.

"I'm glad we met," she said.

"Me too. Can I see you again?"

"I'd like that. Let's exchange numbers."

They did, and he squeezed her hand once more. "You go first," he said. "So I can make sure you leave safe and well."

She squeezed his hand back and said good-bye.

As she drove onto the parkway ramp, it occurred to her that he hadn't tried to kiss her. That was a first for a first date. She kind of loved the fact that he didn't even try. The respect it implied was reassuring, and at the same time, she wondered what it would have been like if he did.

8

Larimar awoke in the morning and stretched her arms overhead. What day was it? Where had she . . . oh. Ohhh. It was Sunday. A smile crept to her lips as every detail of the night before flooded her mind. The warmth of Ray's smile, his gaze, his voice. The way he held her hand when they danced. Diañe . . . what a night.

If only she hadn't agreed to work on a Sunday. She would have liked to spend another couple of hours savoring the replay of those tender moments. But she had to. Mr. Gerges would be at the new storefront at eleven, and she had to be there to open the door for him as well as to approve the fixtures being installed that week.

She checked her phone. It was eight o'clock in the morning. With a sigh, she rubbed her sore calves and set an alarm to give herself another hour to snooze. The effects of the transformation sometimes stayed with her for days or even weeks. It was not easy on her body. It never had been.

Twenty years earlier

"The answer is simple. I will never leave the house again, Mami," Larimar said, exhaling every ounce of air she had been holding in as her mother put the finishing touches on her coming-of-age talk.

Berenice shook her head. "Don't be ridiculous, hija. You can't stay in this apartment forever. And besides, I'm telling you. Once you get the hang of how to move, there's no way you'll get caught. You'll be way too fast."

Larimar gave her abuela, Doña Bélgica, a doubtful glance, and Doña Bélgica nodded her reassurance.

"It's true, m'ija. Trust me. We would not send you out into the night if it would be dangerous for you. Humans are slow, m'ija, If you do what we practiced down by the river, they will never, ever see you, much less catch you. Just keep it moving, because if you stop, they will be able to see you."

Larimar willed her shoulders down and back, and picked up her knit satchel, the one she had sewn Mustard Plug and Operation Ivy patches to by hand.

"Okay, then," she said in a shaky voice that gradually grew more even. "I'm doing it."

"Eso es, m'ija," Doña Bélgica said, clapping her on the back. "You can and will do this. You were born to do this."

Larimar gave her abuela a warm hug, and then her mother a quicker and lighter one. Doña Berenice was not a big hugger, and her entire family had accepted that she probably never would be. Larimar glanced at her watch. The moon would be up in approximately three minutes. The transformation would happen whether she was inside or out, but judging from her first experience, outside would be more comfortable.

She took the elevator to the building lobby and ducked into the shaded parking lot. Being here alone at night was creepy, and she had to remind herself that it would only be a few seconds. She sat down in the corner of the lot, right next to her parents' Ford Windstar. She tucked her satchel, which contained an ankle-length skirt for her return, under the wheel cap. As the light of the moon touched the crown of her head, the torquing began in her ankles. Before her first transformation, she had expected it to hurt, but as long as she was seated, it was more like a firm pressure.

Her feet swiveled from the front to the back, and her curls stretched into long, straight strands. The transformation was complete. Moments later, she started craving butter. But before she could partake, she would have to run the length of the river.

Larimar zipped out of the parking lot, her feet hovering centimeters above the pavement. Was she running? She was aware that her arms and legs were moving, but the movement was so fast, she couldn't be sure. So that was how her abuela and mother ran with backward feet! Their feet didn't even touch the ground.

The most direct route to the river would be the main street, but she wasn't confident enough yet. She wound her way through the side streets, zipping along until she reached the Elizabeth River. When she got to the river, she stopped short, almost sending herself flying. There was a gray animal down on the banks sipping water from the river.

From far away, it looked like a wolf. She didn't dare get closer, and ducked behind a tree to peek around the trunk. The animal sat and began licking its paws. She huffed out a breath. It was just a stray dog.

One of Larimar's greatest assets in life was that she had never been afraid of dogs. She zipped down to the riverbank, slowing as she reached the animal. It glanced up as she came near, and then kept licking its paws. No fear, and no interest, either.

She sat down on a cold mossy stone and inhaled the sweet scent of senescent autumn leaves. There was some crackling several yards away, and she noticed a small group of people descending the banks, beers in hand. Even though they didn't look much older than her, her heart began pounding. She was not up to being seen by them, no matter what her abuela said.

She gathered her courage, pulled her arms close to her body, and took off in a sprint that crossed right in front of them. She trained her gaze on them as she passed, and not a single one looked her way. Elation puffed her chest. Her abuela was right.

What to do? She hardly got to go out alone. On the one hand, this was her only chance to zip over to a punk show without having to get permission from her parents. On the other hand, her mother and abuela would be waiting for her at home. And most likely, they would have butter on hand to celebrate her first solo night run.

It was a snap decision. She whizzed home, reversing the path she had taken to the river. By the time she reached the parking lot, she was panting. She retrieved the black bag, threw on the skirt, and floated into the apartment building hallway.

When she reached Doña Bélgica's apartment, she found her mother turning over delicate slices of steak in butter. Her stomach grumbled as the delectable smell hit her nose.

Her mother removed the steak slices from the skillet and laid them on a porcelain plate. Her abuela was already waiting at the table. Berenice placed the plate in the center of the table and passed out small shots of mamajuana.

Larimar sat, and they all raised their glasses.

"To Larimar!" they said, clinking their glasses together and downing the woodsy elixir.

Larimar reached for a slice of steak and took a hearty bite. Steak and butter had never tasted better.

At nine o'clock, the sounds of boisterous canned marimbas echoed through Larimar's apartment. Larimar rubbed her eyes and checked her phone. Sure enough, the first message was an eye-opener.

MAMI: Come downstairs. I'm making arenque con huevo.

"Damnnnn," Larimar said under her breath. She needed her clothes not to smell like herring for this meeting, but saying no to Mami's arenque con huevo was not an option. It was impossible for her on a cellular level.

She resolved to change her clothes after breakfast, threw a ratty old robe over her black tie-dye pajama set, and padded to the elevator. When she reached the third floor, the aroma of herring greeted her before she reached her parents' door.

"'Cion Mami, 'cion Papi, 'cion Mamá," she greeted her parents and abuela, who she had not seen yet, but she knew would already be there helping her mother.

Her mother greeted her with a grunt. "This girl, fresh as ever. She doesn't even wait until she sees our faces to kiss our hands and ask for our blessing."

Doña Bélgica popped out from inside the pantry and gave Larimar a warm hug. "Dios te bendiga, m'ija," she said, ignoring Berenice's comment.

"We're making a sancocho today," Berenice said. "Can you pass by the Bravo and get some yautia coco?"

Larimar bit her lip. "I can, Mami, but I won't be able to bring it until a little later. I'm working today."

"Working on a Sunday? I've got a few words for that Ms. Beacon—" She stopped talking under her husband's gaze.

"If Larimar needs to work today, we are the last people who should be commenting on it. Thank you, m'ija, for all you do for us," Papi said. She could already feel her cheeks starting to burn. Larimar hated when her father singled her out like this.

"Well, that much is true," her mother said. "If only that Oliver had a little more gratitude—oh, never mind."

They were staring at her now because they had all resolved not to talk about these things in front of Doña Bélgica.

"Mamá, is the egg getting rubbery? Take a look, hágame el favor," Berenice said. When the elder had turned to the stove, Berenice slapped her forehead in self-recrimination.

Suddenly, Larimar was not that hungry. "You know what, I better go and get ready for work."

Her father's face fell. "You will work better after a good breakfast. Stay, and just hazte la loca to all that stuff your mother is saying." Larimar sighed and settled back in her chair, but thought better of it and sprung up to get some plates to set the table.

Her mother brought a heaping plate of herring and eggs to the table, and her grandmother set a large bowl filled with boiled yuca at its center.

"Oh! One more thing," her mother said as she headed into the kitchen. From Larimar's seat, the kitchen was out of view, but she heard a whir of the blender, and a moment later, her mother was back.

"Here," she said, and placed a jug of fresh pineapple juice on the table. They ate in contented silence, not mentioning anything besides how good the arenque was with the onions Doña Bélgica had sautéed.

Water in, coffee out. Larimar made her office coffee using the same simple process every day. It always tasted the same, and yet, each time she was disappointed when it wasn't good. Her mother and abuela probably wouldn't even recognize this as coffee. "Eso es un agua tindanga," they would say. Larimar wandered over to Emerson's desk, a manila folder tucked under her arm, to see if Emerson had any chocolate-coated biscotti to make her Monday coffee a little less dreadful.

Emerson was sitting at her desk, typing furiously. Her desk was adorned with framed photos from her girls' trips to Las Vegas and tiny crystal glasses that looked as if they held Cosmopolitans and Manhattans. Larimar fully expected Emerson to be the first fan in line for the twenty-year *Sex and the City* reunion.

She couldn't launch directly into her biscotti request. Instead, she hitched her hip up and sat on the edge of the desk. "So, Em, how was your first October weekend?" she asked.

Emerson looked up from her typing and gave Larimar a friendly smile. "Hey, Larimar! It was good." She leaned forward and narrowed her eyes, and Larimar knew a real gem was coming.

"Remember that guy, Everett, I told you about?"

Everett . . . Everett. It was hard to keep up with Emerson, but she thought she knew the one.

"The married guy?" Larimar asked.

"Mm-hmm," Emerson said. "I saw him mowing his lawn again."

"You don't say," Larimar said.

"You know what he said to me?" Emerson asked.

Larimar pursed her lips and shook her head.

"He said that if his wife gave him a hall pass, he would use it on me!" She flipped her glossy black hair over her shoulder.

"Ohmygorsh, how romantic!" Larimar rolled her eyes back so far it hurt.

"Oh, stop! Don't be like that. Miss High Road and all that. There's nothing wrong with having a little chat."

"Yeah, okay. Hey, by the way . . . do you have any biscotti left?"

Emerson's lips curved up into a mischievous grin. "Are you sure you want them? They're sinful," she said, fishing some plastic-wrapped packages out of her desk drawer and waving them in front of Larimar's face.

"Oh, can it, Em," Larimar said and snapped one out of her hand, sticking her tongue out at Emerson, who had not been counting on her quickness.

Emerson let the biscotti go with a playful shrug as if to say, "suit yourself," and then focused back on her desktop screen.

"Is Ms. Beacon in?" Larimar asked, and Emerson nodded. "Okay. Do you have time to go over the master list for the Beacon Union opening?"

"Give me a minute," Emerson said, and she typed away while Larimar sipped her coffee, somewhat ameliorated by the biscotti.

"Uff! Done," Emerson said, pushing off and rolling her chair away from her desk. "Okay, whatcha got?"

Larimar pulled the manila folder from under her arm and opened it on top of Emerson's desk.

"Okay. So far, the initial meeting with the architect has been done. City health department inspection is done, paint colors have been chosen, and the fixtures have been ordered. I thought we'd divide it up—I do the legal stuff and order the fixtures, and you order the food ingredients and paper products through one of our suppliers. You will need to compare prices to find the best one. Budget for the grand opening is $30K, and then for the first quarter of next year it's $100,000. Thoughts?"

"Sounds good to me," Emerson said.

"Perfect," Larimar said as she rose to leave. "I'll email you if I think of anything else."

"You want some biscotti for the road?" Emerson asked, shuffling something around in her desk drawer.

"Em, you're priceless," Larimar said, taking the biscotti Emerson handed her and heading back to her desk.

Larimar settled at her desk, but before she had a chance to dunk her biscotti, her phone rang.

"This is Larimar," she answered.

"Hiya Larimar, would you have a moment to pop by my office?" Ms. Beacon asked.

"Sure," Larimar said. She hung up and walked to Ms. Beacon's office.

Ms. Beacon gave her a cordial nod and gestured for her to have a seat in the metal chair facing her desk.

"So, how are things going?" Ms. Beacon asked.

"Site looks good," Larimar said. "Central location, good foot traffic."

"That's exactly what we want," Ms. Beacon said. "I had Emerson do some research for me, and she found there's a small mom-and-pop bakery right across the street, but with any luck, they'll be out of business within the first six months."

Larimar just sat there in response.

Ms. Beacon picked up a file and laid it in front of Larimar on the desk.

She opened the folder and took a look. A glossy photo showcasing a storefront was pinned to the top of the file.

"This is the place. The name is Borrachitos."

At the mention of the name, Larimar's ears pricked up. That was the name on the storefront sign she'd spotted across the street from the new location, the one she'd planned to check out but never did because she went to help Brynne deliver flowers.

"Owner's name is Raymond Antonio Concepción," she said. "Thirty-five years old, local resident." What did Ray say his business was called? He didn't say it was a bakery, did he? Larimar's mouth went dry, and her stomach folded in on itself like someone had punched her. It couldn't be.

Ms. Beacon continued on, oblivious to the tempest whipping up across from her. "I don't think we have anything to worry about."

Those were some choice words. She knew what big, polished corporate chains like Beacon meant for small artisan shops like Ray's. But what could she say? She needed this job. For her. For her parents. For her abuela.

She drew in a deep breath. "Yes, Ms. Beacon. We got this."

How the hell she was going to make this work, she had no idea.

CIGUAPAS' FAVORITE STEAK

Makes 4 servings

1 pound minute steak
Salt and pepper, to taste
3 cloves garlic, minced
(optional)

½ teaspoon dried oregano
(optional)
2 tablespoons unsalted
butter

Season the steak with salt and pepper (and garlic and oregano, if desired). In a cast-iron skillet over medium-high, melt the butter. Add the steak and brown on each side, about six minutes per side. Enjoy.

LARIMAR'S OFFICE COFFEE

¼ cup ground coffee

Percolate 1 cup water and the ground coffee using an office coffee machine. Survey the almond, oat, rice, soy, and pea protein milks on offer, and avoid all. Enjoy.

9

Dawn broke on the following Saturday and with it, buckets of rain. Larimar could hardly convince herself to get out of bed. The skies were gray and overcast, and she was just starting to feel the nip of the impending winter. After two coffees, she was able to give herself a push into the shower.

While she got ready, she put on her Café Tacvba at the highest volume she could swing without getting thumps on the wall from her neighbors. The jangly guitars and gritty vocals soothed her anxiety and ramped up her energy. She dressed in a navy-blue turtleneck and black wool pants, and pulled on a black twill jacket with a fleece-lined hood.

On the drive to Union, she left the radio off. There was parking in the lot behind Brynne's flower shop, and she snapped up the spot next to her best friend's Camry. The rain had stopped, but she grabbed her umbrella, screen-printed with the blazing stars of Vincent van Gogh's *Starry Night*, just in case.

Larimar sighed and shook her head as she passed the front door of Wildflowers and dashed across the street. "What am I doing?" she said to herself, squeezing her fists inside her jacket pockets.

The tantalizing aroma of melting chocolate and robust cinnamon greeted her as she stepped into the bakery. The warmth had her peeling off her jacket within seconds of entering. There was no one at the counter, so she helped herself to a seat at a mosaic-covered table by the window.

Larimar leaned back and inhaled. The little hairs on her arms were standing up at attention. Just beyond the chocolate and cinnamon, there was another smell whose call she could not refuse: butter.

The beaded curtain between the kitchen and sales counter jingled, and out stepped Ray, bearing a tray of freshly baked chocolate cupcakes waiting to be frosted.

"Larimar!" he said, and the warmth of his smile sucked her in. She shouldn't have come here. She was just making the inevitable harder for herself. But in the sunshine of his smile, those thoughts just slipped away.

The rain started again, with such forceful wind that even if she used her umbrella she was still liable to get soaked.

"Not going anywhere for a while?" he asked with a glint in his eye as they both watched the wind bend the scraggly trees planted along the sidewalk.

"I guess not," she said, pulling her phone out of her coat pocket and laying it on the round table. His gaze burned her face, and the thought that he could see right through her turned her chest into a block of ice. A shiver shook her shoulders.

A look of concern knitted Ray's full brows, and he leaned in her direction. "Are you okay?" he asked. "Can I get you a blanket?"

Larimar shook her head vigorously. "No way," she said. "I mean, no thank you."

He held back a chuckle. "Well, how about a steaming hot cup of tea with a little something sweet?" Their eyes met, and the ice in her chest grew thicker. He didn't deserve this.

Larimar pursed her lips and nodded. "It's beyond the scope of my restraint to say no to that," she said, and he laughed as he turned toward the kitchen.

In what seemed like seconds he was back with a steaming hot earthenware mug, a chocolate cupcake, and an oversized coconut cookie with a little pot of jam on the side.

"Conconetes!" she said when she recognized the cookie. "You're speaking the language of my soul here. I haven't had these in forever."

At this, Ray broke out laughing. "The jam is guava," he said when he had recovered himself a bit.

She glanced from the velvety cupcake to the golden-brown cookie to the bracing tea to the torrential rain outside. She wasn't going to be able to leave for a while, so she might as well relax and enjoy. There were worse things than being stranded in a tiny café with a gorgeous man making her tea and offering her cookies. A gorgeous man she wanted to get to know better. A gorgeous man she should be leaving alone and staying away from before she did any damage.

"Fuck my life," she muttered under her breath.

"Did you say something?" Ray asked.

She trained her gaze on the mosaic tabletop. "Um, this is the life!" she amended quickly, gesturing toward the tea and cookies.

He studied her with curiosity, a corner of his mouth turning up. Yeah, he had heard her.

"Are you on a diet or something?" he asked.

"Helllll no. My favorite food is butter."

This garnered another resounding laugh. Ah, if only he knew she wasn't joking.

"I'll be here all week," she said, and instantly regretted the cheesy line. Damn, she was saying the opposite of what she needed to.

The rain continued hammering the deserted sidewalk.

She glanced around the café walls in search of material for a subject change. Sure enough, there were some small wooden plaques with military insignia. They stuck out against the backdrop of burgundy walls and lattice star lanterns.

"Was this, like, a VFW hall before it was a bakery?" she asked.

Ray shook his head and chuckled again. "Those are my plaques," he said.

"Oh," she replied softly. "You were in the Army?"

He nodded. "Yep. I went in at eighteen and I got out at thirty-two. Three years ago."

"I see. How was that for you?"

"A lot of things," he said.

His face was calm, but she noticed him fidgeting with the tea bags. She appreciated him not adding a polite smile on the end of that, the way she had seen Papi do when people asked him about his time in the Army.

She wondered if he had gotten an SBA veterans' loan to open

the bakery, just like Papi had done to open his tailor shop.

Larimar took a sip of the tea. There was a distinctive taste that reminded her of a familiar smell.

"Is there . . . lavender in here?"

"Yes," Ray said, "it's lavender Earl Grey. Do you like it?"

She nodded. "It tastes like body wash in the best possible way."

Ray brought his hand to his face and rested his chin in the crook between his thumb and his index finger. "Hm, I can see that."

She took another sip. It was quite good once she succeeded in convincing her brain that she wasn't drinking soap. "So from the Army to the bakery . . . how did that happen?"

Ray was still standing next to her table, and she motioned for him to have a seat, which was weird since she was in his place of business. But maybe less weird since they had been on a blind date. And maybe even less weird still because the two of them were alone. Yeah, having him standing next to her table instead of sitting was weirder.

He pulled up a chair and pondered her question. "This is my passion project," he said. "When I got discharged from the military, I needed something to lift me up and keep me busy."

That was understandable. She knew that when Papi got back, he opened his shop as soon as he got the loan.

"When I was deployed, there were months on end that I felt like I had nothing to look forward to. I loved to bake, and in my down time I kept up a Pinterest board of recipes. It started out as a joke, some of the guys saying, 'When Ray gets out, he's going to open a bakery.' We had a laugh, but in my loneliest moments, I would think about it, and it brought me joy.

"Years later when I got out and came home, I had no idea what to do. I couldn't focus long enough to sit in the classroom, and the ringing in my ears wouldn't let me concentrate. Then one day I remembered the bakery. I started baking at home and felt like there was something to look forward to again. And that's how it started."

Larimar couldn't even imagine what it would be like to be moored in some remote place wondering if one day she would get a chance to live her passions. Larimar had gone straight into business, which was her passion. She'd never had to wonder.

"Did you always enjoy baking?" Larimar asked.

Ray nodded emphatically. "Loved it. I got the home economics award three times in a row in high school," he said with a wide grin.

She clutched her chest. Imagining a teenage Ray standing next to a table laden with cakes and cookies with a medal pinned to his shirt squeezed at her heart. It was time for a deep breath.

"Enough about me. What's it like being a florist?"

It was the moment she hadn't thought to dread. So he *had* said flowers that night at the concert. But now that she knew what the correction could signal to him, she couldn't bring herself to make it.

"It-it's fun," she stammered, rolling her eyes inwardly at how dispirited that sounded.

How to distract him . . . oh! She hadn't tried the cupcake yet. She grabbed it and took a healthy bite. Velvety chocolate and piquant espresso washed over her tongue.

"These are *amazing*! I try baked goods all the time and—"

Ray's gaze was curious. "Oh, because of your butter craving?"

"Y-yes, because of that," she said. She took another bite and allowed the chocolate to melt over her tongue.

"I'm glad you like them. Hey, Larimar, would you excuse me for a moment? I have a customer coming in to pick up an order later. I'll be right back—I just need to get the dough rising."

"Oh, of course!" she said. "Don't let me keep you."

He stood up and turned to her. "I like you keeping me," he said, leaving her to drown her guilt in lavender tea.

She snuggled into the window corner, which was bolstered with fluffy tasseled pillows. From her vantage point, she could see into the kitchen where Ray was preparing the dough.

He sprinkled his work surface with flour, and it fell like snow over the smooth marble slab. Powdery flour met water, and before long, he had dough to work with. He hummed an old bolero to himself as he kneaded it.

As she watched him so intent on his work, she felt a strange stirring in her chest. With every second that went by, she became sure of one thing: she could not let Beacon put him out of business.

BORRACHITOS' CINNAMON PRETZEL BITES

Makes 60 pretzel bites

FOR THE PRETZEL BITES

5 tablespoons light brown sugar

2 cups warm water

5½ teaspoons active dry yeast

¼ cup vegetable oil

6¼ cups all-purpose flour

7 tablespoons baking soda

1 large egg

FOR THE CINNAMON-SUGAR COATING

⅓ cup plus 2 tablespoons superfine sugar

2 tablespoons ground cinnamon

2 tablespoons unsalted butter

Make the pretzel bites: Grease a large bowl with oil and set aside. In another large bowl, combine the brown sugar and warm water, stirring until the sugar dissolves. Sprinkle the yeast over the sugar water and let stand for about 5 minutes, until foamy. Stir in the vegetable oil and 3¾ cups of the flour until combined, then turn the dough out onto a floured surface and knead in the remaining 2½ cups of flour. The dough will be sticky, but continue kneading for about 3 minutes, until smooth.

Transfer the dough to the greased bowl and cover

it with plastic wrap, then let it stand in a warm place for about 1 hour, until doubled in size.

Meanwhile, preheat the oven to 475 degrees Fahrenheit. Line three large baking sheets with parchment paper.

Punch the dough down and turn it out onto a floured surface. Knead the dough lightly, then cut it into six equal pieces. Roll each section into a rope-like strand around 15 inches long, then cut each section into about ten 1½-inch pieces. Let sit uncovered on the prepared baking sheets for ten minutes.

In a large pot over high, bring 8½ cups of water and 7 tablespoons of baking soda to a simmer.

Lower the heat to medium, and carefully transfer six pretzel bites at a time to the simmering water and leave them for 30 seconds. Transfer each bite to a paper towel to drain, then return to the baking sheets, spacing them evenly apart. Continue the process with the remaining bites.

Create an egg wash by cracking the egg into a bowl and whisking it together with 1 tablespoon water. Brush each pretzel bite with the egg wash. Bake for about 10 minutes, until dark brown.

Make the cinnamon-sugar coating: In a medium bowl, combine the sugar and cinnamon. In a small saucepan over low, melt the butter. Dip each baked pretzel bite into the butter and then toss in the cinnamon-sugar mixture until fully coated. Serve warm or at room temperature.

Recipe Adapted from *The Mermaid Cookbook* by Alix Carey
(Andrews McMeel, 2019)

BORRACHITOS CHOCOLATE ESPRESSO RUM-INFUSED CUPCAKES

Makes 12 cupcakes

FOR THE CUPCAKES

4 large eggs, separated

1 cup sugar

½ cup/1 stick unsalted butter

½ cup strong brewed coffee

1 ounce baking chocolate

2 tablespoons dark cocoa powder

1 cup all-purpose flour

1 teaspoon baking powder

4 tablespoons dark rum

FOR THE FROSTING

½ cup/1 stick unsalted butter, at room temperature

1 cup confectioners' sugar

2 tablespoons dark rum

Make the cupcakes: Preheat the oven to 375 degrees Fahrenheit. Prepare a cupcake pan with cupcake liners.

In a large bowl, beat the egg whites just enough to break them up and add the sugar.

In a medium saucepan over medium, melt the butter.

Add the coffee, chocolate, and cocoa powder and whisk to combine. Set aside and allow to cool.

Whisk the butter mixture into the egg white–sugar mixture. Add the flour, baking powder, and run and mix to combine.

Fill the cupcake liners two thirds full and bake for 15 to 17 minutes. Allow to cool completely on a wire rack.

Make the frosting: In the bowl of a stand mixer, cream together the butter and confectioners' sugar. Add the rum and mix to combine. Frost the cupcakes when they are completely cool.

10

The rain finally let up, and Larimar said goodbye to Ray and crossed the street to Wildflowers. The door was locked. Ugh. Brynne had gone home, surely owing to the lack of foot traffic. Safe and warm in her car, she dialed Brynne's cell. Brynne picked up after the third ring.

"You home already, mama?" Larimar asked.

"Yes," Brynne said.

"Listen, babe. You got any BMW? Just the W will work, too."

Brynne let out a chortle. "Uh-oh. What's going on?"

Thirty minutes later, Larimar was shaking off her umbrella in front of Brynne's door.

She peeled off her soaked socks and left them on the porch. Brynne greeted her out front and ushered her inside. A bottle of cabernet sauvignon graced her kitchen table, waiting to be opened. They each poured themselves a glass and took a seat on the couch.

"So, tell me all about it," Brynne said.

Larimar sighed. "I can't do this project, Brynne, this Beacon project."

Brynne's brow furrowed in concern. "Why not, sweetie?"

"It's Ray."

"Ray?"

"He's going to lose his business."

Brynne mulled it over for a moment and frowned. "But sweetie, you can't know that," she said, patting Larimar's free hand.

Larimar let out a low exhale. "I do know that. I've seen it happen twenty-seven times before. I can't let it happen to him."

They sat together in silence.

"You didn't get to finish telling me about the rest of the date, by the way," Brynne said.

"Oh." Larimar smiled. "He's something else," she said.

"Wowwwwww."

Larimar swatted her friend with a pillow. "Don't make fun! I'm serious. Good choice, querida. Good choice."

"Can you understand why I thought you two could hit it off?" Brynne said.

Larimar inhaled and thought of Ray's chocolate-drop eyes. She thought of his smile and easy laugh, and the way he squinted when he was feeling the music.

"Uh, yeah. Yeah, I can understand it."

"It doesn't make any of this easier, does it?" Brynne said with a frown.

"Nope. Not at all."

Brynne punched her fist into a throw pillow.

"Just tell him."

"That I work for Beacon? Or that I'm a ciguapa?"

"Both."

Larimar shook her head. "Brynne . . . I can't."

"Why not?"

Larimar pressed her lips together. "Brynne. Does the name 'William' mean anything to you?"

Brynne regarded her quizzically before hiding her grin with the back of her hand. "By William, do you by chance mean your sweet baboo?"

Larimar yanked a pillow off the couch and launched it at Brynne. "Fine, make fun of me! It was college, okay? Everyone's stupid in college."

"Maybe everyone is stupid, but not everyone has those cheesy-ass nicknames for their significant others."

"Seriously, though. Remember what happened with him? People in Roselle Park said they could hear him screaming in terror all the way from Passaic."

"Hmm, I get your point. Although, William was William, and Ray is Ray. Just saying," Brynne said with a shrug.

They settled back into the couch pillows again.

"What if they were to find some sort of defect in the building?" Brynne asked.

"What?"

"Yeah. What if some sort of defect was discovered in the building where the new Beacon is set to go? Something that would make it impossible for them to execute their plan?"

Larimar leaned backwards into the couch as she pondered her friend's question, partially hoping to disappear between the soft cushions.

"I see your point. Well, there are a few obvious ones that

would delay a building, like rats, flooding in the basement . . ."

Brynne plopped down next to her on the couch. "So?"

"So?"

"A place can suddenly get rats, no? And basements can flood."

It was true, these things could happen. But could she give them a little nudge? Especially after she had already reported to Ms. Beacon that the coast was clear?

"I don't know if I can do that," she said to Brynne.

Larimar took another sip of her wine. Brynne had a point. Beacon was hell-bent on opening the new location in Union Center, but if the building were some sort of health hazard, they'd have to find somewhere else.

She wasn't the Pied Piper, though. How was she going to summon a nest of rats to the building when it had already been given a clean bill of health?

And the basement was dank, but weren't all basements? How could she convince Ms. Beacon that it was so dank, it was dangerous?

She surprised herself by thinking about this. When in her professional life had she ever thought of doing anything to counteract her goal, which was opening every Beacon location with flying colors? Meeting Ray had already changed the direction of her thoughts. She was feeling wiped just thinking about it.

"And another thing. I can't keep seeing him," Larimar said.

Brynne frowned. "I had a feeling you were going to say that," she said. "Just sucks since you got along so well."

Larimar shrugged. "It was nice feeling that with someone, even if just for one night. Can I stay over tonight, ma? I feel pretty tired."

"Sure, querida," Brynne said. It was one of the few Spanish words Brynne had picked up after so many years being friends with Larimar.

Brynne went to her linen closet and pulled out a turquoise velour comforter and a fluffy pillow.

"Okay, now you're not going anywhere for a while, so let's make some dinner. Penne á la vodka? Extra cream and butter?"

Larimar grinned and took the comforter from Brynne, patting it down on the couch and running her hands over its surface, delighting in its softness.

"You know me too well."

Larimar awoke to the sun shining on Brynne's couch. She stretched her arms overhead. It was Sunday, but she still had a little work to do . . . nothing she couldn't easily do from Brynne's shop. Larimar threw on her navy-blue-and white Beacon Foods T-shirt, the one she'd had since new employee orientation, and a pair of jeans. She and Brynne rode in in Brynne's Camry to Wildflowers. She was entirely tempted to ask Brynne if she would mind popping over to Borrachitos for muffins, but she didn't.

From opening time on, delivery people stopped by with boxfuls of buttery yellow daffodils, brilliant pink camellias, and little sprigs of lavender, and Larimar helped her arrange them all between stints on her laptop. Just when she was about to ask Brynne what she had in mind for breakfast, Larimar saw a familiar leather jacket outside the flower shop window.

"It's Ray!" she gasped.

Brynne looked at her in confusion.

"He can't know about my work! Hide me!"

She dove under the counter, leaving Brynne with an amused expression.

Larimar folded her legs to her chest and hugged her arms tight around them.

There was the creak of metal, and she heard Ray's footsteps as he approached the counter. She peered up just in time to see Brynne shaking her head silently.

Something was placed on the counter—a coffee?

"Morning, Brynne, do you have any purple splendor orchids?" he asked.

Ooh, he had good taste in flowers. She liked that in a man.

"Hi, Ray. Give me one sec, please. I will check in the back." Brynne disappeared, and Larimar prayed Ray wouldn't look around the counter. Wait, why would he look over the counter? That was rude. It was unlikely he would do that to another businessowner.

Brynne's footsteps signaled her return.

"Here are the only two bouquets I have. Nice to see you, by the way. How did it go the other night with Larimar? Did you guys have a good time?"

Larimar perked her ears up. "Yes . . . we had a great time," he said, and there was a softness in his voice that wrung her heart in her chest.

"Glad to hear," Brynne said after a long pause. Ray handed her his card and she ran it through her card reader before handing it back to him with a receipt. "Thank you," she said.

"Thanks for these!" Ray said. "Let's talk more soon. I have to arrange these before opening the shop. Have a good day!" he said, and she heard his footsteps retreating.

Brynne reached under the table and swatted her with an olive branch.

"You can come out now," she said.

Larimar climbed out, sheepishly smoothing the front of the telltale shirt.

"So this is part of the plan, huh. What are you going to do? Hide every time he comes around?"

Larimar shrugged. "Um, yes?"

Brynne shook her head. "I don't see how that's going to work, but okay. So you're not going to tell him you work for Beacon?"

"He can't find out, Brynne! Not now, at least. I will tell him, I promise, I just need to get Beacon off his back first. We won't be able to date long, anyway. Let me at least enjoy this little bubble of joy."

Brynne laid an arm around her shoulders and squeezed her close. "Lari. What if you told him?"

Larimar sighed and leaned her head on her friend's shoulder. "I can't . . . not just yet. Let me see how I'm going to resolve this. I won't keep him in the dark forever. But right now, I need him not to know."

Brynne shifted uncomfortably against the counter. "Alright. Here's hoping this goes according to plan."

"And now I just have to figure out how to get some rats into the basement," Larimar said, twirling a honey spoon in her mug of tea.

11

Fransinatra always wore a fedora. Whether rain or shine, snow or sleet. The brim of his gray wool hat shielded his forehead from the world and his eyes from whoever he did not want to see them. He was king of his hill: the bodega that sat squarely on the street corner where Larimar's apartment building stood. He had to know a thing or two about how to catch rats.

Fransinatra's hat had stories; it was almost as legendary as he was in their neighborhood.

It had an air of mystery, like Fransinatra's real name. "Nobody knows his real name," the elder ladies of Covington Arms would whisper. Larimar found out it was Victor Manuel Rodríguez Castillo by peeping the sanitation certificate hanging behind the cash register, which most people never bothered to check. The tigueres of the neighborhood called him Fransinatra because he played Frank Sinatra from sunup to sundown, and he always, always looked dashing with his fedora.

Larimar popped into the bodega early Monday morning. Most of his friends who hung out in front didn't get up until ten o'clock. This would be a good time to get some advice from Fransinatra without their lewd interjections. She found him twirling in the aisles to Che Che Colé while he stocked the shelves with canned tuna and vacuum-packed coffee containers. He didn't *only* listen to Frank Sinatra.

"Buen día, Fransinatra," Larimar said. It was imperative that she greet him correctly under threat he would call her parents to let them know if she didn't. It wasn't his problem that she was thirty-four.

Fransinatra looked up from his tuna cans. "Buenos días, mijija," he said. He always said "mijija."

Larimar fiddled with her purse. "Um, where's Misu?" she asked.

Fransinatra looked at her like she had grown a second nose. She had never before shown an iota of interest in the scraggly, high-strung cat that terrorized the aisles of the bodega.

"Ehm, he must be in the back. Why? Got a mouse problem? I doubt it. Doña Berenice must have taught you to clean the right way."

Larimar sighed. This was going to be harder than she thought. "No, no, it's not that," she said. "Have YOU ever had rats before?"

Now he looked at her like she had grown a third eye. "Tu ta loca? With Misu here? If rats even dare to come in here, Misu makes them pipián!" He slapped his thigh for emphasis.

Larimar resisted the urge to roll her eyes. That would be another call home to her parents.

She wasn't getting anywhere. "Um, Fransinatra? Do you know any bodegueros who do have rats?"

"If they had rats, I wouldn't be friends with them," he said with a snort. "You know what they say: tell me who you walk with and I'll tell you who you are."

It was becoming clear that Fransinatra lived in a world with no rats. "Okay, then," she said. "Thank you." She turned to leave.

"Gracias de qué?" Fransinatra called from the tuna aisle.

"Exactly," she said under her breath.

When she got back to her apartment, she dialed Oliver's number.

He picked up on the third ring. "Who died? Who died?"

"Don't be like that, Oliver. I call, sometimes."

"Yeah . . . I think the last time you called me, Motorola Razrs were all the rage."

"Whatever, son. Listen . . . do you know how to catch rats?"

The line went silent for a minute.

"You are so dead when Mami finds out you have rats!"

"I do NOT have fucking rats. I actually . . . need to get some rats."

"Need to get some rats? Have you lost your damn mind? Larimar, what is going on over there?"

Larimar heaved a sigh. How had she thought asking Oliver for help with this would be a good idea?

"Um, next question. How do you use Photoshop?"

Prayers and stuff were not her thing, but Larimar said a silent prayer as she clutched the doctored pictures to her chest on Tuesday. She'd had to bribe Oliver with money and Jordans and promises of sancocho. That brat. Muscle shirts and all, he was still the same snotty little brother that peed in her baby pool and drew mustaches on her Barbie dolls.

She thought of Ray to quell the anger. He needed her help.

Knocking on Ms. Beacon's office door and waiting for her to call her in was the best she could do. She didn't have an appointment, and Ms. Beacon's secretary was nowhere to be seen.

Larimar slumped down in the burgundy crushed-velvet chair outside the CEO's office, but jumped straight up moments later when she called her in, her voice tinny and aphonic on the intercom.

"Good morning, Ms. Cintrón!" Ms. Beacon said with a jovial smile.

"Good morning, Ms. Beacon," Larimar said in a more subdued tone.

"What brings you here today?"

She pulled the photos from her folder and laid them on her desk. "There's something we need to discuss about the new location," Larimar said. "If you will please look closely at the pictures."

Ms. Beacon stared at the printed photos, shadows crossing her face now and then. Finally, holding her gaze with a stern expression of authority, she said, "Larimar, I can't believe I didn't say this sooner."

Larimar held her breath.

"We should be getting an exterminator to the premises before we do anything else!" Ms. Beacon said. Her expression was sunny again, and she leafed through a box of cards before pulling out a matte black one. "Here, this is the number for the North Jersey exterminator we have contracted," she said. "And don't worry. They will fix this little problem in no time."

Larimar took the card from her, grinning uneasily. "Thanks, Ms. Beacon. Uh, I-I'll be going now, then," she said.

She grabbed the photos off the desk and marched back to her desk. Seated in her own chair, she let out a long exhale. Was she crazy? Ms. Beacon seemed none the wiser, but what if she'd noticed the rats were cut-and-pasted into the picture?

She didn't, though, and now Larimar had an exterminator to call. She hadn't helped Ray, and she had gotten herself more work. It was time to take a walk down to the river.

With the press of a button, she switched on her phone's answering message and ducked into the elevator. In seconds, she was out on Fifth Avenue and crossing the street to Central Park. She exhaled what felt like five pounds of stress as the expansive Pond space opened up before her.

Throngs of tourists made their way around the Pond, and there were a few people running in the park, others biking and stretching.

When she was sure no one was watching, Larimar descended to the water's edge and took a seat on the mossy rocks. She sat on the bank, took her heels off, and allowed her feet to slip over the wet surfaces. Her feet were going to be muddy, but she didn't care. She needed this time to connect with herself, connect with the earth, and be comforted.

She leaned her head forward on her knees, and before long she felt an arm around her shoulders, light as a feather. The touch prompted her to exhale deeply, letting go of her worries and forgetting her cares. As she heaved a calming breath, the hand stroked her back, and she welcomed the touch. She pulled away, and a friendly face, almost transparent, came into view.

The woman facing her, if she could be called that, had straight hair so long that it covered her body. Larimar could not explain how she could see the woman's face, but she could, almost like a hologram. Her face was weathered, with deep grooves that seemed to glow. Larimar knew the woman couldn't speak, but that didn't stop her, now or in the past, from talking to her.

She gazed into the woman's eyes. "Got myself in a real bind this time," she said.

The woman nodded wordlessly, a smile crinkling her face further.

"I really don't know what to do."

The woman ran her hand over Larimar's hair. She touched Larimar's forehead, and then touched her heart. She gave Larimar's hand a squeeze, and then stood up, firm on her backward-facing feet. In a flash, she disappeared into the water.

She had laid her palm on Larimar's head and heart. From my head to my heart? Larimar pondered the encounter as she pushed up to standing and wiped her feet over a dry patch of rock. Her break was up and it was time to cross back over Fifth Avenue and return to the Beacon office.

Larimar never ceased to be amazed by the versatility of pumpkins. One simple gourd that could be made into pie, cake, bread, and even cookies. And all were delicious. She thought about how people needed to be more like pumpkins as she strolled through the pumpkin patch she had come across on her way to shop for tile for Beacon Union.

Shopping for tile was a fairly straightforward affair; they had to match the color and size of the tiles in all other Beacon locations except for the backsplash behind the coffee bar, which was always navy blue and white, but which they tried to give a different artistic design in each shop. She had brought with her a sample of the tiles from Beacon Cobble Hill as well as a list of measurements from the new location. It had been ten days since she had tried to persuade Ms. Beacon with her shoddily doctored photos, and she hadn't come up with any better ideas in the interim. The project was moving forward.

She went to South Jersey because she got the best prices on tile there. South Jersey Stone and Tile was a single-level standalone building on a busy highway, and the pumpkin patch was right next to it. The woman at the entrance told her it was a strawberry and blueberry patch in the summer.

The October wind was gentler than usual, and the sun warmed her face and hands. She strolled the aisles of the patch, inhaling the sweet, earthy smell of the hay and burnished pumpkins, and made a mental note to visit a pumpkin patch on one of her next ciguapa runs. Being there she felt a peace that only came to her when she was surrounded by nature.

Larimar picked out one pumpkin for her abuela, one for her parents, and one mega pumpkin to place on her kitchen table. That would be another advantage of buying a house for the whole family; only one big pumpkin to haul for them all. She loaded the gourds into the back of the Beetle and crossed the parking lot to South Jersey Stone and Tile.

A staccato bell pealed as she stepped in, and she went right up to the counter. There was a youngish clerk seated there, wearing an olive-green beanie and round glasses, reading *Science Fiction* magazine.

"Welcome to South Jersey Stone and Tile," he said.

"Thanks. I need some off-white subway tile, colonial white if you have, three-quarter-inch thick," she said. "And can I please see your backsplash designs?"

"One second, please," he said, and disappeared into one of the aisles. He came back with five different samples. One of them had tiny gold flecks, another was matte, and yet another had a grainy, almost bubbled texture on the surface. The remaining two were just plain white glossy tiles.

"I'll take this one," she said, tapping the matte sample, "and this glittery blue and white backsplash. For the tiles, how many boxes do I need for a twenty by thirty space?"

The clerk punched a few numbers into a calculator and started scribbling some notes on a sheet.

While she waited, Larimar wondered what Ray was up to. It was a Friday, ten thirty in the morning. He had to be at the bakery, whipping up some cinnamon pretzels. Or some mojito cupcakes for later. Those pretzels were so soft. Just like his lips looked—

"Um, miss?"

Larimar gave the clerk a startled glance.

"Yes?"

"Uh . . . I need the address you want these shipped to."

She shook herself out of it. "Oh, of course," she said, and

hastily scribbled the address on the order form. "Here you go."

"Thanks," he said, eyeing her with a half-smile.

She handed over the company credit card and waited as he ran it through.

All she needed to do was wait for the tile to be delivered. No way 143 boxes of tile were fitting in any part of the Beetle.

When Larimar worked, she listened to jazz. It distracted her less than ska-punk, but still stimulated her ears enough to keep her on task. Dead silence was not her thing. There was too much music to listen to in life. The sweet strains of cello, bass, and piano twinkled in the background as she plopped down on her couch, pulled a crocheted blanket over her legs, and settled her laptop on her lap to work the rest of the day from home.

Once she was settled, she took a sip of apple chai from the teacup she had placed on her side table. Her stomach rumbled—luckily she'd had the foresight to buy a pumpkin muffin at the pumpkin patch. She picked it off its napkin and took a hearty bite. In her inbox, there was a twenty-eight-page statistical report on coffee and baked goods sales in New Jersey. Her goal was to read the entire document without dozing off.

She skipped the acknowledgments and went straight to page five, *Market trends for North Jersey*. Emotional wellbeing was the number-one trend, which she loved because that was exactly how she thought of her coffee. Curated chocolate creations were there again; lately they'd been coming back year after year. And, oh lord. Cronuts were coming back in style. Number six on the list was baked goods with a twist, like alcohol infusions. That didn't really help Beacon, but it was good for Ray. Larimar wondered how much time he dedicated to market research, and how much he just went with the flow of where his passion took him.

This reminded her of a topic she'd wanted to research. Was Borrachitos the only bakery in Union Center, or would they have additional competition? She opened her Google Maps app, dropped a pin at Wildflowers, and searched for "bakeries." Larimar took another sip of chai as the search results loaded. Sure enough, Borrachitos was the first result. The rest on the list were outside Union Center. She frowned. The competition was direct.

Her eyes skimmed the rest of the report with some effort. Once she realized Borrachitos was Beacon's only competition, she had to force herself to keep focused. She found herself gazing out the window and picking the pills off the crocheted blanket. She switched off the jazz and turned her favorite Catch 22 song up as high as it would go. She chucked the laptop into the corner of the couch and got up to dance.

She punched the air and did a few twirls. The blood was circulating through her legs again; that was good. Once the song was over, she sat again and picked up her laptop.

Nope, she wasn't ready to keep working. She popped up off the couch again, threw a black shawl over her shoulders, and let herself out of her apartment. She took the stairs down to the third floor for extra exercise and knocked on her parents' door.

She found Mami standing on a high stool, a tie-dyed bandanna around her head, wiping down the fan blades with a microfiber cloth. Papi was holding the stool with one hand and scrolling through the news on his phone with the other. Larimar gasped. If her sixty-six-year-old mother fell off that stool . . .

"Mami! What are you doing?"

Mami looked down, not letting go of the fan blade in her hand. "This girl. Just comes in and starts yelling." She shook her head with a cluck-cluck of her tongue.

Larimar inhaled deeply and counted to five. "'Cion Mami, 'cion Papi. Why are you up on the stool?"

Her mother looked at her askance. "You going to do it for me? These fan blades won't clean themselves. And it's been a whole five days since I wiped them down last. Right, Roberto?"

"Mm-hmm," Papi said, without looking up.

"I'll do it," Larimar said. "Just get down from there, okay?"

Papi's gaze shot up and he raised an eyebrow as if to say, *Are you sure?*

Larimar nodded. Papi and Mami exchanged a look and he held out his hand to help her down. Mami handed Larimar the cloth, and without another word, she was off to the kitchen. Larimar hopped up on the stool, and one by one, she wiped down the fan blades. The cloth had been dipped in water with a dash of bleach, and the aroma gave her a comforting flashback to her childhood.

Once she had wiped them all, Papi held his hand out to her, and she hopped down. There was a blue bucket on the living room coffee table into which she deposited the cloth.

"Okay, Mami! It's done," she said, walking into the kitchen to wash her hands in the sink.

Mami stuck her head out of the pantry. "What do you mean, it's done? There are three fans in this house," she said.

Papi cleared his throat, and Larimar knew that was his *I told you so.* Suddenly, she remembered the market report waiting for her on her laptop.

"Ay, Mami! I came down in the middle of reading a market report. I have to send Ms. Beacon a summary before the end of the day." She crossed her fingers behind her back in her mind.

Mami studied her face and then lifted her hands to the heavens. "Fine," she said. "You get off the hook this time because you're working from home. This time only, you hear?"

Larimar grinned, gave each of her parents a cheek kiss, and ducked out before Mami had her wiping down every fan blade in the apartment. Leave it to Mami to make finishing the market report vitally interesting.

12

Halloween fell on a Monday, so Larimar rode the New Jersey Transit train home from work with a car full of witches, ghouls, and headless horsemen. She sat next to one particularly creepy horseman and kept her eyes trained out the window to avoid looking at the plastic head he held in his hands. It felt as if it was staring up at her.

Her Halloween plans involved a pumpkin-shaped bowl of Reese's peanut butter cups and her favorite episodes of *Buffy the Vampire Slayer*. Brynne would be at a Halloween party, and her parents didn't celebrate esa vaina. Every year, Larimar had a brief moment where she considered going to a Halloween party as herself, and if it wasn't a full moon, dressing as a ciguapa. Then she talked herself out of it and picked out something "normal," whatever that meant.

She rested her weary frame on the couch. Her body was crying out for a hot shower and an evening of lounging. The knowledge that the doorbell was going to start buzzing off the hook any moment kept her from conking out altogether. She liked having trick-or-treaters stop by, though.

She was just about to close her eyes when her phone buzzed.

RAY: Larimar! What are you doing tonight?

LARIMAR: Probably making like a mole and burrowing down into my couch.

Write . . . erase. Write . . . erase. Ray's thought process was etched into a little gray bubble with three dots that kept appearing and disappearing from her phone screen.

RAY: Today one of my regular customers gave me two tickets to a Halloween party cruise leaving from Hoboken at 9:00. Said something about not being able to make it last-minute. Do you want to go with me?

His question took her by surprise. A Halloween party on a boat?

LARIMAR: Uhh . . . come again?

She reread her text. "Come again?" Jesus. They hadn't even been on the second date.

LARIMAR: I mean, what? Not come again. That's not what I meant. I'll shut up now.

RAY: Is that a yes? 😄

She leaned her head on the couch's armrest to think. On the one hand, there was her sweet, sweet tub of peanut butter cups, and the fact that she had *just* come from Manhattan. On the other, there was an adorable man who wanted to cruise the Hudson with her, drinks in hand and surrounded by people dressed as ghosts. It was a snap decision.

LARIMAR: I'll meet you at the dock.

RAY: Are you sure? I can pick you up, you know.

LARIMAR: You would? You don't even know where I live, though.

RAY: Yep.

LARIMAR: Okay, I live in Atlantic City. See you in two hours.

RAY: Larimar, you do not live in Atlantic City!

LARIMAR: How do you know?

RAY: Brynne told me you lived in Union County.

LARIMAR: Damn it. Fiiiiiine. 8170 Covington Arms Road. Thank you.

RAY: I'll pick you up at 8:15. It'll take us about 30 minutes to get to Hoboken. And Larimar? Even if you did live in Atlantic City, I would still go pick you up. ☺

She shoved her phone between the couch cushions and squealed into a pillow until guilt gnawed at her belly. She sat up straight and tossed the pillow into an armchair. She should not be going out with him. She should not be saying he could pick her up even if she lived in Atlantic City. She should not be going on a second date with him.

The list of should-nots continued to roll in her head as she dashed into the shower and dressed all in black. She drew herself an elaborate cat-eye and slid on a cat-ear headband she still had from last Halloween. There. She was dressed up. And it was only 7:30.

It'd be another forty-five minutes before Ray got there. She thought of going downstairs, but she didn't want her parents to even suspect she was going out on Halloween night. The very first question would be "with who," and she just didn't feel like getting into it. Maybe she had time to watch a *Buffy* episode after all.

An episode later, she was jazzed and it was time for Ray to pick her up. She threw on her black puffer jacket, added a pumpkin-hued chenille scarf, and took the stairs down to the lobby. She waited in the unheated foyer, blowing little clouds out in front of her in the chilly autumn air.

An ancient Chevrolet Bel Air pulled up to the curb. It was sky blue, with shiny round headlights and perfect chrome detailing. She didn't even look to see who was driving because she didn't see Ray as the type to drive a car his grandfather's age. But then the horn beeped and her eyes shot to the driver's seat. A warm smile spread across Ray's face when he saw her waiting inside. He beckoned her with a little wave and got out of the car to open the passenger side door for her.

Her skin tingled as she double-stepped to the car. He leaned over and greeted her with a kiss on the cheek, and she leaned over to return the cheek kiss. His cheek was soft and stubbly at the same time.

"You're a cat!" he said, in a tone fitting for someone who had just discovered cats.

"Rrrrow," she replied. "And you're a—?"

He gestured to a purple wig laying on the bench seat. "Something that has a purple wig," he laughed. "That's what I had at home, so—"

"Yeah, I get it. Hence my last-minute cat costume."

He motioned to the open door and she got in. The seats were covered with a buttery-soft leather. And contrary to her assumptions upon first sight, the car smelled good inside.

She leaned back against the seat and stretched her legs in front of her, all the while feeling his gaze on her as he climbed back in the driver's seat and gunned the engine.

"Hoboken, here we come," he said as they shifted away from the curb and onto the main drag. "So, do you get a lot of clients on Halloween?"

"Huh?"

He shrugged. "I don't know. It just seems like an in-between holiday for flowers."

Oh, shit. The flowers.

"Yes, it's quiet," she said, with a vigorous nod. "Not too many people buying Halloween flowers, nope, not at all." She hoped she didn't sound as nervous as she felt.

"Where's your shop, by the way?" he asked, keeping his eyes on the road.

"M-my shop?" she asked.

"Yes. I figured you had your own shop since Brynne mentioned once that you didn't work together."

She froze. How had she not thought this through? Her heart thrummed in her chest as she thought of what to say. What was a place that was so far away, he wouldn't try to drop in on her?

Her mind jumped to Oliver and Melissa's neighborhood. "Philadelphia! It—it's in Philadelphia," she said.

Out of the corner of her eye, she could see his eyes widen. "Wow. So you drive to Philly and back every day?"

Larimar shook her head. "No. My brother lives in Philly, so I stay with him during the week and come back home on the weekend." She let out an exhale, one ounce at a time.

"Ah, okay," Ray said, his eyes still trained on the road.

Before she knew it, a wooden pier covered in twinkling lights came into view. Ray pulled into a small parking lot next to the pier and parked his Chevy in a corner spot. As Larimar opened the door, music began to stream into the car. There were about three different types of sounds, each playing on a different floor of the boat.

The boat hadn't even left the dock, and already costumed revelers were twirling and dipping aboard. Larimar and Ray exchanged a glance as he closed the car door behind her. The rails leading up to the pier were wrapped in tiny paper lanterns shaped like pumpkins. They gave off an orange glow in the chilly October night.

Larimar and Ray followed the music up the path and onto the pier. At the gate to the boat ramp, a Frankenstein lookalike greeted them and asked for their tickets. Ray handed them over and Frankenstein opened the gate to allow them to pass. The boat had three levels: the rooftop space, the main party space, and the hull.

As they ascended the ramp, Larimar felt the call of the river. The scent of it was on the breeze. It tugged at her arms and legs, inviting her to jump into the water, be with the water spirits who lived there. She took a deep breath and ignored it. She reminded herself that that water had to be about sixty degrees Fahrenheit.

The colorful horns and rhythmic drums straining from within the hull enveloped her, and she forgot about the water's song.

"Would you like a drink?" Ray asked.

"Yes. Let's see what they have," she said.

He nodded and reached for her hand, squeezing it in his. She felt the little hairs stand up on her arms. His grip was warm and solid. Their eyes met, and the corners of his mouth crinkled up into a shy smile. Larimar's breath caught in her throat. It was the first time she had seen Ray looking shy. And it was adorable.

Hand in hand, they walked over to the bar. The brushed-chrome top seemed to glow back at them. A bartender with a zebra costume leaned over the bar.

"What can I get you guys?" she asked.

Larimar glanced over the menu. "Pumpkin mojitos . . . wow. I'll try one of those," she said.

"Make that two, please," Ray said. He placed a few bills on the bar top, and they turned their backs to the bar, gazing out over the scene. All around them, couples and clusters of friends were shaking their hips and swilling their drinks.

"I'm kinda surprised no one looks seasick," Larimar said.

Ray grinned. "It could be because the boat hasn't left the dock," he said.

As if the captain was listening in on their conversation, the gears in the hull of the boat began to creak and grind, and the thrum of the engine reverberated against the backdrop of the music. The boat gave a lurch, and they began zipping through the Hudson River.

The bartender set their pumpkin mojitos on the bar, and Larimar picked up her glass and took a sip. The pumpkin was surprisingly not overpowering. There were notes of cinnamon, ginger, nutmeg, and the faintest tickle of cloves. It was delicious.

The DJ, who was dressed as a vampire, called all the eighties kids to the dance floor. He played Michael Jackson's "Thriller," and half the crowd assembled to perform the famous moves. Next was "The Time Warp" from *The Rocky Horror Picture Show*.

"Do you know any of these dances?" Larimar asked Ray.

"Maybe," he said with a sly grin.

"Come on, let's dance!" she said, pulling on his jacket sleeve.

The next song was "Cupid Shuffle." Neither of them knew the dance, but they just did a combination of boisterous moves that eventually warped into a slow-motion version of a merengue.

"I don't think this is the dance at all," Larimar laughed.

"It's definitely not," Ray said. All around them, partygoers were gyrating and knocking their knees in time to the music.

The song came to an end, and they found their way to the prow of the boat.

"Here comes the *Titanic* moment," Ray said.

Larimar shivered. "I hope you mean the 'I'm the king of the world' and not the sinking," she said, although she could swim just fine if she had to.

The next song to come on was Rancid's "Time Bomb," a boppy ska-punk number from the mid-nineties that reminded her of high school.

"Come on, this is my jam!" she said, grabbing Ray's arm and pulling him back to the dance floor.

They jumped and skipped around in time to the music, and to her surprise, Ray knew ska dancing and didn't miss a beat. They hopped up, punched the air with their fists, and reveled in the moment. When it was over, they stumbled back to the prow of the boat, out of breath and laughing.

"I'm surprised you knew that song!" Larimar said.

"I'm surprised *you* knew that song!" Ray said. The joy evident in his infectious grin made her want to squeeze him.

"I had a punk phase in high school," she said between attempts to catch her breath.

"Me too," Ray said, and his voice sounded thoughtful.

By now, Larimar's breath was becoming more shallow and even. She took a deep inhale as she processed this new information.

"How was that with your family?" she asked.

"Hard," he said with a shrug. "They didn't understand what I saw in punk, what about it could be appealing to me. Oh yeah—and then there was the time my mom had some church ladies come over to exorcise me."

"What?" Larimar asked, her mouth hanging open in disbelief.

"Yep," Ray said. "They made a circle around me and prayed. I think it was the black nail polish."

Larimar laughed out loud. "Yeah, Dominican church ladies have something against black nail polish. My mom's friends would whisper about me when they saw me with it."

Ray shook his head. "It's the evidence you've crossed over to the dark side."

They exchanged a glance and laughed together. "That's the good thing about growing up," he said.

"Kind of," Larimar replied. "I live in the same building as my parents and my abuela. They still look at me sideways when they see me with black nail polish."

A chilly breeze blustered over the river, and Larimar pulled her coat tighter around her.

Ray noticed and leaned in closer. "Can I put my arm around you?" he asked.

"Yeah, I think that would be okay," she said, allowing herself to be enveloped by the warmth of his side.

She found herself snuggling into his shoulder before reminding herself she was going to have to cut this off. With every hand squeeze and snuggle it was getting harder to keep that in mind.

Larimar dug into her purse and pulled out some of the Reese's cups she had squirreled away.

"Would you like some?" she asked Ray, holding out the spoils and waggling her fingers in his direction.

When he saw the peanut butter cups, he shrank back a bit. "No, thanks," he said.

She had never met a human who did not like peanut butter cups. "Are you allergic to peanuts?"

He shook his head.

"Well, then . . . are you an alien?"

Ray laughed and waved his hands in front of him. "No, I'm

human, I promise. I don't eat those, though."

She ran a finger along the cuff of his jacket, wondering if she should probe further.

"Why not?"

He shifted a bit in his seat, and then turned to face her, captivating her gaze. "They were my ex-wife's favorite."

"Ohh." That was not the answer she was expecting.

"Do you think differently of me now? That you know I've been divorced."

"Ray, I'm going to tell you something."

He bit his lip and leaned closer to her. "What is it?"

"I couldn't give a flying fuck."

Ray let out a heavy exhale. "Sweet." He opened his mouth as if to speak, but then closed it, and took her hand. One by one, the questions popped into her head. And one by one, she put them on the back burner for another time. The pumpkin mojitos were too good to miss a drop.

She was about to ask Ray if he wanted another one when his phone rang. He exchanged a glance with Larimar and left it in his pocket. It reached the end of the ringing cycle and Ray still didn't answer.

"Hey, do you want another—" she began to ask, but was interrupted by the beginning of a second ringing cycle.

He glanced nervously at his pocket. "Sorry, I should get this," he said.

"No worries," Larimar said, wondering if it was the ex-wife calling and that was why he didn't want to answer.

Sure enough, when he picked up the phone, she immediately

heard a woman's voice on the other line. The voice was high-pitched and sounded worried.

"Hey . . . tell me quickly. I'm on a—just tell me quickly. A what? A spider? . . . Angely, you gotta be kidding me . . . Use a shoe! You what? Alright . . . fine. I'll see what I can do. I happen to be on a boat." He hung up the phone and took a deep breath.

"Larimar. Would you mind terribly if we made a stop on the way home?"

Jesus. It seemed kind of early to be meeting his ex-wife.

"My sister has a spider in her apartment, and she's too chicken to kill it. She's deathly afraid of spiders."

His sister? Ray hadn't even mentioned that he had a sister.

"Your . . . sister? You have a sister?"

"Yep."

"Oh! Well, sure. No problem."

"Would you rather I dropped you off first? I would understand if you feel like it's kind of awkward to be meeting family and all that."

"Don't be silly!" she said.

"Do you mean it?" he said.

"If I didn't mean it, I wouldn't say it," Larimar said.

"Well . . . okay. My sister can be a bit much sometimes," he said, biting his lip.

"Don't worry. I have a brother who thinks he's God's gift to humanity. I get it."

Ray took her hand. "I look forward to hearing more about that. Thank you. Now let's grab one more mojito. Angely and the spider can stare each other down a while longer."

They pulled up to a newish apartment building. Although, to be fair, every apartment building appeared new compared to Covington Arms. The windows had brushed metal frames, and the lobby had that Pine-Sol smell. Larimar was certain the building was populated by singles in their twenties and thirties with little dogs on leashes and Yetis attached to the back of their Cherokees.

She followed Ray up the steps to a door decorated with construction paper pumpkins on the second floor. He rang the bell and a second later, a thirtyish-year-old woman with an oversized Grateful Dead T-shirt and a tubi covering her bleached-blond hair stood before them, holding a fuzzy pink slipper in one hand. Psychedelic batiks stood in as the curtains of her living room, and the shelves of the bookcase were dotted with quartz crystals and craggy geodes.

"It hasn't dared come any closer," she said, waving the slipper in the air. Her attention fell on Larimar, and all of a sudden she straightened up and lowered the shoe to her side.

Her gaze flicked from Larimar to her brother and back to Larimar again.

"Hiiii," she said in a singsong tone, leaning in to give Larimar a cheek kiss. "I'm Angely."

"She already knows you're Angely, you nut," Ray said, patting her shoulder quickly and then stepping into the apartment. "So, where's the fearsome beast?"

Angely pointed to the corner of her living room, which was decorated in shimmery shades of gold, white, and pink. "It's there," she said in a low voice full of dread.

Larimar craned her neck to see, and her eyes alighted on a small brown house spider. Despite Angely's terror, it wasn't bothering anyone. She would hate to see it killed.

"Those can't do anything to you," she said.

"What do you mean?"

"Do you have a cup and a napkin? I'll put it outside."

"A . . . what? Is this girl for real?"

Ray glared at his sister. "Just get her a cup and a napkin. Please."

Angely scowled at him, but she ducked into the kitchen and returned with the requested items. She handed them to Larimar, who crouched down in the corner, swept the spider into the cup, and walked it outside. She closed the door behind her to keep the almost-November chill from following her in.

Angely held out her arm to her. "Can I take your coat? Sorry. Now that the spider is gone, I can think more clearly. It's nice to meet you."

"Nice to meet you too," Larimar said automatically.

"Thanks, but we won't be staying, Angely. Your home is now safe. Good night."

Angely looked from Larimar to Ray and nodded slowly. "Thank you, and sorry to bother," she said. "Call me tomorrow, Ray."

"Ta 'to." He took Larimar's hand as they walked back out to the Chevy.

Later that night, Larimar cozied into her bed and pulled the blankets all the way up to her chin. She dreamt that she was running alongside the Hudson, watching a party boat from the shore. She awoke without any trace of tiredness. When she checked the time on her phone, it was 3:33. Ugh. Again. And once she turned on the bright phone screen, that was it. Sleep had flown away, as it usually did when she woke up in the middle of the night.

She sighed and sat up in bed. There was a little water bottle she kept on her night table, and she raised it to her lips and took a swig. She was awake—might as well burn her retinas a little. She tapped on the Instagram icon and began scrolling, her eyes flitting over the picture-perfect cakes, cars, and relationships.

On one account, there was a photo of a majestic oak tree against the dark of night, draped with tiny lights that looked like glowing amber pumpkins. It reminded her so much of the party boat that she wanted to send it to Ray. She clicked on the little paper airplane under the photo, then on the next screen checked the circle next to his Instagram handle, and sent. She switched off her phone and set it on the night table.

One minute later, it pinged. She rushed to open her notifications.

RAY: Just like the party boat! Love it. Thanks, Larimar ☺

Holy shit! Ray was awake.

LARIMAR: Ray! OMG I hope I didn't wake you up!

She waited, and seconds later there was a ping.

RAY: No, not at all. I can't sleep.

LARIMAR: You can't sleep tonight? Or in general?

RAY: Both.

That had to be hard. Larimar grew restless and sleepless closer to the full moon, but the remainder of the month, she was able to get a full night's rest. How did Ray function and bake without being able to sleep every night?

LARIMAR: I'm sorry. That's hard.

RAY: Eh. It's okay. I'm used to it.

LARIMAR: Has it always been like that?

RAY: Started in my Afghanistan days.

LARIMAR: Ohh.

She bit her lip and thought for a moment.

LARIMAR: What do you think about when you can't sleep?

RAY: Hmm, let's see. 80s TV shows, new cupcake recipes, mistakes I've made.

Larimar laughed out loud. The sound rang like bells through her apartment.

LARIMAR: Oh, okay. Some light early-morning thinking.

RAY: Yep. How about you?

Her heart dropped a few inches in her chest. The true

answer—bills, how to get back at Oliver for demolishing her Barbie Dreamhouse when she was eight years old, and how to not get found out as a ciguapa—would not do.

LARIMAR: Um . . . I think about the ska punk shows I went to in high school and relive those moments. They were some of the best.

RAY:

She was surprised to feel herself getting sleepy.

LARIMAR: Alright, I'm going to turn in for the night. Speak to you soon?

RAY: Text you tomorrow.

Squee! ☺ ☺ 😄

The following Wednesday, Larimar walked down the darkened hallway of the Iglesia Hispana, feeling slightly creeped out. It needed to be a brighter in these halls. It felt like a wayward usher could jump-scare her at any moment. She exhaled in relief when she stepped into the brightened meeting salon. Anairis, Miguelina, and the other women were already seated on the metal chairs.

Larimar chose a chair and reached out her hand to brush away something that looked like shiny glitter on top of the seat.

"Hi, Larimar! Oh, sorry about that. There was a Halloween party in here this past weekend, and the kids must have left glitter on the chairs."

"Oh! Ta'to," she said, taking a seat. When she turned her hand over, it was covered in tiny glittering pumpkins. Just like the glowing pumpkins from the Halloween party boat. Ray's delight at discovering them came to mind, and she gave a happy little sigh. He was so . . . sigh.

Anairis stood in the center of the circle to update the group on the treatments she'd tried since the last meeting. Larimar caught every fifth word. In her mind, she was back on the party boat. They were twirling on deck, and the warmth of Ray's hand was radiating into her body.

Nobody seemed to notice she was on another planet, and that was okay with her, until she caught the words, "and for that reason, we will be changing the meeting schedule by two weeks. You know, to rake in some full-moon magic," Anairis said with a wink. Larimar snapped to attention. What?

She raised her hand, and Anairis turned to her with a kind smile. "Yes, honey?"

"Uh, why the change?" Larimar asked.

"We took a survey in the Facebook group, and there are more members who would like to join but can't make it on the current schedule."

"Ah," Larimar said, forcing herself to nod along weakly, although her heart was sinking. The rest of the group smiled and nodded to the news of the change. They did not appear to object.

The schedule change set the next meeting square on the full moon. Her hair would be straight, and there wasn't much she could do about it. Besides curl it. But she had never had to curl her hair before. It seemed like a hell of a lot of work.

The other choice would be missing the group. But she was making *friends*, and she really felt like she was making progress with her hair. Helplessness rose up in her throat and threatened to choke her. Would she just keep going through this until she finally accepted being alone?

The rest of the meeting breezed by, leaving Larimar in a daze.

"Hey, Larimar, you okay?" Miguelina asked at the beginning of social hour.

"Yes, I'm fine," Larimar said.

"You want a coffee?" Miguelina asked. "I'm going to get one for myself anyway."

"Uh, sure."

Miguelina got up and came back with two cortaditos. She passed Larimar the cup with a kind smile.

Larimar hardened her resolve. She would come back and keep attending the meetings, even if she had to curl her hair.

PUMPKIN-SPICED RUM CUPCAKES

Makes 16 cupcakes

FOR THE CUPCAKES

¾ cup granulated sugar

½ cup/1 stick unsalted butter, at room temperature

2 large eggs

1 (15-ounce) can pumpkin puree

2 teaspoons dark rum

1⅔ cups all-purpose flour

1½ teaspoons baking powder

¼ teaspoon salt

½ teaspoon pumpkin pie spice

FOR THE FROSTING

1½ cups unsalted butter, at room temperature

2½ cups confectioners' sugar

1 tablespoon dark rum

¼ teaspoon pumpkin pie spice

Make the cupcakes: Preheat the oven to 325 degrees Fahrenheit.

In the bowl of a stand mixer, cream together the sugar and butter. Add the eggs. In a separate bowl, sift the flour, baking powder, and salt. Combine the two bowls and mix well, until there are no lumps. Fill the cupcake liners two-thirds full and bake for 20 minutes. Allow to cool completely on a wire rack.

Make the frosting: In the bowl of a stand mixer, beat

together the butter and confectioner's sugar for 4 minutes. Add the rum and spice and mix until evenly blended.

13

"Oliver! You look just like you're about to give a merengue concert in 1997," Larimar said, showing her brother and Melissa into Doña Bélgica's apartment. They wiped their feet on the macrame welcome mat and handed her their coats.

Oliver replied with a playful tap on her shoulder. "Watch it, sis. I don't want to have to fight anybody on my birthday."

She shoved him back, and then reached out to squeeze Melissa's hand. "Great to see you again, Melissa," she said.

Melissa returned the hand squeeze. "Great to see you too."

Doña Bélgica came out of the kitchen to greet her younger visitors. "Perfecto! You're all here. Now come peel some plátanos for the sancocho." She beckoned them into the kitchen and passed them each a crisp cotton apron. Oliver pulled his over his head and Melissa tied the strings for him, then he did the same for her.

Doña Bélgica divided up the piles of plátanos and root vegetables on her wooden kitchen table. She gave the plátanos to Oliver, the squash to Melissa, and the yuca to Larimar. In front of each of them was a melamine cutting board and a steel knife. She had already begun to brown the meat for the stew, and the sizzling vittles filled the apartment with a savory aroma.

Oliver pulled up a bachata playlist on his phone and connected to the mini portable speaker he had brought.

"Sorry, Larimar. No headbangers," he said.

"Whatever," she said, rolling her eyes.

They fell into companionable silence swaying to the tropical rhythms of the music, and while they worked, Larimar thought of Ray and their Halloween party boat date.

He was so funny, warm, and sweet. She'd had a wonderful time with him. The pumpkin mojitos and wacky music had only been icing on the cake.

She cut the long yuca roots into sizable chunks, then ran the knife under their skin to peel them. His bakery was excellent too, and she knew how much it meant to him. There had to be something she could do to help him compete against Beacon, even if she was simultaneously helping Beacon open its doors. Ugh . . . when she put it that way, it sounded terrible.

"Larimar, get some onions from the bottom of the pantry, will you, hija?" Doña Bélgica called to her. She sprang up, grateful for a distraction, and grabbed some round red onions from the bottom of her abuela's pantry.

"Do you need me to cut them for you, too, Mamá?" Larimar was about to ask, but then she remembered Doña Bélgica's favorite saying: "Lo que se ve no se pregunta." That which is visible does not need to be asked. She laid the onions on her cutting board, peeled back their papery skins, and began to slice them in thin rounds.

"Oh!" She had cut two slices before she remembered the candle trick she had seen in *Chocolate*, a Korean drama on Netflix. She struck a match and lit the small white votive in the center of the table. When she returned to cutting the onions, she was pleased to find that her eyes did not even begin to water.

"Gracias, hija!" Doña Bélgica swooped in and scooped up the sliced onions, adding them to the base she was sautéing for the chicken.

Oliver and Melissa had finished prepping the other ingredients. They passed them, cut into cubes and piled into Tupperware containers, to Doña Bélgica, and in turn she handed them some fresh coffee she had just poured out of the percolator. Oliver leaned back in his kitchen chair, and Melissa rested her head on his shoulder.

Seeing them together made Larimar think of Ray. She started by recalling the cruise and eventually her thoughts landed on his bakery. An idea hatched for her to give Ray some tips to help make his business better. He didn't have to know they came straight from the Beacon manual. And not all of them would. Some of them would come directly from her ten-plus years of experience as a brand manager for a major bakery chain.

If his business flourished in its own right, it would matter less that Beacon was right down the block and across the street. And they also had different target markets. Those seeking artisan baked goods were not going to find what they were looking for at Beacon, no matter what their painstakingly written marketing copy said.

She would pay him one more visit, a final one before extracting herself from his life. As she thought it, she knew she was lying to herself. It was not going to be that easy for her to stay away from him. Only something like having him find out she was a full-moon ciguapa and running away screaming could kill the tiny but growing torch she was carrying for Ray.

"Aha! You come to help your abuela and all you do is sit and daydream! Qué muchacha más jaragana, what a lazy girl, Jesús Santísimo."

Larimar didn't even have to turn around to know who was addressing her. "'Cion, Mami. We already cut everything up."

Oliver shifted out of his seat to stand and greet his mother with a cheek kiss. "Yeah, ma. Larimar did a lot. Take it easy on her."

Doña Berenice gazed at her son, and Larimar could almost see her eyes morph into hearts. "If you say so, Oli. Japi verde, my precious and only son." She enfolded him in a bone-crushing hug.

"Excuse me, I think I just threw up in my mouth a little," Larimar said under her breath, and Melissa shot her a conspiratorial smile. She knew her boyfriend was a mama's boy. How she was okay with that, Larimar had no idea, but she seemed to be managing, so more power to her.

By then, all the meats had been browned, and the water for the sancocho had been brought to a boil. At Doña Bélgica's signal, Larimar added the ingredients to the water and covered the pot with its sizable lid.

Larimar filled another pot with water for the rice, which Oliver was rinsing in the sink.

"Where's Papá, Mami?" Oliver asked their mother.

Doña Berenice raised her eyes heavenward. "That man is still getting dressed. Would you believe it? He takes longer than me." In the forty years they had been married, she still had not come to terms with this fact.

"Ay Berenice, tú sí jodes," Doña Bélgica said with a sigh. In the sixty-two years she had been Berenice's mother, she still had not become immune to her daughter's penchant for melodrama.

A pigeon perched on the fire escape outside Doña Bélgica's apartment, and Larimar watched it preen to its reflection in the glass. She had a sudden desire to bolt from under her mother's watchful eye.

"I'll be right back," she said, grabbing her black puffer coat.

"But muchacha, the rice is not even ready!" Berenice said.

"I'll put it in," Doña Bélgica said, throwing Larimar a wink.

Once down on the street, Larimar sucked in a breath of fresh air and let the choppy November breeze wash over her face. She loved her mother, but sometimes she needed to be in her own space. In times like these, she was grateful for having had the foresight to get her own apartment, even if she was in the same building.

She did a brisk thirty-minute walk around town, and by the time she rode the elevator back to her abuela's apartment, the sancocho was almost ready. That was when she remembered . . .

"Holy shit, bro, we didn't get you a cake!"

Oliver made a dramatic show of draping his forearm over his forehead. "I knew you guys didn't love me."

"That's beside the point," she said. She glanced at her watch. Not like the time mattered, anyway. Her family would wait for the cake.

"Where are you going to get it from, hija?" Doña Bélgica asked, and as the answer popped into her head, she rejoiced and regretted it all at the same time.

"There's a bakery I know not too far from here. They should be open at this time on a Sunday."

14

"You could just get one from Carvel, you know," she told herself as she drove down the busy roads that led to Borrachitos. Maybe this would be a good time to tell Ray she couldn't continue to see him. She sighed and let her shoulder blades drop. Who was she kidding? The best she could do at this point was help him, and let nature take its course. Nevermind Beacon, there was no way he would want to stay with her after finding out she was a ciguapa. The end was bad anyway, so why did she have to hasten it?

Without remembering the drive, she arrived at Borrachitos and parked right outside. She blasted through the door and found several customers cozied around the round tables, sipping fragrant coffee and taking hearty bites of their muffins. Behind the counter, there was an older woman at Ray's side, assisting him with piping turquoise frosting on some vanilla cupcakes.

She came to a full stop at the counter and remained silent, waiting for Ray to notice her. He was intent on making a spiral with the turquoise buttercream. The woman did notice her, though, and she looked her up and down, finishing her off with a stone-cold glare. The longer she rested her glance on Larimar, the more her eyes began to bulge and her nostrils started to flare.

Yikes. With an expression like that, she could double as Ray's security guard.

Larimar had no choice but to break the awkward, tense silence. "Hello, there!" she said in a voice she hoped sounded sprightly.

As soon as her voice echoed across the counter, a luminous smile spread across Ray's face.

"Larimar! I was just thinking about you."

She could feel a blush creeping up to her cheeks. "Oh, why, I—"

Ray nudged the arm of the woman at his side. "Doña Delfina, this is the one I was telling you about. This is Larimar." Larimar stuck out her hand to the woman.

Doña Delfina eyed her again, and her nostrils flared anew. If Larimar could check out her arms, she would guess that the little hairs were standing up. But why? Could she tell something was different about Larimar?

A moment passed, and Doña Delfina did not respond or return the greeting. Ray glanced from one woman to the other.

"Uh . . . do you know one another?"

Larimar began to shake her head when Doña Delfina spoke up. "No! No, we do not. Larimar, pleased to make your acquaintance," she said, without extending her hand.

Larimar took a deep breath and rested her hand at her side. It was not the first time someone had snubbed her for a handshake, and it probably would not be the last. When she glanced back up again, the older woman was staring at her feet.

"Doña Delfina is my mother's best friend. I mean, was."

"Oh," Larimar said softly. "I'm sorry. About your mom."

"Both his parents are dead," Doña Delfina snapped.

Jesus Christ! What was wrong with this lady? It would probably be best to get her cake and haul ass. Save the questions for Ray when Sergeant Scowl was not around.

"I'm so sorry to hear that," Larimar said. "Ray, if you want to talk about it sometime, I am here."

"Thanks," said Ray, and he looked genuinely grateful. He seemed to understand that she didn't want to get into much around his hostile helper. "So, what brings you in today?" he asked.

"I need a cake," she said. "It's my brother's birthday." Her eyes scanned the offerings behind the glass and alighted on a tray of cupcakes with perfect tufts of fluffy turquoise frosting.

"What kind of cupcakes are these?" she asked.

Unless the lights were terribly off, she could swear she saw a blush creeping up to his cheeks this time around. "They're vanilla with coconut rum. I called them the . . . um . . ."

His eyes strayed to the wood-framed blackboard in front of the counter. It read,

TODAY'S SPECIAL! THE LARIMAR. VANILLA WITH COCONUT-RUM FROSTING.

Without thinking, she clapped her hands to her mouth to cover her smile. Not even the fuming of his hostile helper could break this moment for her.

"They're beautiful," she finally said. "But I think my family's had enough of me. What kind of cakes do you have for today?"

His wide grin was melting her heart. "I have a vanilla with

raspberry filling and a chocolate marble with Oreo filling in the back."

"Ooh. The second one is so much closer to what I would like, but Oliver hates chocolate. I'll take the first one."

"Sure," he said. "So, 'Happy Birthday Oliver'?"

She nodded. "Yeah. It must fit better on the cake than 'Happy Birthday, You Annoying Fuckface.'"

Ray's laughter echoed throughout the bakery, and even a few customers looked up and grinned. Doña Delfina cleared her throat, her impatience reverberating through the space.

Ray regarded her and began to open his mouth to say something, then seemed to think better of it and shook his head. "I'll get it."

He returned with a two-tiered cake with pristine white frosting, bearing the birthday message in olive-green gel.

"It's so beautiful, I almost don't want to put it in a box," Larimar said.

"So leave it out of the box and see how that goes on the drive home." Doña Delfina snorted.

God, what was wrong with this woman? Ray ignored her and packaged the cake in a white bakery box, which he tied with red twine and then placed in a large white paper bag with handles.

Larimar decided to take the high road, and then dig for information later. "Doña Delfina, it has been an absolute pleasure meeting you." She couldn't help but leave her with a zing of sarcasm. "Ray, thank you so much. This cake is perfect, and I'll call you later tonight after the party."

"Sounds great," Ray said. "And Larimar? Enjoy," he said,

looking pointedly at the bag.

"Thanks," she said, and gave him her sweetest smile. Hostile helper would have no choice but to eat it all up.

She took the bag, which felt heavier than she expected, and walked out to her car. She came around the passenger side to set the box at the bottom of the front seat, when something blue from within caught her eye.

No, he didn't. Besides the cake, Ray had also gifted her a dozen of the Larimar cupcakes.

"Ahhh, Ray, why are you so cute? Why do you exist to torment me?" she wondered aloud as she ran her fingers over the glossy cardboard box.

THE LARIMAR VANILLA CUPCAKE WITH TURQUOISE COCONUT RUM-INFUSED FROSTING

Makes 16 cupcakes

FOR THE CUPCAKES

¾ cup granulated sugar

½ cup unsalted butter, at room temperature

2 large eggs

⅔ cup whole milk

2 teaspoons vanilla extract

1⅔ cups all-purpose flour

1½ teaspoons baking powder

¼ teaspoon salt

FOR THE FROSTING

1½ cups/3 sticks unsalted butter, at room temperature

2½ cups confectioners' sugar

1 tablespoon coconut rum

5 to 6 drops blue food coloring

3 drops green food coloring

Make the cupcakes: Preheat the oven to 325 degrees Fahrenheit. Prepare cupcake pans with cupcake liners.

In the bowl of a stand mixer, cream together the sugar and butter. Add the eggs, milk, and vanilla, and beat to combine.

In a separate small bowl, sift the flour, baking powder, and salt. Add the dry ingredients to the batter, mixing until there are no lumps.

Fill the cupcake liners two-thirds full and bake for 20 minutes. Allow to cool completely on a wire rack.

Make the frosting: In the bowl of a stand mixer, beat together the butter and confectioner's sugar for 4 minutes. Add the coconut rum and mix to combine. Add the food coloring and mix until the colors are evenly blended in and your desired shade of blue is achieved. Frost the cupcakes once cool.

15

At the office the following Monday, Larimar kicked her heels up on her desk. She twirled a crystal-studded pen in circles with her fingers, looking down at the report in her hands. According to Mr. Gerges, all the fixtures for Beacon were ready. She should've been relieved and thrilled, but instead she just felt uneasy.

She clicked on her email to find Ms. Beacon's missive.

FROM: Regina Beacon
TO: Larimar Cintrón
SUBJECT: BEACON UNION!

Good morning Larimar,
Did you see the great news from Mr. Gerges? You know what this means. Please draw up an ingredient and paper product order. And have you already contacted our hiring partner so they can start placing ads?
Thank you!
R. Beacon

Her stomach sank to new levels. She wasn't going to be able

to stall for much longer.

She took a deep breath and poised her fingers above her keyboard.

FROM: Larimar Cintrón
TO: Regina Beacon
SUBJECT: Re: BEACON UNION!

Hi Ms. Beacon,
Yes, I saw the news. Will get right on it.
Larimar

Stretching her arms above her head, she stood up from her desk and walked to the office kitchen. She made herself a coffee, almost spilling it on her silk blouse as she thought about Ray and Borrachitos.

When she came back, she had a new email from Ms. Beacon.

FROM: Regina Beacon
TO: Larimar Cintrón
SUBJECT: Re: BEACON UNION!

Hi Larimar,
That's it? Where's your passion for the project?

She bit her lip. What was she supposed to say? *Sorry, it started out cool but now it's threatening the livelihood of the cute and thoughtful man I'm dating?*

FROM: Larimar Cintrón
TO: Regina Beacon
SUBJECT: Re: BEACON UNION!

Oh, it's right here! You will see.

What a lackluster answer. She cringed as she imagined Ms. Beacon reading her email. Thankfully, her office wasn't visible from hers.

And that was perfect for moments like this, when she had to text her friends at work.

She pulled her phone out of her black studded tote and began typing out a text to Brynne.

LARIMAR: The new Beacon location is ready to receive supplies. I think I need to start coaching Ray, like we discussed.

She set her phone down on her desk and took a few sips of coffee. She preferred drinking black coffee at work, mostly because the office manager bought ten different kinds of alternative "milks" and no plain-old cow's milk. The closer she got to the full moon, the more she craved cow's milk. Full-fat and delicious. But that just wasn't an option at work.

She stood and did a brisk lap around the office. When she came back to her desk, she found a reply from Brynne.

BRYNNE: Just go for it, grrl. Like you said: asked and answered. We talked about it and you know what you need to do. I support this plan, and I support you. Love you.

Larimar smiled. What would she do without a friend like Brynne?

LARIMAR: You're the best and idk what I would do without you. Now I just have to figure out which casual moment is the best for me to slip in my florist's bakery advice.

She ended her text with a tiny monkey-hands-covering-eyes emoji. Come to think of it, she and Ray hadn't agreed on a next time to see each other. Yes, it had only been one day since she had seen him, but . . . oh. That was her conversation starter. She hadn't yet complimented the cake. Well, that would be easy. Her family had scarfed it down in five seconds flat. And the cupcakes had been next. Melissa had even taken a couple for her parents.

She stuck her phone under her desk in case anyone was watching and opened a new text.

Why did she suddenly feel shy? It was just a text message, for God's sake.

LARIMAR: Hii Ray. The cake was amazing. Muchas gracias. And the cupcakes . . . I don't even know what to say. I'm touched.

She stared at the screen until the little bubble with three dots appeared.

RAY: My pleasure, Larimar. Thanks for the inspiration ♡

He sent a heart! He sent a heart. Why did she feel like she was twelve again? Another bubble popped up on her screen.

RAY: When can I see you again?

She stared at her phone. There had to be something she could say besides "today."
And then he kept writing.

RAY: Oh, wait! Secret show Thursday night at The Stone Pumpkin. 10 pm. 108 Bear St. Roselle Park. Join me?

Ten on a work night. Damn. It was also the full moon; she would be in ciguapa mode. Fuck my life, fuck my life, she chanted to herself. At the same time, there was a part of her that couldn't pass up the opportunity to go to a secret punk show with Ray, no matter how uncomfortable it would be for her.

LARIMAR: Hmm. 10 pm on a work night. Will you think I'm irresponsible if I take you up on it?
RAY: I would think you're irresponsible if you didn't take me up on it Just kidding! 😜

Larimar switched off the phone screen and leaned back in her chair. What was happening?

16

Two days later, Larimar walked into her apartment and tossed her black leather purse onto the kitchen table. The train ride had taken about an hour longer than she expected, thanks to a faulty switch on the train. She had watched an episode of *Absurd Planet* and still ended up with time to organize all the email folders on her phone.

She poured herself a glass of water and settled into one of her wicker kitchen chairs. It was chilly in the apartment, so she moved to her couch and covered her legs with a camel-colored crocheted blanket. It had been a gift from Hale Kimberlin, a boyfriend she had broken up with two years ago after dating for three months.

Hale was a pretty white boy she'd met at a food service industry convention. He had blond hair that was so light, she was afraid it would glow in the dark (it didn't). He had complimented Larimar's curls, and the conversation had gone from there. They had lots of laughs and got along well enough between the sheets, but then when she told him she needed a weekend off during her ciguapa days, he showed up at her house anyway, and that made her blood boil. There was nothing that made her angrier than telling a man her boundaries and having him try to get around them.

She was starting to get agita in her chest just remembering him when her phone buzzed with a text.

RAY: The Larimar cupcakes were a hit at the bakery! Gonna make them again tonight. Wanna learn how I do it? Thursday feels like forever from now ☺

Her breath caught in her throat. Once she could breathe again, she considered this proposition. Baking, alone, with Ray. Her and Ray, alone in his place of business. Just the two of them. Feeling the air crackle with electricity between them. Seeing him do what he loved. Watching his long eyelashes dust his cheeks as he melded butter and sugar . . . wait. Butter.

LARIMAR: Sure.

She was tired and achy from the extended commute, but that was not going to stop her from getting some Ray time and some butter. Mixed with sugar . . . Heaven.

She didn't even bother changing out of her work clothes, a burgundy cashmere sweater, fitted black pants, and black leather booties with suede ankle tassels. On the car ride over, she cranked up the Sublime radio station and hummed along. It would be interesting to see what kind of food coloring he used to make that bright turquoise frosting.

When she arrived at Borrachitos, the front door was locked.

She started to pull out her phone, but instead let it fall back into her pocket and knocked on the glass. The lights were halfway on, and the star lanterns that hung from the ceiling turned idly from side to side. There was a distant jingling, and after a moment, Ray appeared in the aisle that ran from the serving counter to the door, coming toward her, keys in hand.

When he reached the door, he stopped and regarded her through the glass, and she held his gaze. Her eyes focused on his tousled chocolate-brown curls, and then his bottomless eyes. They stayed this way, studying each other for a moment, until Ray gave his shoulders a gentle shake and unlocked the door.

"H-hey," he said.

"Hi," she said.

Her eyes came to rest on his full lips. She had never noticed how bitable the bottom one was. She had to say something, fast.

"Um, are you going to let me in?" she said.

That was enough to bring him back to the here and now. "Ay Dio' mio, I'm sorry. I—yes. Please. Come in." He moved out of her way and gave her full berth to enter the bakery.

"Thanks," she said, and swiped right past him on her way in. Their arms brushed as she did, and little tingles coursed up and down her body. She followed him through the familiar cozy space, behind the marble slab counter and into the prep kitchen.

Larimar set her purse on one of the wire chairs, and then gestured to the stainless steel prep table in the center of the kitchen. "May I?" she said.

"Please," he said, and ushered her behind the counter with a flourish.

She surveyed the small bowls of butter, sugar, eggs, and flour that were set up there.

"Okay, so where do we start? It looks like you're just beginning."

"That's right. So the first thing we'll need is the stand mixer, which I brought out for this small batch. Oh, damn. I left the attachment in the closet. I'll be back in one sec, Larimar," he said, his face apologetic.

Larimar waved away his worries with her hands. "It's okay," she said. He ducked into the closet, while she used a butter knife to nab a thin slice of butter and slide it into her mouth.

"Ahh," she sighed as she felt a sense of calm come over her. Never failed to do the trick.

Ray came back then, bearing the attachment for the stand mixer.

"Found it!" he said.

She swallowed the butter as fast as she could and turned to him, trying to keep her expression neutral instead of showing off the goofy grin that was threatening to make its appearance.

Ray attached the whisk attachment to the mixer and pulled out two cloth squares from the shelf space under the table top, handing her one.

"Here," he said.

Larimar shook it and it unfolded, strings and all. "An apron?" she asked.

Ray nodded. "Flour is going to be flying in a minute. I wouldn't want your nice clothes to get dirty."

Ooh, he'd said her clothes were nice. He touched her again

as he leaned over to bring the vanilla extract and rum closer to the mixer.

"Music?" he asked.

"Of course!" she said, her face lighting up. "Where do you play it?"

"My speaker shows up as BORR-878. You can connect to it on Bluetooth if you have something you want to play."

"Say no more," she said. She scoured the playlists in her phone and settled on one that seemed to fit the moment. With a click, she sent it to the speaker, and ambient grooves streamed into the bakery.

"I like this," Ray said, starting to bop in time to the music.

She swayed in place too, and felt herself shifting into a more sensuous mood.

"Okay, so where do we begin?" she asked, glancing over the collection of ingredients.

He picked up the butter and dropped it into the mixer, and then followed by pouring in the sugar.

"First, we cream the butter and sugar," he said. She watched, mesmerized, as the whisk churned circles in the bowl of the mixer.

The gritty sugar and chunks of smooth butter swirled together to become one uniform and delicious-looking mixture.

"What comes next?" she asked, following his every move with rapt attention.

"Next, we add the vanilla, and the rum . . . the rest of the wet ingredients, really."

"Okay. Can I pass you the eggs, then?"

"Yes, please."

Larimar picked up the bowl with the three eggs and held it out in Ray's direction, and he reached out to take it from her. His hand molded to hers, a gentle and unassuming caress that once again sent tiny shivers up and down her body.

"Do you want to crack them?" he asked.

"Sure."

She cracked the first egg using the sharp edge of the table, and dumped its contents into the mixing bowl.

He reached for the vanilla, and all of a sudden, in her mind they were in *Ghost*: The Bakery Version. She was standing at the marble counter, mixing ingredients in a bowl with a wire whisk (which was funny, because Ray didn't even have one of those), and Ray was standing behind her, the length of his body pressed flush against her back.

As she mixed the batter, he curved into the space where her neck met her shoulders, and planted scorching kisses there. His hands ran down the length of her arms, molding to them—

"Um, Larimar?"

His measured voice shattered her sexy reverie.

"Huh?" Intelligent conversation was far, far away.

"Um, you just dropped a whole egg into the mixer." His face was neutral, but sparks of amusement glittered in his eyes.

Immediately her hand flew to her mouth. "Anda la mierda," she said. She had gotten so caught up in her fantasy of Ray pushing up on her at the bakery counter that she had forgotten she was cracking eggs. Her cheeks flamed with a mortified blush.

"I am so sorry," she said.

"It's okay," Ray said, patting her shoulder.

"But all that butter . . . and sugar. It's wasted now," she said. Tears of shame pricked at her eyes. She hated wasting food; she had been raised to avoid it at all costs.

He looked into her eyes, and his expression was soft and open. "Larimar . . . you forget I'm a baker. There's more where that came from," he said. "It's no big deal."

"Are you sure?" she asked.

"Sure. Now come on. Let's get some more eggs from the refrigerator. I actually have some more room-temperature butter over there," he said, motioning to a smaller round table. She followed him back into the kitchen and he led her to a large metal refrigerator. It did not appear new by any stretch of the imagination, but it was obviously clean and well-maintained.

He opened it, and she was wowed by how everything fit into its own little nook.

"My mom would cry tears of joy if she saw this," Larimar said. "After she finished beating me over the head asking why mine doesn't look like this."

Ray gave a little chuckle. "I have to keep it this way," he said. "Makes it easier to give instructions. I used my experience working in the Army supply room to organize this fridge," he said.

"It shows," Larimar said.

He handed her one egg and this time, she led the way back to the stainless-steel table where they had been working.

"Okay," she said, taking a deep inhale and letting it go one ounce at a time. "Ready to focus. No eggshells in the batter."

A lopsided grin spread across Ray's face. "Sounds good. And,

Larimar?"

"Hm?"

"If it's not terribly rude, can I ask what you were thinking about when you dropped the egg in the batter?"

The traitorous flush crept over her face again.

"No," she said bluntly.

Ray nodded. To his credit and Larimar's relief, he did not press her for more details, but rather slid the butter over and started slicing it into squares. An awkward silence hung in the air. She took a spot alongside him, picked up the butter squares, and started adding them to the mixer. When she looked over at him sideways, he was grinning.

Before Larimar knew it, the batter was ready to be poured into the paper-lined cupcake tins. She doled out the individual portions into the tins, then Ray popped the trays into the oven, which he had preheated before she got to Borrachitos.

He pulled up a chair for her and set it across from the oven, then sat down in another.

"You know, Ray, there's something I wanted to mention to you," she said.

"I'm all ears."

"Well, it's just that the quality of your products is excellent," she said.

"Thanks," he replied in a casual tone.

"It's not just an idle compliment," she said. "My point is that they're so good, they should be reaching more people."

Ray cocked his head sideways and studied her, brushing a chocolate-colored curl off his forehead.

"What do you mean?"

"I mean when I go to, say, Philadelphia, I want to see people buying and eating your cupcakes."

"Oh. You mean like when you go to your flower shop? Ah! Maybe we can do a collab at some point," he said, his face growing animated.

Uh-oh. "Um, yes. That could be a future possibility. But for now, what I'm trying to say is that these are too good to stay in Union, and they are too high-quality for people to be passing them up."

"You mean like if they pass them up to go to one of those big, nasty corporate bakeries?"

Her breath caught in her throat. "That's exactly what I mean, Ray," she said in a low, somber tone.

His eyes widened and for a minute they just stared at each other. "Well, that got serious," he said.

She stuck her tongue out at him, hoping to lighten the mood. And distract from where the conversation had the potential to go.

"All I'm saying is that I think you should make some moves. Think of selling some of your products at other locations, or packaging them. Promote your bakery more on social media. Your stuff is incredible, but I'm not convinced anyone outside of Union County knows about this place."

Ray looked thoughtful, and slowly nodded. It was like she could see the wheels turning in his mind.

"Thanks for that," he said. "You have a smart point, and I'm going to give it some real thought."

"Good," she said. "I hope so."

"Come on," he said. "Let's make the frosting while we wait for the cupcakes to bake."

She nodded in assent. The frosting proved to be easy to mix up; all they needed to do was cream the butter and add the confectioners' sugar one cup at a time. She enjoyed pouring in the shots of rum at the end.

They cleaned the workspace as they waited for the baked cupcakes to cool, and then one by one they frosted them together. And then, they were done. A dozen robin's-egg-blue cupcakes stood on a crystal platform, crowned in perfect swirls of buttercream. If only Ray knew she could eat them all and keep going.

She inhaled their scent with an appreciative sigh, and to her surprise, Ray rested his hand on hers. She glanced sideways at him, and her gaze fell on his lips.

"Great teamwork," he said.

It would be easy for her to lean into him and let their lips touch. It'd only take a few seconds, and it wasn't too far of a distance to go. He gazed at her, seemingly trying to read her eyes, searching for a signal that it was okay to kiss her.

But Larimar froze. She couldn't give any signals. Kissing him would mean she was moving forward with this, and she knew that wasn't possible.

She opted instead to give him a friendly pat on the hand.

"Yes, absolutely. We did good," she said.

Ray looked down at the cupcakes, his lashes dusting his cheeks. Something flashed across his face before he hid it carefully away.

"Well, let me box these up for you, then," he said.

Just then, Ray's phone began to ring. He glanced at the screen and groaned. "Angely Concepción, you do have a sixth sense." He struck the "talk" button with a heavy finger.

"Yes, Angely?"

Larimar chuckled to herself. His sister did seem to have spot-on timing for breaking up the most charged moments. Maybe that was good. Maybe Larimar should be appreciating that about her instead of pining for the moment that had just passed. Lost in her thoughts, she missed most of the conversation and was only brought back to the present when Ray nudged her arm.

He wore a chagrined expression. "As you can guess, that was Angely. She . . ." he sighed. "She feels bad about interrupting our date the other day and wanted to invite us to meet up with her for drinks. On her."

Hmm. So far, that sounded acceptable. "When?" Larimar asked.

Ray grinned. "Um, how's now?" he asked.

Shock colored Larimar's face. "Right now?"

He shrugged. "If you're free."

She wasn't sure how hanging out with Angely would go, but another couple hours with Ray suited her fine. And besides, her first meeting with Angely had taken place in the throes of a spider attack. Larimar may not have been afraid of spiders, but ever since a frog scared the daylights out of her in the woods one day, she had an irrational and immobilizing fear of them. She couldn't imagine what another person would think of her if they met her during the terrifying moments she was facing one of the green menaces. She could stand to give Angely another chance.

Larimar reached out and took both of Ray's hands. "Yes. You driving?"

17

Angely had suggested La Posada, a Mexican restaurant in the suburban hamlet of Maplewood. It was not a place Larimar hung out in often, but she knew it well enough. It was only ten minutes from Union, and it felt like they got there in a flash. They parked out front, and Larimar couldn't help but notice the twinkle of the stars against the dark night above the trees.

They found Angely already seated at a rectangular table all the way in the back. She waved at them as they approached.

"Hey, Angely," Larimar said.

Angely had braided her hair around her head in a halo and wore a sapphire-blue sweater with tiny gold threads. Blue crystal door-knocker earrings swung from her ears as she waved, and an armful of bangles clattered with the movement.

"Qué lo qué, manita," Ray said. He pulled out a black wrought-iron chair for Larimar, then for himself. A tiny votive inside a glass holder flickered in the center of the table.

Angely looked from Ray to Larimar and then back again. "Thank you both for coming out on such short notice," she said with a shy smile in Larimar's direction. Her attitude was definitely more subdued than the night of the spider.

"All good," Ray said, leaning back in his chair and plucking a tortilla chip from the basket next to the tealight.

The three of them pored over the drink menu in silence. There were margaritas, tequila shots, and daiquiris. Larimar had never been much of a tequila drinker, but she could work with a passionfruit daiquiri.

The waiter came to a stop in front of their table. "What can I get you folks tonight?" he asked.

"I'll have the passionfruit daiquiri," Larimar said.

Ray smiled as if appraising her choice. "I'll have a Moscow mule with extra ginger," he said.

"Cool," Angely said.

The waiter turned to Angely.

"I'll have the cactus-water margarita, half-sweet, no cayenne pepper," she said.

Larimar thought to ask Angely if she came to La Posada often, but she held her tongue.

"How's the bakery, Ray?" Angely asked.

Ray took another tortilla chip. "Going well. Larimar has been giving me some great ideas I'm looking forward to working with," he said, glancing in Larimar's direction.

Larimar smiled back and focused her gaze on Angely, hoping she would not ask for more details.

"Cool," Angely said. Her eyes alit on Larimar's ring. "Ooh, lapis lazuli! It's one of my favorite stones. Did you know it has healing properties?"

Larimar nodded slowly. "Yes, I did."

"Good, cause—" Angely launched into an explanation of

where to find lapis lazuli and what it could do for the wearer. "Of course, you know, Larimar is a stone as well. Endemic to the Dominican Republic. You're Dominican, right?"

Larimar nodded. "Yeah. Dominican American. I was born here in Jersey. My dad has been here for a bazillion years, and my mom, too, actually."

"Don't say 'cool,' Ange," Ray said, and Angely kicked him under the table.

"That's not very nonviolent of you," he said, and she rolled her eyes.

"Hey. Yo soy de paz. I am of peace," Angely shot back.

At this, Angely and Ray broke out into a rolling laugh at the same moment.

Larimar glanced quizzically from one to the other.

"Our dad used to say that all the time," Angely explained.

"Yeah, and usually when he wasn't doing something too peaceful, like killing a fly, or throwing the neighbor's wandering trash back into their yard," Ray mused with a mischievous grin.

The waiter brought their drinks to the table. They clinked their glasses together in the name of health and took hearty sips. The daiquiri tasted a little less like passionfruit than Larimar would have liked, but otherwise it was passable.

It occurred to Larimar that this was as good a time as any to ask about Ray's parents and family life growing up. Or it could backfire horribly. She was about to find out.

"What's your dad like, Angely?" she asked.

She saw a thoughtful expression cross Ray's face, but to her surprise, it was not walled off or guarded. He and Angely exchanged a glance, and she leaned in, her earrings swinging along with her.

"Was," Angely said.

"I'm sorry, I didn't know he had passed away," Larimar said in a soft voice.

Both Ray and Angely nodded. "Our parents both passed away five years ago," Angely said.

"Sorry to hear that," Larimar said.

"Thanks," the siblings said in unison. The three of them sat in a silence that stretched on.

Finally, Angely spoke. "Well, he was very much like your traditional Dominican man. Yo soy el hombre. A macho man. A machometro. That type-A thing," Angely said, and Ray nodded along.

"Yeah. He was very much the 'no crying in baseball' type, except by baseball, he meant life," Ray said.

"Interesting," Larimar said. That could explain some things about Ray's reserved nature.

"And what about your mom?" Larimar asked.

"Oh, our mom went along with whatever he wanted, and went wherever he did," Angely said.

Larimar let out a short chuckle. "Ha! The opposite of my parents. Mami is the resident ball-buster, and my dad says yes to whatever she wants," she said.

A look of astonished curiosity crossed Ray and Angely's faces.

"Really?" Ray asked.

"I would love to see that in action," Angely said.

"Heh," Larimar said. Too bad she was going to have to cut things off before they ever got to that step.

18

When Larimar arrived home from work Thursday evening, there was an assortment of Thanksgiving flyers wedged between the doorknob and door jamb, complete with coupons in the shape of turkeys. She unlocked the door, and the paper turkeys fluttered to the floor. Larimar left them just where they fell. She had other things to worry about, like whether her hair would stay curled for the entire Rizos Natural Hair Club meeting. Once the door was locked securely behind her, she zipped to the bathroom and holed up with a duffel bag of hair curlers and a curling iron. She divided her hair into sections and painstakingly curled each one, combing through them and curling them into smaller sections for texture. This had to work. She checked her watch. The meeting would start in thirty minutes. She would get there a lot faster if she ran, but the group members might notice if she didn't bring her car. And besides, if she did, her curls would be gone by the time she arrived.

She groaned to herself. Driving was a pain in the ass when she was in ciguapa form. But it wasn't the first time she'd had to do it. She dressed herself in a marled turtleneck sweater and a floor-length cotton skirt, and locked her apartment behind her.

She eased herself into the driver's seat and the Beetle started up with a purr, despite the cold.

In order to be able to drive, she had to flex her feet, which in turn pressed her heels down against the brakes and gas. She let her foot off the brake and slowly eased the car out of her parking space. She drove slower when she was in ciguapa form, mostly because it took more control to drive with her feet backward.

The streets flew by until she was in the parking lot of the Iglesia Hispana. There were a few other women parking their cars, and she waited till they were all in to get out of hers, just in case her skirt went up while she was getting out of the car.

Up ahead, Miguelina was holding the door for her. She spread her skirt out in front of her, then got up and whizzed across the lot to the door.

"Thank you!" she said, and she truly felt grateful for the kind gesture.

Miguelina looked at her quizzically, but she nodded and ushered Larimar in.

As she entered the room, she felt stares and openmouthed gazes on her. Willing herself not to touch her hair, she kept her hands to her sides. Once Anairis began to speak, she allowed her hands to float up and pat her hair. It was exactly as she thought. Her painstakingly created curls had all vanished and been replaced by the long, straight tresses that were the mark of the ciguapa.

"Damn!" she said under her breath as she stroked the glossy, straight locks.

She dreaded the moment when it would be her turn to speak

about the headway she had made with her natural hair. Miguelina spoke about how it had been hard to keep her curls moistur-
ized for the past two weeks, what with the increasing cold.

Larimar thought ahead to the concert date with Ray, and her
stomach did flips. On the one hand, she couldn't wait to see him
again. On the other, she was going on a date with him in ciguapa
form. There were so, so many ways this could go wrong.

She willed herself to take a deep breath, and that's when she
noticed the entire group staring at her.

"Larimar?" Anairis asked.

"Uh, yes?"

"I've been calling your name. It's your turn to, you know,
share about how it has gone for you with your hair these past
weeks." She gave Larimar's straight hair a pointed glance.

Larimar took a deep breath. She would have to think fast.

"I'll tell you the truth, it's been hard," she said. "My tía Bruni-
lda is staying over my house, and she is going to cosmetology
school. Every few days, she needs a body for training, and since
yours truly is the only one there . . ." She gave a shrug for dramatic effect, and six pairs of eyes responded with a sympathetic
glance.

"I already feel my hair getting drier from all the blow-drying.
But, you know how it is. Hay que ayudar a la familia. You have
to help your family."

The other members of the club nodded, and with that, Larimar's turn was over. She gave an inaudible sigh of relief as the
next member began her review.

19

Hours later, her Beetle squealed into the parking lot of the Stone Pumpkin at 10:15. She was on time by Dominican standards. She checked her lipstick in the mirror and adjusted the knot at the front of her olive-green tie-dyed shirt. The hairs stood up on her arms. There was something about going to a late-night rock show in November.

She fell in line at the door, ignoring the cigarette smoke that swirled around her. There were all kinds of people. Shaved heads, green hair, stretched earlobes, leather jackets. She was probably the only one with backward-facing feet, though. She shook her head in disbelief. Probably? Who was she kidding. Luckily, she had her trusty floor-length skirt to hide her condition. None of these people would know.

The bouncer nodded at her and waved her in. Should she be happy or mad she wasn't being asked for ID? She was thirty-four, after all. But couldn't they card her just a little bit longer?

The club was filling up, and the band was finishing setting up onstage. She took a stool near the bar, sinking down onto its leathery comfort. The first twangy notes floated off the stage and let her know the Fun Bunnies were about to start.

The music began, and she let herself get lost in it. There was a touch on her arm, and she whirled around to find Ray at her side.

"Hey!" she cried. He was wearing a leather jacket, jeans, and Doc Martens. She reached out to wrap her arms around him and leaned in to kiss his cheek. When she pulled away, his eyes were shining.

"Hi. Where do you want to stand?" he asked.

She pointed at the bar stool. "Today, this is my MO," she said. "Seated at the bar with a mule in my hand."

He grinned. "I'm digging your style."

The Fun Bunnies began striking some chords, and a crowd formed at the foot of the stage. That would be fun, but the space and the company were better right where she was.

Ray pulled up a chair next to her. "One whisky sour, please," he said to the bartender. Larimar couldn't help but glue her eyes to his ID when he laid it on the countertop. Raymond Antonio Concepción, it read. She rolled the name over the tip of her tongue in her mind, remembering the first time she saw it . . . on top of a work file. How romantic.

Ray thanked the bartender, then turned to her. For a moment, their eyes met and it felt like they were sharing a secret. In front of all these people. She couldn't think of what to say, so she said what she was thinking.

"This is different."

"What's different?" he asked, his gaze thoughtful.

Me. You. Larimar swallowed hard. "Being out this late on a work night! I almost never do this."

He gave her a little shrug, then reached for a napkin and his jacket fell open. Her breath caught in her throat. No, it couldn't be. No, no, no. On his T-shirt there was a drawing of a figure, a female figure. She had long, straight hair that she wore like a dress. And her feet were facing backward. Larimar was going to faint.

She teetered on the bar stool before she caught and steadied herself. He had a ciguapa T-shirt.

What would he do if he found out ciguapas weren't just a cool T-shirt design? He likely had never imagined it. Would he be more accepting since he already knew about them, and obviously felt connected to them in some way?

She was staring. She shook herself and thought of something to say. The Fun Bunnies were ramping up their oeuvre, their playing getting more frenzied. It was very energizing and a little scary.

"Do you want to get closer to the stage?" he asked.

Larimar considered it for a moment. They would be closer to the music, but the chances that her skirt would get tangled or pulled or lifted were greater. And she wasn't in the mood for that kind of night. She didn't have this problem when she was going to punk shows as an early teen. The grim thought clouded her thoughts until Ray gently brushed her arm and dispersed them with his touch.

She shook her head. "I just want to chill here for a bit."

He nodded. "Okay, so we'll chill here." She smiled inwardly.

Coño. If it was any other time besides the full moon, they could have danced together.

And then that was it, she couldn't take the curiosity anymore. "Nice shirt," she said.

"Oh, thanks!" He turned to face her more fully. "It's a—"

"I know. It's a ciguapa."

"You ARE Dominican!"

Her laugh rung out almost louder than the Fun Bunnies' riffs. "Yeah, it's not only something I put in my profile."

They stared at each other long and hard. What were the chances?

"Why do you have this?" she asked.

Ray gazed straight into her eyes and looked almost nostalgic. "I just always thought ciguapas were cool."

Wake me now, wake me now. This can't be real. "What?"

A patron next to her leaned a little too far over, and Ray pulled her out of the way. Her skirt got stuck under one of the legs of the stool and she quickly lifted her feet. Whew, close one. The man next to her steadied himself and she leaned back into her place, her skin burning where Ray had touched her.

"Wow, I thought that only happened in movies," she said out loud before she could catch herself.

Ray leaned his head to one side and asked, "What's that?"

She glanced around frantically. Thank God, the bassist was slamming his guitar on the stage, sending tiny splinters careening through the air. "That people broke their guitars onstage!" she said. "What the fuck! Those things are expensive, right?"

He nodded. "Yeah, they are definitely expensive," he said, his gaze thoughtful. "Do you want to dance?"

Larimar sighed inwardly. Another bullet to dodge. She hoped to get to the end of the night in one piece.

"Um, I have two left feet," she said, a grin creeping up around her lips.

"You certainly do not, Larimar. Remember the bodega and the party boat?"

Damn it. "Vaguely."

Ray smiled and the corners of his eyes crinkled.

Right then, there was a tap on her shoulder.

"Larimar? Is that you?" She had definitely heard that voice somewhere before.

She whirled around and found herself face-to-face with Mr. Gerges, the architect for Beacon Union. The blood rushed to her head before she could control her reaction. She felt her cheeks flame as she glanced from Mr. Gerges to Ray. In a split second, she uttered a frantic prayer that Mr. Gerges would say a professional hello and get the heck out of her way, as one would when running into a business contact at a ska punk show. And whatever he did, Lord, may he not say anything about the Beacon project.

"Mr. Gerges! Funny bumping into you here," she said, trying to keep her voice as neutral as possible. He had traded his usual dress shirt and jeans for a Mustard Plug T-shirt and a gelled faux hawk. He fit right in, and she would never imagine him as a straight-faced architect. Good for him, she thought, and then she remembered her predicament.

"I know!" he said. "Hey, man," he said with a nod in Ray's direction.

Ray nodded back, and his face was pleasant, but she could tell he was definitely curious how they knew each other. Would his first thought be that Mr. Gerges could be an ex of hers? Hopefully, the use of "Mr." would make it clear that he wasn't. The truth was, she didn't know Ray well enough yet to even guess what he would assume. Her chest grew a little tight as she let this realization sink in. And she knew she wanted that to be different. She wanted to know him better.

But what could she say that would make it clear that they were business contacts but not prompt him to talk about Beacon at all? Damn, that was a hard one.

"So, are all the numbers adding up?" Mr. Gerges asked. An icy finger of fear tickled her heart. It would only take one comment from him to blow her cover and reveal her as the disgusting liar she was. This was a problem, a real problem. But she needed more time with Ray.

She leveled her gaze and tried to inject some icy professionalism into it.

"Yep, sure are," she said. "How about I'll give you a call from the shop on Monday? The Fun Bunnies are one of my favorites." She gave a meaningful glance at the stage.

Mr. Gerges's gaze shifted from her to the stage, to Ray, and back again. The realization that she was on a date seemed to dawn on him, and he took a step backward.

"Yeah! Yep. Monday sounds good. Excuse me," he said, and as quickly as he had popped up to scare the bejesus out of her, he disappeared back into the crowd.

She let out the breath she had been holding. Then Ray said, "Oh, man! My friend Victor is here too. Come on, I gotta introduce you, Larimar."

Her stomach dropped to her knees. Another meet and greet? She was going to be sick.

Anxiety over whether she would be able to reach Victor's post without tripping or revealing her feet swept over her.

"Do you think he'd be able to come over here? My, uh, my feet are a little tired."

Ray looked at her with a drop of curiosity, and it didn't surprise her, since they had been seated since they got to the concert. But he shrugged and said, "No prob, I'll get his attention."

He stretched up and waved until he caught the eye of a bearded man with round glasses and a lumberjack shirt. It was an unusual choice for a Fun Bunnies show.

In seconds, the man was striding over to the bar. He stopped right in front of them. Larimar stretched her feet to the edge of her skirt and could not make contact with the floor. At the risk of appearing rude, she was going to have to remain seated.

Ray reached out and gave Victor a quick hug, clapping him on the back. "Hey, man," he said. Victor reached around and clapped him back, then turned to Larimar. "Hello!"

Victor had a kilowatt smile, and he seemed perfectly comfortable in his surroundings.

"Larimar, this is Victor. Victor, this is Larimar."

Larimar stuck out her hand and Victor shook it vigorously.

"Nice to meet you. I'm Ray's only friend."

He and Ray broke out in laughter, and Ray punched his arm. "Shut up, man."

Victor shrugged and gave Larimar an apologetic smile. "Well, maybe not his only friend. But the best of them."

She managed a polite smile through her anxiety. "Nice to meet you, Victor." *Please God, don't let him ask what I do.*

Victor glanced from Ray to Larimar, and Ray gave him a small nod. "Well, I'll leave you two to it!" he said quickly, taking a step back. "Enjoy your da—the concert." He gave them another little wave before turning away and joining a group of dancers.

She let her shoulders sink down and forced herself to take a deep inhale. The shock of running into Mr. Gerges with Ray had left her dizzy. She felt herself wobbling a little and stuck her hand out to steady herself. Instantly, Ray's expression shifted to one of concern.

"You don't look so well," Ray said.

"I don't feel so well," she said.

"Do you want to go outside?" he asked.

Hmm. Would she be able to get outside without tripping on something, getting her skirt caught on something, tumbling over in a mess and revealing herself as a mythical creature to the world? She decided it was worth taking the chance.

"Yeah," she said. Next came the big task: pushing through the crowds.

"Let's go out the fire exit," he said. "It goes right to the parking lot."

Was he psychic too?

Ray held his hand out for hers, and with her heart in her throat, she hopped down from her stool, and thanked God that she didn't pitch forward and fall on her face.

They squeezed through the crowd and reached the exit. Ray opened the door and they stepped out. The parking lot was empty of people, but there was nowhere to sit.

"Wanna sit here?" Ray asked, gesturing to the stoop.

Larimar thought for a second. That would be better than sitting in her car with a man she wanted to jump and shouldn't. And also, she needed a few minutes to calm her heart, which had only just stopped pounding in panic.

"Yeah. Let's sit here."

"Should I get us a couple beers?" he asked. A few leaves fell onto the stoop from the oak tree above, making a sweeping sound as they drifted down the steel stairs of the fire escape above them and settled on the ground.

Perfect timing.

"Sure!"

Ray turned back toward the club, and Larimar took a moment to breathe and settle herself on the stoop.

Ray returned with the beers and sat down next to Larimar. He reached for her hand and held it tightly in his. With his other hand, he passed her a beer wrapped with a paper napkin. When she glanced up, he was smiling at her.

"What?" she asked. She couldn't help but smile back.

"It's, well . . . I have such a great time with you. We don't have to even be doing anything. Just sitting here is perfect."

Larimar inhaled, the sweet aroma of senescent autumn leaves tickling her nose. The conversation was taking a turn that skated dangerously close to a place she was not ready to go. Especially after almost being exposed by Mr. Gerges.

Ray set his beer down on the stoop.

"See, I like you and . . . I want to date you, Larimar. Do you want to? To—date me?" He glanced up from their joined hands and his gaze searched hers. He looked scared. She knew this wasn't easy for him—to say how he felt.

Every fiber in her body froze. The truth was that she did want to date him. But she also knew she would hurt him.

She did the only thing she could do. "I have to go," she said, and she whizzed to her car with a speed she could only hope Ray wouldn't realize was superhuman.

On the way home, she cried. "I'm sorry, Ray," she whispered.

20

That night, Larimar dreamt she was at Cipriani and she saw Ray across the room. She tried to call out to him, but when she did, her mouth filled with water—they were somehow also underwater. He looked lost, like he was searching for her but couldn't find her. The impossibility of calling to him underwater was too much for her, and she broke down in tears.

She woke up with hot, fat tears streaming down her face. She clutched her blanket closer. She needed to call Ray and make things right. But it was seven in the morning. Ugh. Her legs ached. She needed to swim . . . and it was November. Jumping in the river in northern New Jersey was not really an option. *The river.* It never failed to calm her and set her thoughts on the right path.

She forced herself to get out of bed, and pulled on sweats and her black jacket.

The Elizabeth River passed not far from her house, and there was a small park where she would be able to park her car and sit on a bench. She took the elevator to the ground floor and hopped in the Beetle.

It was a five-minute drive to the park. She parked her car

and darted down to the river, where instead of sitting on a park bench, she found a perch right on the water's edge. It was there that she let the rest of her tears go. Between running away from Ray and the emotions from her dream, she had a lot of them. A couple walking their dog looked at her, startled, and several squirrels dropped their acorns and ran away.

She had never felt so alone in her life. And that was saying a lot, growing up a full-moon ciguapa, never finding a place to fit in, finding it hard to be herself with anyone besides her abuela and Brynne. Her mother, even though she was a ciguapa herself, didn't make her feel any more connected, with her strict attitude and constant eagle eye ways. Her father made her feel less alone, but he was always busy, working to keep their family afloat in a country that never quite felt like home for him even though he'd once been willing to die for it.

Larimar stared at her hands. Her almost-black burgundy nail polish was starting to chip and crack. Just then, she felt a feather-light touch around her shoulders. She didn't have to glance up to know who or what it was. The ciguapa had found her, and didn't want her to be alone.

She felt a tickle across her eyelids, light as butterfly kisses. The ciguapa was wiping her tears. For some reason, this only made her cry even more, and she rested her forehead on her knees as the ciguapa pat her back. She couldn't bring herself to look up yet.

When she finally did, she saw the woman's holographic image, so transparent and light that if she studied it from a different angle, it was barely visible. The ciguapa took Larimar's hand and placed a glossy blue stone in it. The stone was familiar, although it wasn't the turquoise-colored stone Larimar was named after.

The ciguapa drew close again and wrapped her in the lightest hug that somehow still filled her with strength. The ciguapa was right. She had this. When she opened her eyes to give thanks, the ciguapa was gone.

She had only been present for a few moments, yet she had turned Larimar's day and the direction of her thoughts around. She pressed her hands to the ground and whispered words of thanks, and then whirled back into millennial mode, pulling out her phone and snapping a picture of the stone the ciguapa had gifted her. She sent it to Brynne, and moments later, Brynne sent back a Wikipedia article.

Lapis lazuli, a glossy blue stone renowned for its connection to wisdom and truth.

She sucked in a breath. The ciguapa was telling her to tell the truth. Ay . . . why couldn't she have just given Larimar the winning lotto numbers? This was a lot harder. She turned the stone over in her hand, its cold smoothness tickling her palm.

It was 8 a.m. Luckily, she didn't have to report to the Beacon Union location until ten.

Ray had to be up, right? He sold coffee, for God's sake. She began typing a text.

LARIMAR: Ray. I'm so sorry about how I acted last night. I just . . .

Write . . . erase. Write . . . erase. How was she going to explain this to him? Maybe there was no time like the present to start telling the truth.

LARIMAR: I just flipped because I feel so strongly for you and I'm afraid that once you know the real me you won't want me anymore.

She promptly erased that message and began a new one.

LARIMAR: I'm sorry I ran away. It's not easy for me to be myself with anyone, and with you I feel like I get close and it scares me. Can we talk about this in person?
RAY: Sure.

One-word answer. Yep, he was upset. And he had every reason to be. She racked her brain for the right time and place for the conversation. If she were to do it on a full moon night, she could show him her feet and that would explain a lot. But she also had to be honest with herself. She was not ready for that.

LARIMAR: Meet me at the Asbury Park convention center on the boardwalk tonight at 8:00. We'll talk. I'll bring blankets and a thermos of hot chocolate.

She watched the little gray bubble appear and disappear, then appear again.

RAY: I'll be there.

When Ray arrived on the boardwalk, the wooden planks creaking under his Doc Martens, Larimar was already waiting for him under the painting of the octopus lady.

His gaze was a little distant at first, but then he met her eyes full-on, and she took that as a good sign.

"Walk with me," she said, and without asking, he took a macrame bag stuffed with blankets from her and they descended the boardwalk onto the beach.

They found a spot far enough from the tide, and Larimar spread out one of the blankets, a fluffy blue velour one she had borrowed from Oliver a few months back and kept.

When the blanket was spread smooth, she took a seat in the center and motioned for Ray to join her. He looked a little tentative, but he sat down next to her, crossing his legs.

The wintry breeze blew in from the ocean, and she pulled her puffer jacket tighter around her. Ray began to reach out his arm, then seemed to rethink it and brought it back to his side. Seeing that hurt her. She knew he would warm her if she would let him.

To her surprise, he was the first to speak. "I feel like an ass after yesterday," he said, staring out over the waves.

She pressed her lips together and rubbed her hands to warm them up.

"Ray, that's literally the last thing in the world that I want," she said.

"That's why I'm telling you this. I don't know why you ran away, but I have a feeling it's not the whole picture about how you feel," he said.

She breathed a heavy sigh. "No, it's not. It's so not. But—I got scared."

Ray's eyes grew wide. "Scared? Of me?" His features contorted as if the thought brought him physical pain. He reached for her hand and pulled it to his chest so her palm covered his heart.

Little tendrils of warmth flowered down her arm. He was so beautiful, and she had to make this right.

"It's just that . . ." She heaved a deep sigh. "I can never be all of myself around anyone. There's always something to hide. There's always a part of me I can't be." She wiped a tear off her cheek, and before she knew it, Ray was reaching out to take her other hand.

Ray looked into her eyes, and his expression was gentle and at once afflicted. "I know how you feel, in a way."

"You do?" *Are you a supernatural being too?*

"Yes. I feel like I can never be all of who I am either." Oh.

"Who are you?" she whispered.

"Scared," he whispered back.

The meaning of his words sunk in, and suddenly Larimar wanted to squeeze his hand so hard that she was afraid she'd hurt him. She thought about the things she had overheard Papi say throughout the years. "I couldn't be afraid." "I wouldn't allow myself to be scared."

She leaned into him. "You can be scared with me," she said, and her stomach twisted as the multiple meanings of those words dawned on her. She was offering him the ability to be scared with her, but she still didn't know if he would be scared *by* her. Maybe it was time to tell him.

She sat up straight, startling him from the coziness of their moment. "There's something you should know about me," she said, well aware of the irony of those words, knowing full well that her big reveal would be a half-reveal at best.

"Oh?"

"I don't really know how to say it."

"Just say it, Larimar."

"So . . . you know that T-shirt you have? The one with the ciguapa on it?"

"Yes."

She relaxed her posture and could see some confusion on his face, mixed with curiosity.

"Well, you've found a real one."

"Larimar, I know you're a real one."

"No, I mean a ciguapa. You have found a real-life ciguapa. A full-moon ciguapa, at least."

Ray leaned his head to the side, his expression wary.

"If you're trying to make me feel better . . ."

"No, I mean it. I know it sounds unbelievable, but I turn into a ciguapa at every full moon. It's been happening since I was a teenager, and it runs in my family. The women . . . of my family."

"What?!"

"Mm-hmm."

"How is that possible?" he asked.

She shrugged and stretched her arms out behind her to lean back. "Wish I knew. You can't tell by looking at me unless it's the full moon," she said.

"How is that—?" He sat in silent thought for a minute, and then he spoke again. "I . . . I never imagined—"

"I know," she said. They sat in silence for another long stretch. He gazed out over the ocean, then turned back to face her.

"Larimar . . . would you let me see you? At the full moon, I mean?"

Larimar's jaw dropped. Running away, she would have expected. But this?

"Uh . . . I haven't really thought about it."

"Well, think about it. I want to see you. You don't have to be alone."

His words were a knife in her heart. Here he was, thinking she should not be alone, and she still had secrets left. What if she just told him about Beacon? Then there'd be no dark and shady patches left between them, all would be known and he could make a true decision.

"I don't know what it's like to be a ciguapa, but I know what it's like to feel alone and feel like you can never show your true self to anyone. In my family, everyone expects me to be tough, "be a man", be a soldier. Look at my sister! For God's sake. I'm not allowed to be scared , and sometimes, that's what I am. But I can't ever show it. To them, it's weakness. Therapists don't understand me," he scoffed. "They haven't been to war. My buddies don't understand me. They have one idea of me—Ray the soldier—and that's all they want to see."

He heaved a heavy breath once he finished speaking, and she could tell he'd been holding that in for a while.

"Ray . . ." she said softly, leaning forward and placing her palm on his chest. He looked up, and his gaze was pained.

"That's a lot to be carrying," she said. This wasn't the right time to bring up Beacon, not when he was baring his soul like never before.

He let go of her other hand and smoothed a curl off her face.

"But with you, I feel less alone," he said. "I don't care if you're a ciguapa or a werewolf or whatever other being our culture comes up with. I'm falling in love with you, and I just want *you*."

He leaned in closer, cupping her face with his hand and lightly touching his lips to hers.

They tasted of mint, and she'd be damned if she was imagining it, but she tasted the faintest hint of caramel. She angled herself closer to him to deepen the kiss. Her heart fluttered as their tongues touched for the very first time. The kiss was tender, but with a heated core that made her wonder what else Ray had been hiding behind the closed doors of his extroverted personality.

She was the first to pull away, and with a tender sigh, she laid down on the blanket, facing up to the stars. He followed suit and pulled one of the heavier blankets from the macrame bag to cover them. They found each other's hands under the blankets and interlaced their fingers.

They stayed like this, staring up at the stars, for some time. Before Larimar knew it, she was drifting off into a pleasant sleep.

21

Larimar awoke to the sound of birds screeching at the top of their lungs. With her forearm, she rubbed her eyes. She almost screamed when she opened them and saw a seagull inches from her face, craning its neck to get a better gander at her. Then she felt a firm hand on her shoulder and let out a long sigh. Right. She had fallen asleep on the beach with Ray.

She turned to Ray, who was lying just inches from her. There was enough space between them to set a small picnic basket, though. She loved that he had given her space.

As her eyesight got sharper, her stomach twisted with worry as she saw that he was sporting two dark circles under his eyes.

She raised her hand to touch his face. "Good morning," she said softly.

He caught her hand and pressed a kiss to the back of it. "Good morning," he whispered.

She zeroed in on his undereye circles. "Did you get any sleep at all?"

Ray smiled and nodded. "About five minutes, I think," he said.

Guilt gnawed at her belly. "Ray, you don't have to watch over me," she said.

His relaxed expression narrowed a bit. "Yes, I do," he said.

"I may not have superhuman strength, but I'm fast . . . I can be fast if I need to."

Ray cracked a smile at this. "Okay."

"You don't believe me, do you?"

He nodded emphatically. "Of course I do. Now, how about we get some breakfast from the boardwalk and do a little picnic?"

Hm. Breakfast would be a good idea. She pushed off the ground and stood up, stretching her arms overhead. To his credit, she did not catch him looking at her feet. They folded the blankets and put them in the macrame bag.

A glance at her phone revealed that it was 7:15. Some cafes had to be open already. Fifteen minutes later, they were back at their spot with a veritable spread. Between the two cafes that were open, they had been able to find muffins, orange juice, coffee, and bananas.

They spread it all out on the heavy wool blanket. Larimar took a bite out of one of the muffins.

"Mmm, they're good. Not as good as your baking, of course."

Ray cracked a smile. "You know just what to say."

A swell of courage filled her chest and suddenly she did know exactly what she wanted to tell him.

"Hey, Ray . . . have you given more thought to making your liqueur-infused cupcakes into a line you can sell outside the bakery? Like, at a liquor store maybe? Or places like Whole Foods?"

Ray thought for a moment. "Well, no. I hadn't ever thought about that."

Larimar took another bite and washed it down with a sip of the quickly chilling coffee.

"I think that would be a dope move. And it gives you another income stream."

He nodded. "Hmm. True. Although . . ."

"Although what?"

". . . I don't know," he said. "I feel like a lot of small, artisan products lose their quality when they start being produced on a larger scale." He leaned his head against the heel of his hand and rubbed the back of his neck.

"I hear that," Larimar said. "You'd have to set things up so that you would be in charge of quality control, at least until the line is expanded out and operational to the degree you'd be comfortable with."

"Yeah. I don't know . . . I'll think about it. Thanks for the idea though," he said.

She bowed her head and gave a little flourish with her hand.

"Is that something that's worked for you in the floral business?" he asked.

She froze, then shook her head with vehemence.

"No, but it just seems like it could work for you given that you have a standout product already. Nobody makes cupcakes like yours in the tri-state area."

She reached down for her coffee, and when she looked up, he was studying her.

"What?"

His smile spread wide across his face. "You're amazing, that's all. Even if you were to give me the boot tomorrow, I'd be happy

I met you."

His words were like nails scratching on a blackboard. Did he have some kind of premonition or something? Did she have the right to blame him if he did? She willed her shoulders, which had crept up to her ears, back down to their resting place.

"Well, that's not in my plans," she said finally, and gave him a wink she hoped came off as casual.

"Good. Do you want to lay down with me and watch the clouds go by?"

She gave him a curious glance. "Is that something you like to do?"

"Yeah. It reminds me that no matter what I'm feeling, life is still going on around me, and if I don't pay attention, it's going to pass me by."

"Ah."

She was the first to lay down, amassing a small roll of blanket under her head for her comfort.

Ray laid down next to her and threaded his fingers through hers. He brought their interlaced fingers to his lips and pressed a kiss against the back of her hand.

Her heart swelled with all sorts of swoony tickles, and she leaned over to touch her lips to his, rolling onto her side to stretch her body against his.

He rolled onto his side too and wrapped an arm around her as he slid her lower lip into his mouth.

Desire was welling up in the pit of her belly, and she thrust her tongue between his lips, causing him to let go of her lower lip and deepening the kiss.

Their breath was coming in shallow pants, until Larimar felt a wet, slobbery thing on her forearm. Jesus, that could not be from Ray unless something was seriously wrong. She pulled away from Ray and whipped around to find a goofy, curly-haired giant poodle nudging her back with his nose.

Several feet behind him, an elderly couple stood, open-mouthed.

"Um, maybe we should sit up," Larimar whispered to Ray, feeling her cheeks beginning to burn. They propped themselves up and this seemed to shake the couple out of shock.

"I'm so sorry," the lady said.

"It's okay," Larimar said, pulling her jacket close to her.

"Here, Twinkles!" the man called, and the dog bounded over to them. They uttered a couple more apologies and walked away.

"Damn, how long were they standing there?" Larimar said.

"I don't know, but thank God for the dog or that would've been even more awkward," Ray said.

An awkward lull had fallen over them at being discovered by the couple.

"Maybe we should start heading out," Ray said, glancing at his watch. "I'll call Doña Delfina and ask if she can open the shop for me."

At this, Larimar recalled a question she'd wanted to ask Ray. "About Doña Delfina. She was your mom's best friend?"

Ray nodded. "Yes. They'd known each other since they came to this country as teenagers. They shared a boarding room when they first arrived in New York."

"Wow."

"Yeah. She's become like a mother to me since my parents died."

"About your parents, how did they . . . ?"

He gazed out over the ocean, his expression growing overcast. "They were killed in a car accident while I was deployed. A drunk driver crashed into them at a stoplight."

She reached for his hand, and he took hers but kept looking out into the distance. "Oh my God, that's horrible. I'm so sorry."

He squeezed her hand back. "Thanks."

Knowing how his parents died made her want to stand up for him even more. He and Angely were alone in the world. Maybe he understood how she felt more than she thought.

"Were you and Cari still together back then?"

He gently shook his head. "No. Cari and I have been divorced for seven years already."

Larimar cocked her head to one side as she considered this. "And how long were you married?"

"Eight years. We got married at nineteen, right when I got out of basic training."

"Wow. Did you two date in high school?"

"Yeah. Classic, right? No wonder we grew apart."

She stroked his hand, and turned to face him, wrapping her arms around his waist and enveloping him in a hug. She rested her head on his chest, and he smelled of vanilla and the slightest hint of bourbon.

He gazed down at her, and his eyes were shining. It would be so easy to start kissing him all over again, but it was getting late and they both had to go to work.

"I know it's not easy for you to talk about these things. But promise me that if you need to talk, you'll call me." She was so far gone by now. Gazing into his chocolate drop eyes, feeling his arms around her. The promises she'd made herself were bubbles popping by the minute.

"I promise," he said, bestowing a soft kiss on the tip of her nose. "And Larimar?"

"Mm?"

"Same for you. Don't ever feel alone. You're not alone anymore . . . you have me."

He was tapping on the glass of her composure, and she was pretty sure any minute it was going to come crashing down.

She pressed her lips together, choking back the tears that wanted to come. "Okay."

BORRACHITOS' DOMINICAN HOT CHOCOLATE-INSPIRED CUPCAKES

Makes 12 cupcakes

FOR THE CUPCAKES

3 tablespoons cocoa powder

½ teaspoon ground cinnamon

¼ teaspoon ground cloves

¼ teaspoon ground ginger

¼ cup hot water

1¼ cups all-purpose flour

½ teaspoon baking powder

½ teaspoon baking soda

¼ teaspoon salt

2 large eggs, at room temperature

¾ cup granulated sugar

½ cup sour cream

½ teaspoon vanilla extract

¼ cup/½ stick unsalted butter, melted and cooled to room temperature

FOR THE FROSTING

6 ounces bittersweet chocolate

1 cup/2 sticks unsalted butter, at room temperature

1 tablespoon rum (optional)

2 cups confectioners' sugar

Make the cupcakes: Preheat the oven to 350 degrees Fahrenheit. Prepare a cupcake pan with cupcake liners.

In a small bowl, combine the cocoa, cinnamon, cloves, and ginger. Whisk in the hot water until the cocoa dissolves.

In a separate small bowl, sift together the flour, baking powder, baking soda, and salt.

In a large bowl, whisk together the eggs and granulated sugar until well combined. Whisk in the sour cream and vanilla until combined, then add the cocoa mixture. Whisk in the melted butter, then the flour mixture until combined.

Fill the cupcake liners half full and bake for 15 to 20 minutes, until a toothpick comes out clean. Let cool completely on a wire rack.

Make the frosting: In the top of a double boiler, melt the chocolate, stirring occasionally, over barely simmering water. Let cool to room temperature.

In the bowl of a stand mixer, beat the butter, rum, and confectioners' sugar until creamy and smooth, about 3 minutes. Beat in the melted chocolate until well combined. Frost the cooled cupcakes, then refrigerate the frosted cupcakes until 30 minutes before serving to set the frosting.

22

The mid-November sunshine was bright and cold, like light shining through an icicle. The trees had just about shed all their leaves, and little bursts of gusty wind blew through the air, ruffling the edges of Larimar and Ray's jackets. They walked down the gleaming, pressure-washed sidewalks of Church Street in Montclair, gazing in the colorful shop windows without losing sight of their destination.

One block up, they reached Lulu's Thrift Shop. The first thing Larimar noticed were the lampshades in the display window, stacked one over the other in every color imaginable. There were chartreuse ones with hanging crystal tassels in the same color, zebra-print ones with black ruffles around their bases, and velvet magenta ones with tiny pink rhinestones.

"I'm gonna pop some tags, only got twenty dollars in my pocket..." Ray sang and held the door open for Larimar. It wasn't until they stepped through the doorway that they could see the layout of the space. Larimar cheered as they walked in, and she and Ray turned to each other, eyes wide. The lampshades were only a preview of the kaleidoscopic fabulousness that was Lulu's.

Racks and racks of multicolored clothing extended as far as

the eye could see, bracketed by dish sets from 1975 on wooden stands and display cases showing off estate jewelry from the last hundred years. There was a staircase to the second floor, where the shoes and bags lived, and each step held a pair of stilettos or platform heels.

"Ray, come look. Records!" Larimar said as she stooped down to check out a box of 45s sorted by decade. Ray dropped to his knees, sliding into the space next to Larimar. "They've got Nina Simone, Jimi Hendrix, the Isley Brothers . . . oh! Mami would be in heaven," she said.

They leafed through the entire box before Larimar settled on Jimi Hendrix's *Electric Ladyland*. The cost was a meager $1.49. Ray stood up and held his hand out to Larimar, who popped up by herself but gave his hand a squeeze anyway. They moved on to the clothing area, where Larimar picked a neon-pink boa up and draped it over Ray's shoulders.

He grabbed a feathery end and reached out to tickle her arm with it.

"Ah!" she giggled.

Ray smiled and started to pull the boa off, but Larimar stuck her hand out to stop him.

"Wait. I gotta get a picture of this."

"I charge for pictures," Ray said, but leaned in and draped the other end of the boa over Larimar's shoulders. She held up her phone and snapped away as they made silly faces and poses with the boa. When she whirled around to grab a hat to add to their getup, she bumped right into the person turning the corner.

"Ow!" she said, and quickly brushed herself off. When she

looked up, she found herself face-to-face with a relic from her past. The original Mean Girl. Her high school frenemy turned business rival Candy Coulter. Delicate bristles of rage rose up in her chest. She hadn't felt this since the last time she'd run into Candy at the last National Conference of American Bakeries. Larimar was there to represent Beacon Foods, and Candy was there as head of brand for Blue Creek Coffee, Beacon's main competitor in the tri-state area.

Larimar gritted her teeth, accidentally biting the edge of her tongue. She pressed her lips into a flat line. Blood trickled into her mouth, but she held her poker face. Candy wasn't going to see her falter.

"Hello, Candy," Larimar said.

Ray seemed to sense the change in her, and he stood up a little straighter at her side, although he kept the boa on.

Candy flipped her bleached-blond hair over her shoulder and gave Ray a saucy smile.

"Nice running into you here, Larimar. Literally," Candy said with a snicker.

"Mm-hmm," Larimar said. Running into Candy would be a pain in Larimar's rear any day, but today, it was dangerous.

"And not surprising. I mean, I'm here too, right? But I mix my vintage with my couture." Yep, that was Candy. Always looking for a way to one-up her.

"Awesome, Candy. You're so smart for doing that." Out of the corner of her eye, she saw Ray do a double take. Good. Odds were her caustic tone was on point.

Candy shrugged off the comment with another hair flip and

a simpering smile.

"And who's this?" she asked, her eyes glittering.

"Ray, meet Candy. We went to high school together. Candy, meet Ray." She'd be damned before she explained how she knew Ray.

She scanned the shop for the nearest exit. It would be seconds until Candy was asking her about Beacon.

"So, how's the autumn launch—" There it was.

Larimar grabbed Ray's arm. "You know what, Candy? I forgot to put quarters in my meter. Can you go with me, Ray?"

A look of surprise crossed Ray's face, and he looked from Larimar to Candy and back.

"Yes, I'll go with you. Nice meeting you, Candy," he said.

"A pleasure," Candy said. Her voice was sweet with a bitter edge of irritation.

Outside on the pavement of Lulu's, Ray scratched his head. "That wasn't about the quarters, was it?" he said.

"Nope. She's an old high school 'friend,' and let's just say I finished with her in high school."

She told herself she had said enough. That was the crux of it, right?

23

The following Saturday, the first thing Larimar did when she woke up was dial Ray, which said a lot since she was allergic to phone calls.

"Hey, Larimar!" he said after picking up on the second ring.

"Hey, yourself," she said, a smile spreading across her face. "Whatcha up to today?"

"I'm packing up some donations for the Iglesia Hispana's Thanksgiving weekend soup kitchen," he said.

"Oh, at the bakery?" she asked.

"No, at my house," he said.

A shiver moved through her, and she decided to take the leap. "Do you need any help?" she asked.

The line went silent for a second. "Yes, I could use some help. What time did you want to come by?"

"Hmm. I could come by in about an hour. Does that work?"

"Sure."

"What's your addy?"

"707 Spring Garden Road."

"Okay, cool. Should I bring anything?"

"Just your beautiful self."

Her beautiful self? She resisted the urge to squee into the phone. Ciguapas were known for the high-pitched sounds they were capable of making, and in Larimar, this had manifested itself in the form of the squee. "Okay, see you soon!" she said.

Finding Ray's house proved simple. It was a white A-frame with a painted brick face and a big black 707 right above the door. She parked the Beetle in the driveway next to his Chevy and got out of the car. She supposed parking next to him was okay since he lived alone and no one else would be needing the driveway. The house was very big to be alone in. She wondered if it had been his parents' house, and if living in it made him miss them more.

When Ray cracked the door open, a rush of delicious muffin smell flooded the space between them.

"Mmm!" she said, inhaling the heady scent. "Whatever you're doing in here smells amazing."

Ray grinned and ushered her into the narrow main hallway.

"Welcome to my house," he said.

She smiled back and squeezed his hand. "Thank you. It's nice to be here," she said.

The left side of the hallway opened into the living room, whose centerpiece was a brown microfiber couch and coffee table made from an actual slice of wood.

"Sweet coffee table," she said.

"Oh, that? Thanks. I made it myself."

"Impressive," she said. The living room opened into the dining room, and there her eyes alit on a mahogany table stacked high with trays of muffins, boxes of Ziploc bags, and loaves of bread already wrapped in plastic wrap.

"These are the donations?" Larimar asked.

Ray nodded.

"This is a shit-ton of stuff. You're a good person, Ray," she said.

To her surprise, his face fell. "No, I'm not."

Larimar raised an eyebrow. "Yes, you are. Look what you do for people."

"I'm telling you I'm not." He sank onto the couch, and she sat down next to him and rested her hand on his arm.

"What do you mean?" she asked.

"I mean I'm not as good as you think. I've killed someone, Larimar."

Larimar bit her lip. She didn't want to ask too many questions, knowing he had been in the Army and all. She knew from growing up with Papá that this was a sensitive subject.

"In combat?" she asked gently.

He shook his head, and then wrung his hands in front of him. "No, it was an accident. But it's still my fault."

She studied him, and the shadows under his eyes seemed to grow deeper. "What happened?"

Ray stared at his hands in his lap for a good long moment before he began to speak.

"I wasn't always destined for the supply room. First, I trained to be a paratrooper."

Her eyes widened. Ray had never mentioned this before.

"I was in Airborne school and we were doing a practice jump. I was with my best buddy, Pete. He was from Georgia, and we had gone through basic and advanced training together. Whenever I felt low, he would tell me, 'keep going, you can do this.' And I would do the same for him."

Larimar nodded and touched his arm, urging him to continue.

"The week before graduation, we went out to do a jump. I wore a medium harness and Pete wore a large, but when we were handed our parachute packs, he got a medium, and I got a large. I asked him if we could switch, and he said yes. We got in line to jump . . . and when it was Pete's turn, his parachute didn't open."

She tightened her jaw to keep it from flopping open.

"I'm so sorry," she said.

He glanced up at her from his hands, and his gaze was tortured. "I didn't even get to say goodbye. By the time I landed from my own jump, the medics had taken away the body."

"Oh, my God."

"I killed him."

"Ray . . . you didn't kill him."

"Yes, I did. If I hadn't asked him to switch parachutes, he would still be alive."

Larimar inched closer to him and threaded her arm through his. "Ray, there's no way you could've known that."

They sat in silence for a stretch.

"You're a good person, Ray. You didn't kill Pete. And also, if you hadn't switched, you would've died."

"So? I don't deserve to be alive more than him."

"Well, I for one am glad you're alive."

"Really?"

"Uh, yeah."

"You mean it, Larimar?"

"Truly."

He squeezed her hand. "I just wonder what his life would've been like had he lived."

Larimar blew out a long breath. "There's no way to know," she said. "But I do think that when you do something that makes you feel alive, you can remember him, and do it for the both of you."

His expression grew thoughtful. "I love that idea, Larimar. Thank you. You know, you have so many good ideas," he said.

"That's why they pay me the big bucks," she joked before she could catch herself.

Mirth danced in his eyes. "I'm glad to hear. I wasn't sure how lucrative the floral business could be."

"Um, yeah," she said, laser-focusing her gaze on the Ziploc bags. "So, what can I do to help?"

"You can keep me company while I finish packing these," he said.

"That's it? Easy."

He shrugged. "I can make it harder if you like."

She couldn't resist a challenge. "Oh, really? How?"

"You can taste-test these muffins and tell me which one you think should go into rotation at Borrachitos," he said.

"Wow, yes, you're making it terribly difficult for me," she said. She got up and then settled into a seat at the dining room table. "I'm ready right now."

He brought her a tray of muffins and set it down in front of her.

"I told you you were a good person," she said.

At this they both broke out into laughter. The spell of guilt was broken. It was time to move on to important things, like eating muffins.

"Do you want to come with me to the soup kitchen? To give out the muffins?"

Larimar's eyes widened. "Oh! I thought this was a drop-off kinda deal. So you actually hand them out at the church?" she asked.

"In the parking lot," Ray said with a nod. "We'll definitely need our jackets. But . . . I've been doing it every year since I opened Borrachitos. It's a good time, and a great chance to connect with the community."

Larimar took another bite of an apple-bourbon muffin. "How can I begrudge these stellar muffins to the community? Yes, of course, I'll go with you."

Ray stopped what he was doing and turned to face her with a look of shock on his face. "Really? You'll stand outside with me all day giving out muffins to whoever wants to take them?"

She stood up and faced him as well. "With you, yes."

"Larimar, that's the best news I've gotten all day!" he said, and with a triumphant whoop, he swept her off her feet, lifting her in the air. She slid down under his grasp until they were eye to eye.

He raised his hand to cup her jaw and brought their lips together. It was a kiss that made her feel closer to him than any before. It was a kiss that nearly had her forgetting her name, until she remembered Beacon and what she was going to have to do. At some point. With a sigh, she broke the lock they had on each other's lips.

"The muffins . . . the church," she said.

"Right. Right. The church." He smoothed down the front of his shirt, and they pulled apart. Larimar took a deep breath and a mental cold shower, and it was back to the task. Together, they packed the wrapped trays of muffins into six cardboard boxes Ray had made up for the occasion, and loaded the boxes into the bed of Ray's Chevy.

"Do you know the Iglesia Hispana?" Ray asked on the drive over.

Larimar nodded. "Yes. It's where I go for my natural hair group meetings."

Ray glanced at her with curiosity. "Natural hair group?"

She nodded. "Yes. All of us women who were raised being told 'péinate que pareces una abandonada' get together and support each other in celebrating and caring for our curly hair."

"Ahhh. I should tell Angely about that! Our mother was of the 'péinate' camp as well."

"Ufff," Larimar sighed. "I feel for Angely, then."

The drive from Ray's house to the church was only about ten minutes. When they arrived at the parking lot, they found several food trucks and restaurant vans unloading their contributions and setting up their tables. There was a Southern comfort food restaurant giving out plates with mac and cheese, cornbread, and ribs, a Brazilian restaurant doling out rice and feijoada, and a Vietnamese restaurant putting together plates of barbecued chicken and rice noodles.

Ray and Larimar claimed a folding table right next to the Vietnamese restaurant and spread out the boxes of muffins according to their flavor. There were Larimar's favorite, apple-bourbon, and there were also carrot-cranberry, zucchini, blueberry, and chocolate chunk.

A blustery wind blew, causing Larimar to pull her jacket tighter around her. The unseasonable warmth that had allowed them to sleep on the beach had faded, and it was feeling like a true November. As soon as they finished setting up, visitors searching for soup and warmth came by their table, scooping up muffins and adding them to their plates.

The church staff had set up a couple picnic tables across from where the food trucks were parked, and slowly they filled up with congregants and others who had come to partake in the generous meal. Larimar watched as people took their seats and tight, worried faces transformed into expressions of relief and contentment.

Ray nudged her shoulder. "Hey, Larimar. While we wait, do you think we can talk about 'the thing'?"

Larimar looked at him with a blank gaze. "What thing?" she asked.

He pointed to his feet and tried to turn his toes in as far as they would go. "You know," he said. "The thing."

Larimar swatted his arm and stifled a laugh. "Oh, that thing. What do you want to ask?"

Her chest began to grow icicles, but the steadfast acceptance in his gaze warmed them away.

"Well . . . how does it work?" he asked. An elder woman

stopped in front of their table, and Ray filled a plate with one muffin in each flavor for her.

Larimar leaned forward, resting her hands on the table. "When the full moon comes out—"

"Like werewolves?" he asked.

"Um, I guess?" she shrugged. "My mother and grandmother transform every night. But I was born here in New Jersey." She paused for a moment. "The force is weaker," she added in a playfully craggy voice.

"Ahh," he said. "Was it always like this?"

She shook her head. "Nope. Didn't start till middle school."

A white man in a black hoodie and jeans stopped in front of their table.

"These muffins are amazing!" he said.

"Thanks!" Ray said, and Larimar hung on the moment to see what Ray was going to do. He simply nodded at the compliment, gave the man another one, and watched as he walked away.

"Um, Ray, not to change the subject, but we need to have a talk."

"What?" he said, with a look of alarm.

"That would have been the perfect moment for you to give him your business card, tell him where Borrachitos is, and drive further business."

"But, it's a soup kitchen—"

"Doesn't matter! You don't know who is here. Every event like this is a major opportunity to get your name and your face out there.

Ray glanced out over the crowd. "You're right. I don't know what I was thinking. I was distracted by a lovely cig—woman," he said as some congregants neared the table.

She reached behind the table and squeezed his hand, and he squeezed it back.

"You have a way of keeping me on task, Larimar. I love that you help me with that."

"And I love helping you with it," she said. "I'm not good at a lot of things . . . but this, this comes naturally to me."

She picked up the empty muffin trays and carried them to the Chevy to store them in the back so they would have an easier time cleaning up at the end of the event. When she turned around, Ray was right behind her. He pinned her to the side of the pickup truck, kissing her neck, running his hands down her sides, and bringing them to meet behind her back.

"Ray! It's the parking lot of the church," she gasped, loving the sudden feel of his lips on her neck but also being half terrified of being caught by the pastor or his deacons.

"I know," he said, his breath coming in shallow bursts, "but I want more. I want more of you."

She ran her arms behind his back and stuck her cold hands in his jeans pockets, bringing him closer. They were teetering on the edge. And she couldn't allow herself to go over.

"Ray," she whispered. "I want a time for this, too, but I don't feel right here."

At this, he stepped back completely, pulling his sweater down as far as it would go to cover what the parishioners didn't need to see.

"I'm sorry, I just . . . I get turned on just by looking at you. I . . . I said too much."

"No, you didn't," she said, her smile spreading wide. She

popped the collar of her jacket to hide it. "Come on, let's go back to the table." They walked back hand in hand, Ray tugging at his sweater.

Larimar eased into her bed, her mind racing. She was ready for a restful night of sleep . . . until she woke up at three in the morning. Damn it. She really needed to get some rest.

Her fingers began reaching for her phone of their own accord.

LARIMAR: Can't sleep tonight either. What are you thinking about?
RAY: You.

She tossed the phone across the bed and squeed until she remembered Ray might actually be waiting for a response.

With a huff, she rolled over, retrieved the phone, and settled back down. Her mind was blank on how to respond except for with the truth.

LARIMAR: Thinking about you too.

She added a kiss emoji for good measure. Ugh, what was she doing? This had to stop. She stuffed the phone in the drawer of her night table and popped a melatonin gummy into her mouth.

Larimar walked into Borrachitos later that Sunday morning, shaking the rain off her umbrella at the front door. There were a few patrons seated at the round tables, enjoying the first brew of the day. The aroma of pumpkin muffins and dark-roast coffee pervaded the air, an intoxicating perfume.

When she reached the counter, she saw that Ray was nowhere to be found. Only Doña Delfina was there.

"Good morning!" Larimar's voice sailed straight over the counter.

Doña Delfina responded with a surly glare.

"Morning," she said, staring Larimar down hard.

"Is Ray in?" Larimar asked.

"No," Doña Delfina replied tersely.

Larimar didn't know how much time she had until Ray came back, but there was something she had to ask.

"Did I . . . do something to you?"

Doña Delfina looked up from the coins she was counting and narrowed her stare until she had Larimar in its hold.

"It's not me I'm worried about. You haven't been truthful with my Raymond."

Larimar's heart skipped a beat. "What are you talking about?"

Doña Delfina's nostrils flared, sucking in a breath of air. She knew she had her.

"You're one of the Luna women, aren't you?"

"Excuse me?" Larimar stuttered.

"My family is from Barahona, too. I know all about you ciguapas."

"H-how?" Larimar asked.

"I can tell, starting with the white streak on the right side of your hair. Your mother and grandmother must have the same one."

Larimar shrugged. She was not going to let this lady get her goat. "Ray already knows I'm a ciguapa, so I don't see a problem there," she said, forcing her shoulders back.

Doña Delfina twisted her mouth into a smug grin. "That's not all. I've seen you working in the empty bakery across the street. I walk past that shop every day to get to work."

Larimar cursed her blood as she felt it draining from her face. "Come again?"

"Así mísmo. I asked the architect, too. What was his name? Very nice man. And he told me you're the brand manager for the people who want to put Raymond out of business!"

Her voice rose several octaves on the last words, and Larimar cringed.

"So you better tell him. Because if you don't, I will."

Larimar's pulse thudded in her ears. What could she say?

"That's right. You tell him, or I will. And I have proof." She fished a Motorola flip phone out of her pocket and waved it in the air.

Larimar stumbled backward. There were no snappy comebacks that would fix this, and there was no point in denying it. The woman had probably gone full-out paparazzi on her while she was supervising the installation of the fixtures. And dang it, why did Mr. Gerges have to spill the beans? She turned on her heels and walked to the door, and once she was sure she was out of sight, ran to her car.

Once safely inside, she speed-dialed Brynne.

"Brynne? I have a problem."

APPLE-BOURBON MUFFINS

Makes 14 muffins

2 large eggs	¼ cup orange juice
¾ cup granulated sugar	2 cups all-purpose flour
¾ cup packed brown sugar	2 teaspoons cinnamon
⅔ cup vegetable oil	2 teaspoons baking powder
½ teaspoon vanilla	½ teaspoon salt
½ teaspoon bourbon	1 cup chopped apples

Preheat the oven to 350 degrees Fahrenheit. Prepare a muffin tin with paper liners.

In a large bowl, combine the eggs, both sugars, oil, vanilla, bourbon, and orange juice. Add flour ½ cup at a time and stir to combine. Add the cinnamon, baking powder, and salt and stir to combine. Fold in the apples.

Fill the paper liners two-thirds full and bake for 25 minutes, or until the tops are golden. Allow to cool completely on a wire rack.

24

Larimar sank into Brynne's corduroy couch, wishing she could sink so far in she'd never be able to climb out. She had a leopard-print fleece blanket pulled up to her nose, which she lowered only to take sips from a hot toddy Brynne had made her.

"What. A. Mess."

"Lari," Brynne said quietly, "I hate to be the one to tell you, but this was always going to be a mess, from the moment you hid under the table."

Larimar sighed and pulled the blanket back up to her nose. She knew Brynne was right, of course. She just didn't think it would hurt so much.

"It feels so much worse," she said. "I didn't think we would get this far. I never imagined I would tell him about . . . me, and furthermore, that he would accept me."

Brynne patted her hand. "I know, honey." She reached for a scented candle sitting on top of the coffee table and lit it. Soon, the aroma of cinnamon and amber filled the living room.

"It's not what I had in mind when I set you two up, either. And about that . . . I have a little confession to make."

Larimar glanced up from her hot toddy. "What's that?"

Brynne shifted her weight on the couch. "Remember when you sent me the Instagram photo?"

Larimar took another sip. "What Instagram photo?"

"Of a kid at a concert, in 1999?"

"Oh, yeah."

Brynne bit her lip and squeezed her eyes tightly closed for a second before she continued talking. "I knew that was Ray."

"That was Ray?!"

"Um, hello. You've been dating him for what, two months now? You hadn't noticed?"

A whirlwind of emotions swirled around Larimar's head.

"Wait . . . you saw the photo and knew it was Ray, and that's when you decided to set me up with him?"

Brynne shook her head. "I'd been trying to set you up with him before that, remember? But when you sent me that picture, it was like, the last straw. I knew I *had* to do it." She bit her lip. "Are you mad at me?"

Larimar sifted through this new information. Brynne had known Ray was the guy in the photo. Brynne was worried that Larimar would be mad, but she understood. After all, she knew herself. If Brynne had told her she was going to introduce her to the guy in the photo, all grown up, Larimar probably would've chickened out on being set up. And even though it hurt, she couldn't regret getting to know Ray and spending time with him.

"Mad for what?"

"For not telling you he was the guy from the picture?"

Larimar set her drink down on the coffee table and allowed her body to sink back into the couch.

"Mad? No, I'm not mad, honey. If anything, I have to give you points for craftiness."

Brynne let out a sigh of relief.

"But now everything is messed up beyond belief," Larimar said. "And it's my fault."

Larimar forced herself to breathe, and as she inhaled, little by little the scent of the cinnamon amber candle calmed her senses.

Brynne sighed and turned to face Larimar fully. "What are you going to do, Lari?"

Larimar took a deep breath, steeling herself. "I think I just have to tell him," she said. "It sucks, but I think with this kind of thing, the best thing is to face it. I fucked up and I want to know if there's any chance our relationship can be saved. And if it can't—"

Her throat grew thick and woolly. She didn't have to finish the sentence, which was good, because she couldn't. Brynne moved closer and put her arm around her.

"You don't know that yet," Brynne said, squeezing Larimar's hand. "If he understands, I mean—there's no way he's not going to be angry . . . and hurt . . . and betrayed—"

"I deserve that," Larimar said.

"Ya do," Brynne said. "But yes, after he processes that, he may be able to understand why you did it."

Larimar leaned her forehead onto her knees. She wasn't so sure about that.

"And if he doesn't?" she whispered. "Brynne, I've never connected like this with anyone I've dated."

"I know, I know. If he doesn't, we'll deal with it then. One step at a time, hon. Don't psych yourself out."

Brynne was right. It was all she could do.

he week. If you would like to leave a message with
will stick it to her corkboard."

paused to consider this. "I'll write a brief note on
en. Thank you."

e your order?" Giselle asked. Ms. Beacon pointed
lished digit in Larimar's direction.

he sancocho," Larimar said.

t two," Ms. Beacon said.

ight up." Giselle smiled and took off in the direc-
tchen, and Ms. Beacon focused her attention on

step is for us to set a date for the grand opening.
think of December eighth?" she said.

ook a sip from her glass of water. Would she and
talking by then? Where would she be, and where

ety in her chest crackled and hummed as Ms. Bea-
r an answer.

ember eighth is fine. It gives us time to complete the
d of quality assurance checks," Larimar said.

on clapped her hands together in front of her. "Per-
ber eighth it is. What are your plans for the color
decorations for the grand opening party? Larimar?"

stared out the window at a passing couple. The man
leather jacket, and the woman, who had her arm
h his, wore a floor-length charcoal-colored skirt. She
Ms. Beacon tapped her nails on the tabletop. That

BRYNNE'S HOT TODDY

Makes 2 servings

**2 teabags ginger tea
juice of 2 lemons**

**2 shots/6 tablespoons
bourbon
2 tablespoons honey**

In a saucepan over high heat, bring 2 cups water to a boil,
then divide between two mugs. Add a tea bag to each
mug. Squeeze the juice of one lemon into each mug. Add
one shot of bourbon and one tablespoon honey to each.
Let steep for 5 minutes. Enjoy.

25

"Thanks for agreeing to meet me here on a Monday, Larimar. I had to check on Beacon 72nd Street, but meeting somewhere besides the store is a nice change of pace," Ms. Beacon said. She pulled out a mahogany wood chair and sat down at the rectangular table with a turquoise and gold tablecloth, and Larimar did the same across from her.

"Lumi's Kitchen UWS?" She picked up the menu and turned it from side to side in her hand.

Ms. Beacon nodded. "I love this place, and I thought you might too since it's Dominican fusion."

Larimar read over the menu—it was small and curated, and everything sounded scrumptious. The décor in the place was also beautiful, and the staff were friendly. As soon as the women sat down, they were brought lemon water and a small basket with fresh pan de agua.

"So, let's get down to it," Ms. Beacon said, smoothing the menu down on the tabletop. "First of all, OMG! We are almost at the finish line!" Her brilliant smile spread wide, causing Larimar to force a plastic grin in response.

"Let me grab my files . . . well, you're the manager. You don't

"Oh. Sorry, I thought I saw something. Just the usual decorations."

"You sound thrilled, Larimar."

Larimar studied Ms. Beacon with interest. Sarcasm got her attention. "Well, Ms. Beacon, it's been a lot of work, as you can imagine," she said.

"Of course I can imagine," Ms. Beacon said, her voice warm, "and that's why I'm excited for your surprise. Anyway! Let me say no more."

Larimar lowered her gaze. No need to make any assumptions about the surprise.

"Okay, then! Let's dig in," Ms. Beacon said as Giselle placed two steaming bowls of sancocho before them.

Decorating the Beacon grand opening party with a holiday theme had seemed like a great idea in Larimar's office. It'd made sense, since the grand opening fell on December eighth. But with enormous crêpe Christmas trees and Hanukkah menorahs twirling on strings from the ceiling and overfilled Santa Claus balloons festooning the tables, Larimar hoped she hadn't committed a grievous mistake.

"Larimar! You're staring off into space. Think fast," Emerson said, tossing her a package of napkins.

"Huh?" Larimar glanced up and caught them right in front of her. "Nah, Em, it's just that . . . in my head, this presented itself as more holiday glam and less like the seasonal aisle at Walmart."

Emerson let out an uproarious giggle. "I hear that, I certainly do. But you know what? Everyone will be here for the free giant caramel coffee with whipped cream, not for the Santa balloons. I doubt they will even notice. Check out that line." Emerson gestured to the storefront, where a queue was visible all the way down the block.

Larimar drew in a jagged inhale. Looking at that line was the last thing she wanted to do. What if Ray was on that line? What if he decided to check out the competition, to see if he should be scared or not? Would she have time to hide if he stepped into the store? If he saw her, would he immediately know that she was the mastermind behind this Santapalooza . . . and behind the glossy corporate bake shop that was going to be competing with him, coffee for coffee?

She had to get a hold of herself. Before she knew it, patrons were going to be streaming in, and people were going to be giving her accolades for her great work in putting Beacon Union together. Her great work that could ruin Ray's livelihood and life. Her chest tightened to the point she could hardly breathe.

Damn it. There was no joy for her in her work anymore. There couldn't be, not when she felt it could harm Ray. She honestly didn't even care about her job at this point. Before she could hardly wait to climb the corporate ladder. Now she was at the point where she secretly wished it was greased with WD-40 so she could slip off and never come back.

"Larimar, you ready?" Em's voice jolted her from her rabbit hole of thought.

"Uh, I guess," Larimar said. Better to get this over with. Thankfully, Ms. Beacon would not be gracing the grand opening with her presence.

Emerson unlatched the door, and people began streaming in.

Larimar and Emerson had set up a station where waiters would be serving sleeved paper cups of the Caramelatto, Beacon's signature coffee drink. The napkins stamped with Beacon's coffee-and-muffin logo were stacked perfectly, and the carafes of coffee were so high the waiters had to crane their necks to look over them.

"Hi, I'll take a medium Caramelatto!" an overly enthusiastic woman in an ugly Christmas sweater chirped.

"Good, 'cause that's all we got," Emerson said under her breath to Larimar with a snicker.

"OMG, I cannot wait for there to be a Beacon here. I only wish you had a drive-through," another woman gushed.

Larimar's eyes kept darting to the door. And at last, as if she had called him with her thoughts, a familiar form with curly hair and a black leather jacket stepped to the back of the line.

Her heart thudded so hard in her chest, she thought she was going to black out.

"Larimar, are you okay?" Emerson asked.

"W-why?" Larimar said.

"You . . . you look so pale all of a sudden."

Her brain told her to move, but her body was not responding.

There was a loud cell phone ring, and just as quickly as Ray had stepped onto the line, he stepped out to take the call.

She kept holding her breath, waiting for the moment when he would come back and she would have to duck under the table or hightail it to the back room. But they ran out of giveaway coffee twice, and still, no Ray. They reached the end of the giveaway hour, and he did not show his face again.

She packed up as fast as she could, and drove down the street, where she gunned the engine and collapsed into her seat. There. It was done. Her portion of the job was done. She would only have to come back to this place for routine checks, and with any luck, she would be able to send Em.

There was a still a chance that Ray would never know she worked on this project. If she could talk to Doña Delfina, and maybe gift her a lifetime supply of free coffee or something, he wouldn't have any other way of finding out she put Beacon Union together. And then it would be in the past, and there would be no need to talk about it ever again.

Yeah, it could work that way. They could still have a chance.

26

Nails tapping on a desk had long been one of Larimar's pet peeves. Nevertheless, she found herself sitting across from a particularly loud tapper, Mrs. Crosby, the kind front desk receptionist from when she was in college. The creepy thing was, Mrs. Crosby had died fifteen years ago. But in her dream, she still wore her gray hair in pin curls and a starched white blouse with a lace collar. Larimar and Mrs. Crosby sat across from each other and stared. Neither spoke.

When Mrs. Crosby opened her mouth to speak, what came out were bubbles, and Larimar realized they were underwater. How disturbing. She had been underwater all along and didn't know it. Somebody tapped on her shoulder, and when she whirled around, she woke up. Larimar sat straight up in bed, a cold sweat coating her arms and neck.

It took a minute for her shallow breathing to become deeper and more drawn out. Ugh, that had been too creepy. She slipped her feet into her black plush slippers and padded to the kitchen for a glass of water. Moments later, she settled between the cushions of her couch and forced herself to breathe. There was still a day to organize.

If she prepped herself early enough, she would have time to stop by Borrachitos and then jump a train from Union to the city, to review the details of how the grand opening had went with Ms. Beacon. She finished her glass of water and walked to the bathroom, where she twisted the shower knobs until the water was bracing enough to make her forget her eerie dream.

After her shower, she dressed herself in a wine-colored turtleneck, wool pants, and heeled black booties. She skipped coffee so she could buy one from Ray. She checked her watch. It was seven. If she moved with purpose, she would be able to get to the office on time.

On the drive to Borrachitos, a dull ache needled her in her chest. She ignored it and chalked it up to not having had coffee and not having seen her abuela over the weekend. It was rare that Larimar and Doña Bélgica went an entire weekend without sharing a meal. She arrived in Union Center and parked in front of Borrachitos, making a mental note to cross Morris Avenue and check on Beacon Union if she had extra time.

The lights were on at Borrachitos, and there were a couple patrons sitting at the window seats. She opened the glass door and stepped in. Ray was in front of the counter, and as soon as she saw him, she knew something was wrong. Behind him was Doña Delfina, a smug smile on her face.

Ray held a folded newspaper against his chest. With trepidation, she drew closer until she was only a few feet away from him. He studied her, pressing his lips into a flat line, still clutching the newspaper. She gave it a pointed stare.

Ray stared straight past her, and for the first time, she saw something in his eyes she could only describe as a hard coldness. Finally, she couldn't take it anymore.

"What is that?" she asked.

A look of astonishment came over Ray's face, like he couldn't believe she was asking that.

"This is you, right?" he said. He handed her the newspaper, letting go of it before she grabbed it so that she had to catch it from the air.

Larimar took the newspaper and unfolded it.

There was a full-page ad. Beacon's famous logo was emblazoned across the time, and right in the center was a black-and-white print of her headshot.

**GRAND OPENING OF BEACON CAFÉ UNION
CENTER: WEDNESDAY DECEMBER 8.
CONGRATULATIONS LARIMAR CINTRÓN FOR A
FABULOUS JOB OPENING THIS LOCATION! YOU
DID IT ALL, AND WE ARE SO PROUD OF YOU.
—REGINA BEACON AND THE TEAM.**

Her mouth dropped open. There was nothing to say.

"Is this what you've been doing, Larimar? A little recon to help your business?" Ray asked. His voice was soft, but there was an ocean of hurt under his words.

Her mind went blank. Somehow in all the what-if scenarios she'd dreamed up, she'd never gotten to this moment. She'd never expected things to get this far, and she'd never expected she could tell Ray she was a ciguapa. And even more so, that he would be accepting of her.

"I—" she stuttered. The words would not come. No pithy barbs would fix this.

"Told you there was something about her," Doña Delfina said.

"Yeah, but it wasn't what I thought," Ray said.

Larimar glared at Doña Delfina. She hated that the elder woman would be correct in Ray's eyes.

"Ray, can we—talk without an audience?" she said.

Ray looked doubtful, but he followed her outside till they were standing on the sidewalk in front of the bakery.

"I don't know what to say, Larimar. All we talked about, about being honest and revealing . . . was that a joke to you? Were you laughing at me on the inside while telling me you were telling the truth?"

Larimar shook her head vehemently. "No, it's not like that at all."

"Why should I believe you?" His voice rose an octave on the last word.

She fumbled for an answer. Why should he?

"Ray, I know this looks terrible, but—"

"Looks? What about your flowers, Larimar? I didn't see any mention of a flower shop in that full-page ad," he said.

She sighed. Now was as good a time as any to start telling the truth. It was her only hope. "There is no flower shop," she said quietly.

"Yeah, that's what I thought," he said. "Excuse me." He grabbed the door handle and headed back inside, and Larimar let him go. She had no excuse, no grounds to call him back on. All she could do was watch him walk back to the counter. To her surprise, he didn't storm up to it. No, he walked at an even pace and picked up the newspaper, which Larimar had dropped on one of the round tables. He threw it in the trash bin behind the counter. Okay, that was fair. Still, it hurt her to see it.

It was getting late, and if she stayed longer, she would be late for work. Work. She realized she had no desire to go into the office, and didn't really care what happened. She pulled out her phone and shot a quick text to Ms. Beacon.

LARIMAR: Not feeling well. Going to work from home today.

A moment later there was a ping.

REGINA BEACON: Aww, feel better soon. Btw, did you see the surprise?

A wave of nausea surged in Larimar's stomach. The surprise, indeed. The surprise was going to take a lot to fix . . . if it could be fixed at all.

On Saturday, two days after the newspaper ad was published, Larimar was still working from home, and Ray hadn't answered any of her texts. She decided to take a drive at lunch and see if she could at least glimpse his face. She jumped in the Beetle and drove the route she could now navigate with her eyes closed.

When she turned onto Stuyvesant, she slowed down as

much as the busy city center traffic would allow, but when she tried to peer in, all she saw was a black-and-white CLOSED sign hanging on the door.

Closed? At noon on a Saturday? Her heart sank to a muddy place in her chest.

The next day, she drove by at the same time. The same sign was still hanging on the door. Despair threatened to overcome her. There was always driving to his house. He still hadn't answered any of her texts.

She didn't want to just show up, especially if he was making it clear that he didn't want to see her or talk to her. The sad part was she couldn't blame him.

Larimar sat on a metal bench at the Roselle Park train station on Monday, burrowing down into her puffer jacket to fight the wind. She could wait inside the vestibule, she knew, but the icy air helped wake her up. It snapped her out of the funk she'd fallen into and reminded her to keep going.

There was a plunk on the other edge of the bench. "Larimar, is that you in there?"

She recognized the voice instantly, and for a second wished the ice on the cement platform could keep cracking until the earth opened up and gave her enough space to jump in.

"Candy."

"Yes, it's me. Are you okay? You look like you're shrinking into your jacket."

Larimar blew the breath out through her nostrils one ounce at a time. "Well, it's cold as balls out here, Candy."

Candy rolled her eyes. "Obv. Why don't you come inside the vestibule? They don't charge extra to wait in there, you know." Larimar glanced up at Candy's face. Her blond hair was tucked into a burgundy beret and she wore a camel coat with a plaid collar. Was Candy actually trying to be helpful?

Her glance swept from Candy's face to the vestibule. Damn, why did she have to be right?

"Fine," Larimar said, and followed Candy into the vestibule. She plopped down on the black metal bench, and Candy sat too, leaving space between them.

Immediately, the heat from the radiator lamp on the ceiling began to warm Larimar's face.

"Better, huh?" Candy asked, holding out her hands and wiggling her fingers in front of her face.

Larimar stretched her hands out, too. "I can move my fingers again, so, yeah. Not a bad development."

A moment of silence stretched by.

"How's your boyfriend?" Candy asked.

Larimar sighed. "He's not my boyfriend, Candy," she said, measuring each word.

A frown spread over Candy's face.

"Oh, sorry," she said. "I got the wrong impression the day I ran into you—physically—at the thrift shop."

Larimar winced. "No . . . you didn't get the wrong impression. But, uh, we broke up this week."

Candy dropped her gaze to the floor, and her expression grew cloudy. "Sorry to hear that," she said.

"Thanks," Larimar murmured.

Another moment passed, and Candy said, "My boyfriend and I broke up two months ago. I keep waiting for life to feel 'normal' again."

Larimar shot a glance at Candy. This was the first time Candy had ever said something that implied anything besides being perfect about herself. Candy wouldn't be her first choice for a heart-to-heart, but she really needed someone to talk to. And so far, Candy was being kind.

"Um, can I get you a coffee?" Larimar asked. Her eyes darted to the tiny coffee stand next to the ticketing booth.

Candy gave a small smile. "I'd like that," she said.

Larimar popped over to the stand and returned with two coffees. She handed Candy one and blew on the other to cool it down.

"It sucks. It really sucks," Larimar said.

"It does," Candy said, letting out a sigh it sounded like she'd been holding for a while, and taking a small sip from her coffee.

"How's work going?" Larimar asked.

"Uh . . . not doing as good a job as you, but I'm trying," Candy said with a rueful smile.

Candy thought she did a good job? This breakup seemed to have really gotten her in touch with her feelings. All of a sudden, Larimar felt sad for Candy. It must have been tiring to constantly exert a message about how great she was at everything when on the inside she was actually insecure about her performance.

"You do a good job, Candy," Larimar said.

"You think so?"

Larimar nodded emphatically. "You do. We have to work

around the clock to compete with you guys."

The train pulled into the Roselle Park station. "This was nice, Larimar. Maybe we can do it again sometime, outside of the train station." She ventured a shy smile.

"I'd be down for that, Candy," Larimar said, and stepped onto the train.

It was a chilly December Saturday, and somehow Larimar still felt the river calling her.

She went down to the Elizabeth River and sat by its banks. She smoothed out the leaves under her, creating a comfortable seat for herself. There was a chill in the air, but she still wanted to be by the river, to feel its currents flowing near and taking the crackling burrs of her pain with them.

Memories of the past week, and the past two months— everything since she had first met Ray—spun freely through her mind, and one by one, the tears began to flow. She sobbed to herself for a few quiet moments, and before long she felt the ciguapa at her side. When she closed her eyes, she sensed a light pressure on both of her temples, and felt herself being drawn back, threaded through a needle in her own subconscious.

The first change she felt was thick heat and humidity pushing up against her skin. There was a house set back on a hill, fringed with palm trees and lush tropical plants. Adjacent to the house, there was a spring that flowed out of the mountain. This was Doña Bélgica's house in Barahona. She recognized the pink-painted villa from her summer visits as a child. Someone had constructed a pool since then to catch the spring water as it flowed down.

Larimar hadn't been to this place for more than twenty years, and nevertheless she felt a sort of familiarity. She stood by one of the spring-fed pools, and a rustling next to her drew her attention to the ciguapa. The ciguapa took her hand, and as she did, one by one, more ciguapas started coming out of the foliage. They each took a place around her, forming a circle next to the pool. As she glanced around the circle, each of them met her eyes. They were not holographic the way her guardian ciguapa had always appeared to her in New Jersey. They appeared to be solid flesh and bone, with long, flowing hair that for some of them, reached their backward-facing feet. Some of them were big, others were small. Some old and some young. She was surrounded by ciguapas of all ages, shapes, and sizes.

Slowly, they began to close the circle until they were all around her, embracing her. There had to be at least fifteen of them. Her heart leapt and surged as they began to hum a low melodious tune. It wasn't in English or Spanish, but in another language her mind couldn't capture, and yet with another part of her consciousness, she understood the message: *You are not alone. You have never been alone.*

Tears flowed freely down her cheeks as she felt the ciguapas' feather-light touches on her shoulders, the unbearable lightness of the weight of their hands on her hand. Time passed, and she wasn't sure if it was hours or days. Her guardian ciguapa took her face in both hands and bestowed a light kiss on the center of her forehead. Before she knew it, the house and ciguapas slipped away, and she was back at the Elizabeth River.

She blinked her eyes and stretched her fingers and hands in front of her. The ciguapas had taken her home. But now she knew. Right by her abuela's old house, there was a home base where there were so many others like her, and her mother, and Doña Bélgica. This knowledge was a bracing tonic for her spirit. It gave her roots, and she needed roots to soar.

27

After her astral trip to the cíguapas' home, she felt a little low on energy. She needed sugar and butter, and there was nothing she wanted to do besides bake a delicious cake. She could only hope it would raise her spirits. On the drive home, she mentally reviewed the ingredients she had and compared them with the ones she needed.

Luckily, she had everything. She drove straight home and took the elevator up to the fifth floor, making a mental note to stop by Doña Bélgica's once the cake was done.

She stepped through the door of her apartment and hung her puffer jacket on the coat rack. Things were different now. She knew she was not alone, and that changed everything.

On her kitchen counter, she set out flour, eggs, sugar, butter, vanilla, and bourbon. The butter, eggs, and sugar went straight into the mixing bowl, and she watched as the mixer arm whipped them into a fluffy confection. She added the vanilla and scoured her pantry for whatever else she could add. She spotted a lime in her fruit basket and grated the zest into the batter.

What it could not be missing was the bourbon, because that was what reminded her of Ray and his baking.

She measured a shot of bourbon and poured it into the batter, its scent reminding her of Ray's baking. She would later add a little to the frosting, since the alcohol in the cake batter would evaporate during baking.

After she popped the cake in the oven, she sat on her couch to wait as it baked. As the rich aroma of butter and bourbon filled the air and tempted her taste buds, she thought over everything.

What she felt for Ray was so strong, it made her terrified of being rejected when she brought him the cake. She didn't know which was the more likely reason she'd get rejected, being a ciguapa or being the brand manager for Beacon. But she had also assumed from the beginning that their relationship wouldn't get far.

Why was that? Maybe because no other ever had. Or because she didn't know how someone could love her. Love her? Is that what Ray did? It seemed to be too late, but she was starting to think she loved him, too. She couldn't imagine the coming days, weeks, or years without him. And when she forced herself to, it hurt.

He had to love her, right? He said he didn't care if she was a ciguapa. And who wouldn't care if their significant other was a supernatural being . . . unless they loved them?

Now she had to know. She had to know if he loved her.

She nabbed a blanket from the opposite end of the couch and spread it out, pulling it up to her chin. What a difference from the ciguapas' tropical home. A thought came to her mind, screeching like nails on a blackboard. Even if he loved her, it wasn't a guarantee that he would forgive her. She shivered and pulled the blanket a little tighter around her.

Even if he had fallen in love with her over the past two months, she might have lost his trust. Ughhhhh. This was why Brynne had warned her not to lie. Coño. She smacked her forehead with chagrin. Now there was nothing she would be able to do to make him trust her again . . . besides offer a sincere apology and hope he would accept it. Thinking about putting herself out there and not knowing if he would forgive her was terrifying. She wasn't sure if she could take that chance. Her punk heart might shrivel up into a raisin if he said no.

The stove timer buzzed. She put on the black oven mitts Doña Bélgica had crocheted for her and opened the oven door to pick up the cake and place it on her cooling rack. She queued up a ska punk playlist from her phone and put it on in the background as she set to make the frosting. She whipped the confectioners' sugar into the butter and sighed with delight as the mouthwatering, rich aroma reached her nose.

She briefly contemplated adding food coloring to the frosting, but then decided not to, opting for plain white. A gentle brush against the side of the cake revealed it was still warm. Well, there was always dancing around the living room while she waited for it to cool. She cranked up her favorite Sublime song and whirled circles around her coffee table. One album later, the cake was cool and ready to frost.

A spatula dipped into the mixing bowl came out perfectly coated with delectable snowy frosting. She painted it over the surface of the cake, not leaving out a single spot. Then she picked some edible orchids from the plant Brynne gave her and sprinkled them over the surface. There. It was beautiful. If only Ray could see it.

She dozed off and was awakened by the buzz of her phone ringing next to her on the couch.

ANGELY

Larimar froze. Angely had to have heard what happened by now and was probably calling to berate her and tell her what a terrible person she was. She considered letting it go to voice mail, but an impulse swept through her and she tapped the "talk" button.

Oops. Now that she had answered, she had no idea what to say.

"Uh, hey, Angely," she began.

"Larimar."

The line was silent for a second that stretched into infinity.

"What happened?" Angely asked.

Larimar sighed and threw herself back against the couch pillows. How could she explain?

The truth was there was no good explanation. She had messed up, and there was no way to fix things.

"What did Ray tell you?" she asked.

"He told me about Beacon," Angely answered in an even tone that hung on the last word.

Larimar waited for the rest.

"And he told me there was something he couldn't tell me, but that you were gifted and hadn't wanted him to know about that, either."

"Gifted?" That was a charitable way to describe what she was.

"Mm-hmm," Angely said. "You mind telling me what that's about?"

A block of ice formed in her chest. She had already revealed herself to too many people. And she didn't know if she could deal with one more rejection.

"Uh, I'm sorry, Angely, I can't," Larimar said, her voice strained across the syllables.

Angely took a deep breath and sighed. "Okay, I had a feeling you were going to say that."

"You did?"

"Yeah, and it doesn't really matter. I can't believe I didn't see this coming, not even in my platinum-powered crystal jade ball."

"What?"

"Look, girl. You shouldn't have lied about Beacon. That was a shitty thing to do. And I don't know what kind of gift you're talking about. But what I gather from this whole thing is that you were afraid of losing my brother."

Larimar clutched the phone in her hand.

"He's upset that you lied to him, of course. But he's crushed by the thought that you guys are over. And it seems to me that it doesn't have to be that way."

"How?" Larimar said in a voice barely above a whisper.

"Talk to him. Tell him why you did it," Angely said.

"What? How can I do that?"

"Just do it. Don't think about it too much," Angely said.

Larimar sighed. Angely was right. She wasn't ready to go

through with it yet, but Angely was right.

"Y mira, if you need some courage, I can lend you my raw garnet bracelet," Angely said.

Larimar smiled. Angely and her stones. She would miss them if she were to lose touch with Ray. Angely was a little kooky sometimes, but her passion for living and getting the best out of the natural world touched Larimar's heart.

"Thanks, Angely," Larimar said. "I'll let you know on that. And . . . I'll let you know how it goes."

Angely let out a triumphant whoop. "Epa! That's the attitude. Great. I look forward to hearing it. I love that fool brother of mine, and I don't think I can deal with seeing him hurt again, especially when it's so obvious that you guys love each other."

"Um, it is?"

Angely let out a snort. "Bye, girl."

Larimar hung up and laid the phone on her lap, a small smile spreading over her face.

An idea flashed through her head, and she knew it may not be the best one, but it was all she had. How could Ray say no to bourbon? And vanilla? And edible flowers? He wasn't a barbarian. It was worth a try.

Her hands moved as if of their own accord, as they transferred the cake to her cake-taker, secured the plastic cover. She threw on her jacket and scarf.

Out of pure impatience, she took the stairs instead of waiting for the elevator, bounding down two at a time until she reached the lobby. She dashed to her car, buckled the cake box into the back seat, and sped out of the parking lot.

She skipped Borrachitos and drove straight to Ray's house. She didn't have the heart to see the shuttered bakery again, at least not this soon. Larimar killed the engine right in front of his house, and in a flash of movement, unbuckled the cake, ran it up to Ray's door, laid it on the doorstep, rang the bell, and ducked into the bushes.

The thorny brambles scratched the sleeves of her puffer jacket, but she still crouched down to wait and watch, and see if he would receive her gift.

Nobody came to the door. She waited and waited. There was not a single peep. His Chevy was in the driveway, though. After about ten minutes, her heart began to sink. She watched out for another five minutes before she slunk back to her car and drove away.

After dusk had fallen, she drove by his house again to see if he had taken the container in. It sat on his doorstep, covered in fallen leaves. Tears pricked her eyes when it came into her line of vision. And it became real that Ray might not want to ever talk to her again, and she was going to have to accept it.

28

"Oiga, Papá, where's the beer?" Larimar called, staring at the empty bottom shelf of Doña Bélgica's fridge.

Papá looked up from the crocheted doily he was fiddling with on the coffee table.

"It's not there?" he asked in disbelief.

Larimar shook her head. "No. And Oliver and Melissa will be here in about fifteen minutes." Lord knew Oliver would drain the beer supply.

They exchanged a glance. "I'll go down to Fransinatra's," she said.

"Thank you, m'ija," Papá said.

She snatched her keys off the coffee table and her jacket from the hook behind her abuela's door.

The elevator was up on the eighth floor, so she took the stairs, skipping every other one until she got to the ground floor. In a flash, she was at the door of the bodega.

There was Fransinatra, restocking the tuna section, the brim of his fedora sharp as ever, humming along to Hector Lavoe blasting over the speaker.

"Larimar! Haven't seen you for a few days," he said when she stepped in, tipping the brim of his hat to her.

She nodded in his direction in return and lifted a case of Corona out of the sliding-top fridge. She placed it on the counter and waited for Fransinatra to reach the other side of the counter, which wasn't too long since he was still pretty spry. He eyed the twenty-four-pack, then Larimar, then the twenty-four-pack again.

"We're having a party tonight at Abuela's," she said by way of explanation.

She was all grown up and still felt like she had to explain what she was doing with beer to the bodeguero. He nodded in silent understanding and rang up her purchase. She fiddled with her wallet and fished out a pair of bills.

"Alright, enjoy the party and give Berenice y el don my regards. And Larimar?"

Here we go. Fransinatra could not let a person go without one of his famous pearls of wisdom.

"Yes?"

"Beyond fear is every other thing you've ever wanted," he said with a gentle bow of his head.

The little hairs stood up on her arms. Fransinatra had hit the nail on the head. He now had a track record of once every thirty-four years.

"Thanks, Fransinatra," she said, and hoisted the beer off the counter. She gave him a little nod as she headed out.

She wondered if Ray grew up with a bodeguero who would rat him out to his parents whenever he got together with friends to have a beer or smoke a joint in the park. If things weren't so messed up, she could have texted him to ask.

Larimar trudged back to her abuela's apartment carrying the heavy box of beer. It was Oliver who opened the door for her.

"Hey, Lari-nerd!" he said, taking the case from her and ushering her in. Oliver had a little gleam in his eye. That was interesting. She wondered what that was all about.

"Where's Melissa?" she asked, casting her eyes around the apartment.

"She went to lay down in Mami and Papi's apartment," he said. "She had a late night last night. A pipe broke in the salon; it flooded and she had to go in at almost midnight. They didn't finish fixing it until almost three."

"Damn," Larimar said. She made a mental note to check out Melissa's nail designs when she woke up. She always had something new and pretty.

"Larimar!" Doña Bélgica called from the kitchen. Doña Bélgica was waiting for her so they could make pastelón de plátano maduro, ripe plantain casserole, together. She had already boiled the ripe plantains, and Larimar mashed them in a ceramic bowl with lots of butter and evaporated milk. In a glass baking dish they layered the plantain mixture with a mixture of sauteed broccoli and onions Doña Bélgica had prepared, making this version meatless for Melissa.

They topped the dish with a boatload of shredded mozzarella, and Larimar stuck it in the oven. They sat down on the couch next to Papá, who was watching a football game on ESPN.

"Oh! I knew I wanted to show you something," Doña Bélgica said almost as soon as they sat down.

Larimar helped her abuela up again, and Doña Bélgica waved Larimar into her bedroom. "Guess what?" she said, her face lighting up and casting a girlish glow on her elegant features. "I found my memory box!" She sat down on the bed and motioned for Larimar to bring a floral-printed box from her vanity table.

"Oh!" Larimar exclaimed. Her abuela had been looking for it for quite some time. Larimar picked up the box and carried it over to Doña Bélgica's bed. Of course, the box had been immaculately wiped down and was not covered in dust bunnies like it would've been if Larimar had been squirreling it away all this time. It was covered with rose damask wallpaper that was cracking and fading in the corners.

Doña Bélgica removed the lid and laid it down next to the box on her lavender paisley bedspread. Out came an aged photo album, also crackling around the edges.

"Found it!" she said triumphantly. "Mira, m'ija, this was my mother." She handed Larimar a sepia photograph, laying in on her palm with the softest touch.

Larimar took the photo from her. She could not control the sobs that followed. It was like all the stress of the past few weeks gushed out of her when she saw that woman's face. It was a face that had buoyed her through many a moment by the river. She cried, and Doña Bélgica leaned in to comfort her.

"What's wrong, m'ija?" she asked.

Larimar smiled through her tears. "I know her," Larimar said.

Doña Bélgica nodded politely, patting Larimar's arm. "Of course you do, mi amor," she said.

Larimar rested in Doña Bélgica's embrace. "Come on, let's go take out the pastelón," Doña Bélgica said, drying Larimar's tears with her lace handkerchief. Larimar fingered the edge of the photo, not wanting to put it away.

"I'm making a copy of this, Mamá," she said.

"Sure, m'ija," Doña Bélgica said.

Larimar placed the photo on top of the album, not wanting to put it away just yet.

"Can I leave it out for now?" she asked.

"Of course, mi amor," her abuela said.

She traced the edges of the picture lovingly one more time, then followed Doña Bélgica back to the kitchen. With her abuela's lace-print oven mitts, she removed the pastelón from the oven and set it on a cooling rack.

"Hey, guys!" Melissa came into the kitchen, rubbing her eyes.

"Hey, Melissa!" Larimar said. She gave her a friendly hug, and then stepped back to take her hand and check out her nails. She almost fainted when she found an emerald-cut diamond solitaire on Melissa's ring finger.

"Oh, my GOD! You guys got engaged!? Oliver, were you going to SAY anything? You little . . . congratulations!" She pulled Melissa in for another hug, then turned to hug Oliver and clap him on the back.

"What? My son is engaged?" Doña Berenice said, pushing her way into the kitchen at exactly the right moment.

"Yes, Mamá! I proposed to Melissa last night," he said.

"Ohhhh, the salon flooded, huh?" Larimar gave Oliver a conspiratorial wink, and he winked back.

Doña Berenice thumped him on the back. "What kind of bullshit is this? Were you not going to tell us?" she exclaimed.

"I was. It was a surprise!" he said in his defense.

"This calls for more beer," Papá said, beaming from ear to ear while he pulled on his jacket.

"Congratulations, m'ijo," Doña Bélgica said. She wiped her eyes as she leaned in to hug Oliver.

Larimar sat down on the couch and watched the hugging frenzy with a touch of sadness. Oliver and Melissa looked so happy together, and she was happy for them. They made a good couple and they complemented each other well. She hated to be that person who thought of herself when others were celebrating a milestone, but she couldn't help but think of Ray.

She would have wanted something like this for them. She could imagine bringing Ray home, introducing him to her parents. Ray was the type who would ask her father for her hand, even if it wasn't necessary in these times. He was just classic like that.

Things with Ray were over, but it wasn't entirely possible for her to let go. She wiped a tear from the corner of her eye before anyone could notice. Her mom would beat her ass if she saw her crying at the family gathering that had turned into Oliver's engagement party.

The celebration around her seemed to go on in slow motion. She thought of Ray's curls, the way his voice got low when he talked about his fears, the molten heat of his kiss. She was there, but she was with Ray . . . only Ray wasn't with her.

There had to be something she could do to make things right. She had to try again.

LARIMAR'S BOURBON SPICE NAKED CAKE WITH EDIBLE FLOWERS

Makes one 8-inch layer cake

FOR THE CAKE

3 large eggs, at room temperature

4 tablespoons unsalted butter, melted and cooled

1 cup granulated sugar

¼ cup packed brown sugar

1 cup buttermilk

1 ounce/2 tablespoons bourbon

2 teaspoons baking powder

½ teaspoon baking soda

½ teaspoon salt

¼ teaspoon cinnamon

¼ teaspoon cloves

¼ teaspoon ginger

2 cups all-purpose flour, sifted

Orchids or edible flower of choice

FOR THE BUTTERCREAM

1 cup/2 sticks butter

2 cups confectioners' sugar

1 ounce/2 tablespoons bourbon

Make the cake: Preheat the oven to 350 degrees Fahrenheit and grease two 8-inch cake pans.

In the bowl of a stand mixer, beat the eggs until frothy. Add the butter and both sugars, and beat together. Add the buttermilk and bourbon and beat to combine. Add the baking powder, baking soda, salt, cinnamon, cloves, and ginger, and mix to combine. Add the flour in three additions, mixing until combined after each addition.

Divide the batter between the two greased pans and bake for 30 minutes, or until a toothpick inserted into the center comes out clean. Allow to cool in their pans on a wire rack for at least 15 minutes.

Make the buttercream: In the bowl of a stand mixer, cream the butter for 4 minutes. Adding the confectioners' sugar and bourbon and beat to combine.

Remove the cakes from their pans. Allow to cool completely before frosting. Spread a layer of frosting over one of them, top with the other cake, and lightly coat the sides with buttercream using a silicone brush. Spread a thin layer of frosting over the top of the cake. Affix the edible flowers to the cake as pleases the eye. Enjoy.

29

Leaves were falling on Ray's street, to the point where it was raining gold, red, and green as Larimar drove to his home. Strapped securely in the back seat was bourbon cake 2.0, a seatbelt crossing the cake taker she used to transport it. Tucked into the Beetle's center console were the secret ska show tickets she had been able to secure with Brynne's help. She had given him two tickets. If he wanted to give the other one to someone else, she would accept that. But her fingers were crossed that he would share it with her.

Ray's Chevy was in the driveway. She was going to have to be fast for this to work. Once she parked the Beetle next to his truck, she grabbed the cake and tickets and placed them squarely on the middle of the doormat. She rang the doorbell and dashed back to the car at stealth speed, jamming the key in the ignition and jolting the Beetle's engine to life.

Right as she was about to leave, an Amazon truck pulled up and blocked the driveway. Anxiety welled up in Larimar's chest, and she screamed silently in her mind. Ray was going to find her sitting in the driveway. This was not how she planned her getaway at all.

The front door cracked open, and Ray appeared in the entryway. He was paler than the last time she had seen him, and dark circles ringed his undereyes. He glanced down, and moved in slow motion to pick up the cake box and tickets. She watched him read the outside of the envelope, and as soon as he did, he looked up and met her gaze.

He motioned for her to get out of the car. She froze, with nowhere to go and no way out.

The Amazon driver had crossed the street and was chatting with Ray's neighbor. She seemed to have no choice but to get out of the car. She climbed out of the driver's seat and forced herself to throw her shoulders back and stand in front of Ray without cringing. He stared at the cake long and hard before he spoke.

"Why are you doing this to me?" he said.

Her heart twisted in her chest.

"Ray . . . I really didn't mean for things to come out the way they did," she said.

"Why did you lie then? And lie about lying?"

"I was afraid."

"Of what?"

She stared at the cake taker in his hands, unable to answer.

"Larimar. If you don't want to talk to me about this, why did you come?"

She raised her gaze to meet his. "Do you want me to leave?"

Dead silence hung in the air and pressed against her lungs from all sides.

He sighed. "No, I don't want you to leave." He picked an imaginary piece of lint off his cuff. "Why couldn't you tell me you worked for Beacon?"

Larimar rocked back on her heels before she began to speak. "There were so many reasons. I was sure our relationship wouldn't make it to you finding out about . . . me. I wanted to enjoy it, enjoy the connection I felt with you, before it was over. Because I was sure it was only a matter of time before I had to end things so you wouldn't find out who and what I was."

At this, his face turned overcast. "Enjoy it? What about me? So your plan was to make me fall in love with you and then toss me out before I could find out you were a ciguapa? Or that you worked for Beacon?"

"Wait. Did you just say *fall in love* with me?"

He looked down before he raised his gaze to meet hers. "Yes. I said *fall in love* with you. What about me?"

She pressed her lips together to keep from grinning while she thought about his question.

"I've never met a man like you before, Ray. My expectation was that you would care less than I did."

"Well, that's pretty sad."

"Yes, it is."

She slumped down onto his front steps. After a moment, he surprised her by slumping down next to her.

"You said you loved me," she repeated to herself, tracing the gold gel pen lettering on the outside of the ticket envelope.

"Yes. And I don't care if you're a ciguapa, or a werewolf, or whatever else you could be. Just don't lie to me from now on, okay?"

"From now on?"

"Mm-hmm."

"You mean . . . we're not done?"

"Larimar, I could never be done with you," he said, gathering her into his arms. "I want to be with you. But I need to know I can trust you."

"Well, now you know all my secrets," she said. "Except for one."

"Oh?"

"Yes," she said and leaned in to whisper into his ear. "I love you too."

Ray smiled and squeezed her tight. She drew back enough to see the shadows on his face, and he brought their lips together, touching his to hers gently, and then kissing her more deeply.

She pulled away for a moment to catch her breath. "What about Doña Delfina?" she asked.

"So . . . about her. She was my mother's friend and has good intentions for me. But she's also my ex-wife's mother."

Larimar's eyes became round as saucers. "What?"

Ray nodded. "Yeah. Even though Cari and I ended things on friendly terms, she hasn't quite given up hope that we may get back together someday."

Larimar thought for a long moment. "I'm sorry if this comes off as mean, but isn't that sort of a boundaries issue?"

"I see what you mean. But it was never really a problem because I didn't date after the divorce. Until now," he said with a shy smile. "I don't want to take away her job, but I will have a talk with her and let her know she's going to have to be professional and respect my personal life, or we won't be able to continue working together. Besides, she's not my chastity keeper."

Larimar couldn't help but laugh at this. "So who is your chastity keeper, then?"

"Nobody."

"Nobody?"

"No."

"I don't believe you."

"Alllll right, come in," he said, with mock exasperation. "I'll show you."

Inside Ray's house, Larimar, as it was her custom, made herself cozy in the corner of his couch. Suddenly, she felt shy. She had never been the subject of his offer to show her how not chaste he could be.

"Do you have to be somewhere anytime soon?" he asked.

Larimar shook her head. "Nope. My entire plan for the day was ringing your doorbell and running away," she said.

"Sweet. Do you want to watch a movie?"

"Sure. Let's see what's on."

They flipped channels until they came to a film where a man was kissing a woman's back, one inch of skin at a time. They exchanged nervous glances, and Ray changed the channel. The next channel was playing a demure nature film about winter birds of Japan, which they watched in soundless rapt attention for a stretch. Then Ray turned off the TV.

He reached across the couch and pulled her to him, and she touched her lips to his. She leaned into him to deepen the kiss, and they melded into each other until they were both breathless. They broke apart to draw in air, and instead of returning to her mouth, he trailed his lips down her neck, pressing ardent kisses into her skin.

"What do you want, Larimar?" he said, his voice strangled.

"Do the thing from the movie," she said.

He broke away so he could see her face. "The what?" he asked.

"The movie. The one we just saw."

"Ohhh."

His eyes were dancing as he waited expectantly for her to roll over onto her stomach. She did, but could hardly find a comfortable position to lie down on the couch.

She sat up, and their eyes met.

"Do you want to go to my bedroom?" he asked.

It was an awfully weighty question.

"Yes," she said, and she followed him down the tiled hall to a cozy room.

She laid down on the soft gray bedspread and peeled off her black turtleneck sweater. There was an audible gulp of air from Ray when she shook out the sweater and folded it next to her. When she was lying down, she unhooked her bra and folded it neatly in half, then placed it on the wooden night table. Mami would have been proud.

Larimar stretched out over the bedspread, and Ray sat right next to her supine form, his hip aligning with hers. He placed both hands on either side of her back and leaned down to give her the gentlest kiss in the space between her shoulder blades. He moved over her back, one inch at a time, kissing all the way down to where her waist dipped and then rose to fill out the waistband of her jeans. His lips lingered over her back in a slow, languorous motion, turning her joints to jelly.

She sighed happily as he gave her one last kiss and used his arms to push back to sitting.

"How was it?"

"Terrible. You're going to have to do it all over again."

His lips curved up as she rolled over.

She sat up and leaned forward to stroke his face and touch their lips together. Her body was liquid under her skin, and the kiss was different than any kiss they'd had before. Their tongues twisted in hunger, and his hands were rough and heavy on both of her hips.

"I want you," she whispered.

"I've wanted you since day one," he whispered back.

There wasn't much more that needed to be said.

30

"Another year gone by, another Christmas party," Larimar said to Emerson. They reclined in two gold-painted chairs, Christmas decorations swirling in the air above them.

Em shrugged and took a swig of her Negroni, her dangly earrings swinging with the movement of her head. "Next year in Jerusalem ... or something like that." Larimar held back a chuckle.

"Is Ms. Beacon going to speak?" Mason, the mailroom manager, asked.

"Looks like it," Larimar said, eyeing the podium where Ms. Beacon was getting ready to ping a glass with a fork. For the occasion, Ms. Beacon had dressed in a black suit with gold threads and black velvet pumps. Her shoulder-length chestnut hair was flipped inward at the ends so that they perfectly grazed her shoulders, and her bangs were curled so they did a perfect twirl in the center of her forehead. Her earlobes held two gold door knockers.

She tapped the side of the glass, and silence fell over the staff of Beacon Foods.

"Good afternoon to you all, and happy holidays. Before we start, I want to take a moment to recognize Larimar Cintrón.

Great work on the Beacon Union opening in Union, New Jersey. Let's have a round of applause for Larimar."

The room resounded with deafening clapping, and Larimar did a small head-bow while she attempted not to blush.

"That's great. Thank you all. Now moving on to the fourth-quarter promotions."

Larimar's chest tightened. Oh my God, it was too much in front of all these people.

"Juan Perez, Mason Vance, Lilly Linklater, Waverly Greene . . ."

Larimar listened for her name, but Ms. Beacon reached the end of her list.

Booming claps resounded again, but they rang hollow in Larimar's ears. Her work was so great but she had been passed over for a promotion again?

"Thank you all!" Ms. Beacon called with a plastic smile, and then stepped down from the podium.

Larimar and Em exchanged glances. "Well, dang," Larimar said.

Em nodded slowly. "Uh . . . yeah. I don't know what to say other than you deserved a promotion, Larimar."

She felt eyes on her from all around the room. With one simple action, Ms. Beacon had hollowed out her praise of the last four months.

It was then that Larimar made a decision.

The next day, Larimar emailed Ms. Beacon right after her first morning coffee.

FROM: Larimar Cintrón
TO: Regina Beacon, CEO
SUBJECT: meeting today

Please let me know when you are available to meet, as
soon as possible.

Two minutes later, Ms. Beacon called Larimar's desk phone.
"Larimar?" she called, her voice echoing through the tinny
speaker. "I am free now if you are ready."

Larimar wasn't ready, but it didn't matter. She took a deep
breath and steeled herself for what was to come. She smoothed
the front of her white button-down blouse, threw her hair back
over her shoulders, and pressed the soles of her feet into the floor
through her black suede flats.

She walked to Ms. Beacon's office, controlling her breath the
best she could.

Ms. Beacon was all sunny smiles behind her desk.

"Good morning, Larimar! What can I help with?"

Larimar did her best to keep her face a neutral mask. "Nice
party yesterday," she said, her voice even.

Ms. Beacon nodded. "Yes, of course," she said. "You know we
always go all out for the holidays," she said.

Larimar nodded. "Right."

There was a drawn-out pause as Larimar collected her
thoughts, during which Ms. Beacon regarded her with a quiz-
zical gaze.

Well, there was no use in beating around the bush. "I'm putting in my two weeks' notice," Larimar said. "I'll be certain to leave everything in place before Christmas."

Ms. Beacon's jaw dropped. "Excuse me, what?" she said.

Larimar narrowed her eyes at her almost-former employer. "That's what I said," she said. "I will prepare everything before Christmas for whoever follows me. I'm guessing Em," she said with a shrug.

Ms. Beacon continued to stare at her with an open-mouthed gaze. Finally, she regained her ability to speak.

"Larimar . . . I'm shocked. What—why do you want to leave? Especially after the special recognition I gave you?" She squinted at Larimar as if she truly and positively couldn't understand it.

Larimar squared her shoulders and took another deep breath. "The recognition you gave me was not the one I was looking for," she said. Not to mention the other troubles it had caused her.

"Is this about the promotions?" Ms. Beacon said.

"That's certainly part of it. I've wanted to go into business myself for a while, and being passed over once again may prove to be the push I needed." She willed herself not to falter as Ms. Beacon continued to stare at her in disbelief.

"Excuse me . . . I have some paperwork to fill out," Larimar said.

She turned to walk back to her office, leaving Ms. Beacon pondering in her wake.

She printed out the resignation paperwork and took her potted plant down from the filing shelf. She wasn't ready to pack yet, but it was one step in the right direction.

Larimar's Beetle squealed into her parking space at such an angle that the potted plant nearly went flying off the backseat. How was she going to tell her mother and abuela that there wasn't going to be any promotion, and there wasn't going to be any down payment for a house for them after all? She had no idea where to start.

In a weak effort to buy time, she paced over to the bodega instead of entering the apartment building. There was nothing she needed to buy, but she was not quite ready to face the barrage of questions that would follow her announcement.

The hinges of the bodega door squeaked as she entered, and Misu scurried away.

"Fransinatra, qué lo qué!" Larimar called into the empty bodega.

"Epaa!" Fransinatra responded from the cookie and cracker aisle. "Be right there. Stocking up the cookies."

"Got any mantecaditos?" she asked.

"No, but I have these Danish butter cookies," he said, proffering a round tin decorated with photos of cookies.

"Ah, looks like Mamá's sewing kit," she said. Doña Bélgica had just such a tin where she kept all her spools of thread, measuring tape, and needles.

"Of course it does," Fransinatra chuckled.

"I'll take it," she said.

She dug her hand into the bottom of her purse and pulled out a couple of folded bills, then handed them to Fransinatra.

"Gracias, hija," he said. "And may the force be with you."

"Um, ok, Fransinatra. Been watching *Star Wars* much lately?"

"Y esa vaina? What is that?" Fransinatra asked in an innocent tone.

"Never mind," she said, and took her round tin of butter cookies. "Gracias."

"You are very welcome, hija," Fransinatra said. "Say hi to my friend Roberto, please."

"I will."

She trudged to the apartment building, the round tin tucked under her arm. She took the stairs one at a time, in no hurry to reach the second floor.

She sighed. She could already hear the kilometric speech her mother was going to give her.

She rang Doña Bélgica's bell, not bothering to fish the keys out of her purse. Exactly as she expected, it was her mother who opened the door.

"Oh! You're home early," Berenice said.

"Um . . . mm-hm," Larimar said nervously.

She followed her mother into the living room, where Doña Bélgica was sitting on the couch, embroidering a commemorative blanket for Oliver and Melissa's engagement.

It was probably better to get this over with quickly, much like ripping off a Band-Aid.

"Look, I have something to tell you both," Larimar said.

Doña Bélgica glanced up from the blanket, and Berenice settled in beside her and crossed her arms.

"I quit my job," she said.

The two elder Dominican women gaped at her. It was time to be scared.

To her surprise, her mother let out a heavy sigh. "That's great," she said. "That Beacon lady was working you too hard."

"What?" Larimar gasped.

"Así mísmo," Berenice said. "I've been telling you that."

"But Mami, you always told me to work hard."

"Sí, but without being a pendeja! She takes too much advantage of your hard work and doesn't share the benefits. Hmph," she said, uncrossing and recrossing her arms.

"Y-you're not disappointed that we won't have a down payment to buy a house for you, Papi, and Mamá?"

"Pffft. That job was not the only cold soda in the fridge, Larimar. We can still work together to get that deposit." Larimar heaved a heavy sigh.

Doña Bélgica patted the space next to her on the couch, beckoning for Larimar to come and sit. "M'ija, there is something I want to tell you," she said.

Larimar sank into the couch next to her abuela and rested her hand on her elder's.

"When I made the decision to move to this country, it was not easy. I knew our energy would be weaker here. I knew it would affect us in ways I couldn't predict, and I was right. Look at you and your full-moon change." Larimar nodded and squeezed her hand.

"In Barahona we had the run of the forest. But I knew I wanted a better life for myself and my descendants. I didn't want us to live in a place where we would always be labeled "creatures.""

"Sí señora," Berenice chimed in. "We're much more than that."

"I wanted . . . the ciguapa to finally get her happy ending . . . for a change," Doña Bélgica said.

Larimar's eyes brimmed with tears. Out of the corner of her eye, she glanced over at her mother, who was wiping her own eyes.

"You're not living the dream I dreamed, Larimar. You ARE the dream I dreamed."

"Oh, Mamá," Larimar sighed. The tears were flowing freely down her face, and Doña Bélgica reached out to wipe them away with the blanket.

"Now this blanket can go forth into the world blessed," she said. "It has already seen tears of joy. What I want to say with all this is, no comas jaiba. Live your best life, m'ija. And take chances on yourself. I cried tears of blood to get you here."

"I know, Mamá. And I will never not value it." She leaned in for a hug, and Berenice leaned in from the other side to create a group hug. The soft cotton of Doña Bélgica's knit sweater was a caress on Larimar's cheek. The warmth of her mother's embrace was a balm to Larimar's heart.

"Ah, la vida," Doña Bélgica sighed. "What a life this is."

NEGRONI CUPCAKES

Makes 16 cupcakes

FOR THE CUPCAKES

¾ cup granulated sugar

½ cup unsalted butter, at
room temperature

2 large eggs

2 tablespoons Campari
liqueur

1 teaspoon vanilla

1⅔ cup all-purpose flour

1½ teaspoons baking
powder

¼ teaspoon salt

FOR THE FROSTING

1½ cups unsalted butter, at
room temperature

2½ cups confectioners'
sugar

2 tablespoons gin

1 teaspoon orange extract

zest of 1 orange

Make the cupcakes: Preheat the oven to 325 degrees Fahrenheit. Prepare cupcake pans with cupcake liners.

In the bowl of a stand mixer, cream together the sugar and butter. Add the eggs, Campari, and vanilla.

In a small bowl, sift together the flour, baking powder, and salt. Add the dry ingredients to the batter, mixing until there are no lumps.

Fill the cupcake liners two-thirds full and bake for 20 minutes. Allow to cool completely on a wire rack.

Make the frosting: In the bowl of a stand mixer, beat

together the butter and confectioners' sugar for 4 minutes. Add the gin, orange extract, and orange zest, and mix until evenly blended. Frost the cupcakes once cool.

31

Larimar parked her car on the side of the Elizabeth River and descended to the water as slowly as she could make herself. It was dusk, and Ray was waiting for her on the mossy riverbank, right where she had asked him to. She had chosen the river because it was the place she felt most like herself. It was the place she felt the protection of her ancestors and her sister ciguapas. She couldn't think of a better place to share her secret with him . . . besides Barahona, but that would have to wait for when they could make the trip together.

She pushed her straight hair back over her shoulders and pulled her puffer jacket tighter around her. When she got close enough, he took her hand and leaned forward to give her a welcome hug and kiss.

"Okay, this is it," she said, and Ray nodded in agreement.

"There's no running away now," she said. "I will find you."

"Just do it, Larimar," he said with a laugh.

Slowly, she lifted her skirt to reveal her backward-facing feet. If he was surprised, he did not show it. To Ray's credit, he kept his face perfectly neutral.

"I will never tell anyone," he said in a solemn voice. "And I will protect you as long as I live."

Larimar smiled sweetly. "I can protect myself, you know . . . but I appreciate that." She leaned in and pecked him on the lips.

"So . . . how does it work?" he asked, eyeing her feet.

"How does what work?"

"You know . . . walking."

"I'll show you," she said, and putting down her skirt, she whizzed from the riverbank to her car.

That was enough to make him do a double take, and slowly, a wide grin spread over his face.

"Oh, man! You're doing the grocery shopping from now on!" he chortled when she whizzed back to where they had been standing.

She gave him a playful punch in the arm, and they sat down by the river to drink from the thermos of cinnamon-spiced hot cocoa he had brought for them. Larimar allowed Ray to pour her a cup of hot cocoa, and she leaned against his shoulder to sip it. Showing him had gone better than she had thought. They sat at the riverbank for a while, drinking hot cocoa and staring at the water, content to be themselves together.

A couple hours later, Larimar punched the weathered Covington Arms elevator buttons. She smiled, even welcomed, the familiar stomach drop when it gave its nauseating lurch. She tapped her foot as the elevator ascended. On a whim, she punched the third-floor button right as they passed the second. Why not stop by her parents' for a bit and see how her dad was doing?

She knocked, then unlocked their front door. Larimar found

her mother sitting on the couch.

"'Cion Mami," she said. "Where's Papi?"

"Dios te bendiga, mi hija," Berenice replied. "He went downstairs to get something from the bodega."

"Oh."

She picked at an imaginary spot of black nail polish outside her nail.

Berenice cleared her throat. "So, what was all that about a box you found with Mamá?" she asked, her keen gaze on Larimar.

Larimar took a seat on the couch next to her mother and turned to face her squarely.

"We found a box with pictures of Mamá's mother," she said. "Along with a painting she did of a ciguapa."

Berenice raised her eyes heavenward. "Oh, that nonsense again," she said.

"How can you call it nonsense?" Larimar said, her eyes flashing. "This is who we are! Why do you always want to pretend you're something else and like this doesn't affect you?"

Berenice cast her gaze down. "I don't know what you're talking about," she said.

"Oh, come on, Mami."

Berenice's gaze shot up to her daughter. "I didn't ask to be this, okay?" she said, her voice rising an octave. "I didn't want this life. I still don't want this life. Every night, having to deal with leg pain, feeling out of it after changing back, being afraid to go out. I didn't want it for myself, and there was nothing I could do not to pass it to you!" She let out a heavy breath after she finished her speech. It appeared she had been holding this in for about thirty-four years.

"Having my husband look at me like a freak," she said, in a lower tone.

"What do you mean? I mean, surely Papi has accepted you by now," Larimar said.

Berenice leaned in closer, although there was no one else around. "Your father has never seen my ciguapa feet," she whispered in a voice so tiny Larimar had to lean in likewise to hear her.

Larimar stared at her mother, her mind going blank. She had to be messing with her.

"What do you mean he hasn't seen them?"

"I mean exactly what I said. I explained my . . . situation to him and told him we couldn't be together at night, and he said okay," she said.

"What? How could you hide it all these years?"

"I told him that's what I needed, and he gave me my space."

Larimar nearly had to use her hands to push her jaw back to where it belonged.

"Wow. I—wowww." The words would not come. So she and Ray had bridged in a couple months what her parents hadn't been able to in thirty-five years? "And Oliver never lifted up the hem of your skirt to show Papi your feet?" That was nearly impossible to believe in itself.

Berenice shook her head.

"Mami. What do you think would happen if Papi saw them?"

Berenice wrung her hands together in her lap. "I don't know," she said in a small, squeaky voice. It was at that moment Larimar saw her mother not as the booming, imposing figure she had always been in her life, but as a scared child, terrified of losing the affection of those she loved. It hurt Larimar to think her mother lived in such fear, and in that moment, she wanted her to be free.

"What's the worst thing that could happen if you told him?" Larimar asked.

"He could leave me."

"And then? You'd have the TV all to yourself! All novelas, all the time. No more baseball," Larimar said, trying her best to keep a straight face.

"Oye, muchacha!" Berenice said, giving her a playful punch in the arm.

"Just think about it," Larimar said. She wasn't ready to tell her mother about Ray and showing him her feet, but the experience assured her that she wanted the same thing for her mom.

"Just think about it, Mami," she repeated, and with a kiss on her mother's cheek, she was off to plan her next steps.

32

After leaving her parents' apartment and going home to change, she headed to the Iglesia Hispana. The Rizos Curl Club had announced a late-night holiday pajama party where they would also do an angelito, a secret Santa, to gift each other hair products. Larimar got Anairis as her angelito recipient, and instead of buying her a commercial product, she whipped her up a hair mask made of egg yolks, mayonnaise, avocado, and rosemary. It stunk, but it was sure to give her good results.

In a wooden bowl, she had mixed all the ingredients and then sprinkled the rosemary on top for good measure. She had then spooned the mask into a glass jar she'd saved and tied a green and red velvet ribbon around the top. She'd appraised her handiwork with approval. It looked pretty cute, if she said so herself.

As her luck would have it, the angelito fell on the full moon. Having shown Ray her feet, she wondered how it would go if she told the women the truth about her hair.

On the one hand, they were Dominican American like her. No doubt they too had grown up hearing countless stories of the ciguapa, el cuco, and the infamous zángano. On the other hand, growing up hearing legends of ciguapas didn't mean they would be prepared to find out a member of their group was a real life one.

When Larimar walked into the meeting, wearing a checkered flannel pajama top paired with her floor-length skirt and her straight hair cascading down her back, the other women were already sitting around in a circle, glasses of ponche in hand, eating empanadas from tiny paper plates.

"Larimar!" Miguelina called out from the buffet table, and Larimar waved back as she pulled up a chair in the circle. She felt one or two curious glances on her, but nothing she couldn't deal with.

Anairis waved at her and passed her a small plate with two empanadas.

"Welcome everyone to the holiday meeting of the Rizos club. We are going to go around quickly, and then we'll get right to the angelito. Who wants to go first?"

Larimar stuck her hand up in the air, and Anairis nodded in her direction.

"I have something I wanted to share. It's about my hair and why I'm coming here again with this hair texture."

Anairis looked shocked, and the women in the circle exchanged a meaningful glance. "You don't have to explain. It's your hair. And you don't have to have curly hair to be part of the club."

Miguelina nodded. "Yeah, we like you, Larimar. It's not for us to judge if you feel like straightening your hair sometimes. We're here to support each other on our natural hair journeys . . . but that journey will look different for each person." She added a friendly smile at the end of her speech.

Larimar was speechless. Maybe she didn't have to tell them she was a ciguapa at all. Maybe she only had to receive the acceptance they were offering her . . . and allow herself the not-so-small joy of making friends.

"I . . . well . . . thank you," she said. "I really don't know what to say."

"Say you'll try the ponche!" Miguelina exclaimed. "I made it myself."

Someone passed Larimar a glass of ponche, and she took a sip. It was sweet . . . all of it.

The next afternoon, Larimar got back to her apartment after last-minute Christmas mall shopping and flopped on the couch. She covered herself with a fleece Christmas blanket she had gotten on sale at Bed Bath and Beyond, and was about to flick on the TV when the doorbell rang.

"Aghhh," she grumbled to herself as she left her cocoon. She peeked through the peephole and saw her punkass brother staring back at her. Ugh, the last person she wanted to see now that she wouldn't be able to come up with the down payment and he didn't freaking want to help.

Reluctantly, she opened the door.

"Hey, Oli-nerd," she said. "I didn't know you were by Mami and Papi's today."

Oliver stepped in and gave her a quick air kiss. "I wasn't," he said.

At this, her gaze shot up. "Oh?"

Oliver nodded, helping himself to a seat on the couch. "I

heard about your job, Lari."

Well, there was no point in denying it. "Yes?"

He nodded and pulled a folded envelope out of his pocket, passing it to her. She unfolded it, pulled out the paper, and her jaw dropped.

"This is a check for $40,000," she murmured.

Oliver smiled. "I know."

"What the hell is this?" she asked.

Oliver sat up straight in his seat. "It's the down payment for a house for Mami and Papi."

Larimar gasped.

Oliver nodded again. "Melissa and I decided it was way more important than having our wedding in the ice palace."

"What? Oh, your plans. . ." So that's what he was talking about when he'd said he had plans. She remembered him mentioning them before he and Melissa had even announced their engagement. "But then where are you going to have it? And this is enough for the whole down—"

"You've been helping them with their rent for years. Consider that your part of the down payment. And we'll find another venue. There are tons of them in Philly."

Oliver took a deep, jagged breath. "I've been a selfish ass. I know how hard you worked for that promotion, and Melissa helped me see that I've been leaving the responsibility for our parents up to you. We're going to pitch in more from now on. Both of us."

"Ahh!" Larimar lunged at him and gave him a squeeze. "Oliver, I'm so proud of you. And Melissa's the best thing that's happened to you, oh my God! Did you tell Mami, Papi, and Abuela yet?"

Oliver shook his head. "No. Let's go tell them."

Larimar jumped up and grabbed her keys. "I'll race you down the stairs," she said.

The first thing Larimar told herself when she awoke was not to check the time. She was able to hold off for about three minutes before she caved and powered on her phone screen. It was 3:42 a.m. Damn. This time, she didn't even think about what to do or whether to do it.

LARIMAR: I can't sleep.

She laid her phone back down on her night table and was not at all surprised when two minutes later, her phone pinged.

RAY: Hold on. I'm coming over.

In twenty minutes, Ray was at her door. She unlocked it and he stepped inside, burying his face in her neck.

"It's okay," he said, and he let her lead him to her bed. The air between them was charged, but more than anything Larimar felt relief with him at her side. They sat on the edge of the bed.

"Larimar?" he asked.

"Yes?"

"Is it okay if I don't stay up all night watching over you tonight?" he asked.

She glanced up to meet his eyes, and the fire she saw there had her melting. She pulled him to her, and with her touch told him all the things she hadn't been able to say. And when they were done, for the first time in a long time, they slept.

PONCHE (DOMINICAN HOLIDAY EGGNOG)

Makes 2 liters or 20 servings

5 cups sweetened
  condensed milk
10 cups evaporated milk
8 large egg yolks

2 sticks cinnamon
¼ teaspoon nutmeg
¾ cup white rum

In a large bowl, combine the condensed and evaporated milks and the egg yolks. Strain to remove any egg pieces. Stir in the cinnamon sticks and nutmeg. Transfer to the top of a double oiler over simmering water and cook for 40 minutes, stirring frequently.

Remove from the heat and stir in the rum. Allow to chill and remove the cinnamon sticks before serving.

33

"Alegre vengo de la montaña, de mi cabaña, qué alegre está . . ." Oliver crowed an aguinaldo, or traditional Christmas song, at the top of his lungs. Larimar and Melissa exchanged a concerned glance. With his singing voice, the windows of Doña Bélgica's apartment were in peril of breaking, and well, then they'd truly be out in the cold.

"Oli-nerd, could you please save it for when we're all drunk?" Larimar said.

Oliver laughed, but he did lower his voice.

It was the Cintrón family's custom to sing the aguinaldos together on Nochebuena, but they did have a sort of unspoken agreement to save them for the end of the night, when, they were in fact, drunk.

"Larimar, I'm ready to prepare the pastelitos," Doña Bélgica called from the kitchen. Larimar pushed off the couch and whizzed on her human feet to help her abuela, who was waiting with a stack of dough discs and ground beef filling. She floured the surface of her counter, and one by one, they stuffed the pastelitos then folded them and crimped the edges with a fork.

Larimar turned the stove on and waited for the oil to heat.

The flames jumped and danced in time to the holiday merengue music playing in the background at the lowest volume her father had ever played it in her life. She had told him about Ray, and he understood. After all, he had been in the military himself, and although he tried not to show it, he had his scars.

Once the oil was shimmering, she lowered in the pastelitos and fried them on each side until they were golden. As she took them out, her abuela went along arranging them on a sizable round tray, until it was covered in Christmas pastelitos. Larimar and Doña Bélgica stuck sprigs of rosemary between the pastelitos for a decorative accent. That was not traditional, but it looked pretty.

Oliver and Melissa had finished setting the table, and Larimar placed the pastelitos on the table together with the dish of Christmas fruits, mainly apples and grapes. For her, they were the most boring fruits in existence, since they were the ones readily available in New Jersey since she was a child.

The doorbell rang. "He's here!" squealed Melissa, and she nudged Oliver toward the door. Oliver swung the door open . . . to find Fransinatra on the other side of it, his fedora jauntily adjusted and adorned with a tiny sprig of holly.

"Felíz navidad!" he called into the apartment, raising the bottle of rum he carried with him.

Larimar smiled good-naturedly, then turned away to hide her disappointment that it wasn't Ray.

"Eyyy, Fransinatra, qué lo qué?" Her father clapped him on the back and offered him a plate with several pastelitos.

They got back to decorating the table and preparing dinner

when the bell rang again.

"Who is it?" Larimar called from the kitchen, where she was spooning Christmas potato salad into a blue glass bowl.

The door cracked open again, and in popped Enércida, their well-intentioned but nosy upstairs neighbor.

"Oh, great," Larimar muttered under her breath while forcing a plastic smile.

Now Doña Enércida would be checking Ray out and reporting to all their other neighbors. Not that it mattered. Larimar never cared much for what her neighbors thought of her and it had never stopped her from coming home late and parking right in front of their building because "people will talk."

It was true, "people" would talk, but exactly for that reason, it wasn't worth worrying about. "People" didn't pay her bills, and "people" didn't buy her food. "People" could kick rocks.

The doorbell rang again, and this time, Larimar went to answer it herself. When she swung the door open, Ray was standing in front of her, a huge bouquet of red roses in the crook of his arm and a bakery box dangling from his wrist.

"Ray!" she exclaimed, lunging at him. He managed to catch her without dropping the flowers or the bakery box, which was no small feat.

"Heyyy," he whispered, bestowing a small peck on her cheek, surely seeing the nosy neighbors watching.

He handed her the bakery box, and she set it down on the dinner table before whizzing back to his side and turning to face her family.

"Everyone, this is Ray," she said, resting her hand on his arm.

"Ray, this is my Papá, Mami, Abuela, brother Oliver, and his fianceé"—she gave Melissa a big, cheesy wink here—"Melissa."

Ray brought his hands together in front of his chest and gave a slight bow before going down the line and greeting each family member with a cheek kiss.

Her father and Oliver clapped him on the back, and Papá gestured to Oliver to get Ray a rum on the rocks.

Her mother patted him on the shoulder, and Doña Bélgica motioned for him to be the first one to sit down at the table and try her famous pastelitos.

Ray didn't sit down, but he took a crispy pastelito with a napkin and bit into it.

"Wow, this is amazing. My compliments to the chef," he said, and Doña Bélgica beamed back at him.

"So, do we have any dancers today?" Papi asked.

"Uh, maybe after another drink or two," Ray said with a grin. "Can I help with anything?"

Larimar handed him a stack of paper plates. "You can put these out," she said, "because I sure as heck am not doing dishes after that ponche is gone."

"Fair enough," Ray said, and he began to set the table. "Are you expecting many more people?"

Larimar shook her head.

After another rum on the rocks, Ray was ready to dance. Papi and Larimar had scooted all of Doña Bélgica's living room furniture out of the way to create a makeshift dance floor, and Mami had mopped the floor until it sparkled. Larimar and Ray moved to the middle of the dance floor, and Ray laid his hand on

Larimar's hip. He took her other hand in his, and they began to sway in time to a boisterous holiday merengue beat.

He twirled her in circles, and slowly, the other family members came onto the dance floor, first Mami and Papi, then Oliver and Melissa, followed by Doña Bélgica and her dance partner, Fransinatra. Larimar had to stifle a giggle at the sight of Fransinatra dancing, with his chest puffed out and his knees bent at an improbable angle.

Larimar pulled Ray close and hugged him before the end of the song. When it was over, she called to Oliver, "Play a ska song!"

"Here we go," Oliver said. He rolled his eyes in jest, but seconds later, Save Ferris's rendition of "Come on Eileen" was streaming through the speakers.

The rest of the family cleared the floor for them as they pumped their fists in the air and whooped in joy. They danced alongside one another, running in place, flailing their arms, and having a grand old time.

"Whew!" Larimar landed in a chair when the song was over, and Ray sat down next to her. The music changed to a classic bachata song, and her parents and Oliver and Melissa kept dancing. Doña Bélgica went into the kitchen to check on the lechon, and Fransinatra fanned himself with a magazine while answering Enércida's questions about what to do about the mice in her real estate office.

Ray looked at Larimar, and she grasped his hand.

"That was fun," he said.

"Yeah," she laughed.

She remembered she hadn't told Ray about leaving her job

yet, and a shadow fell over her face before she could stop it. Of course Ray would see it.

"What is it?" he asked.

She took a deep breath. "I have something to tell you," she said. "I . . . I quit my job."

Shock transformed Ray's features. "What?" he whispered, glancing furtively around the room. "Do your parents know?"

She shook her head. "Papi doesn't. Mami and my abuela do."

He shifted the ice around in his highball glass and watched it slide from one side to the other, then raised his gaze to hers. "What does this mean for you?"

"Well, to start with, it means I'm done with being passed over for a promotion no matter how hard I work," she said, twisting her mouth.

"Oh. Had that happened often?"

"Yes. More often than it should have in ten years," she said.

"Mmm." He nodded in understanding. "Well, good for you for standing up for yourself, Larimar. You deserve better. I'm proud of you." He finished his speech by squeezing her hand.

"So what will you do now?" he asked.

A glint sparkled in Larimar's eye. "Well . . . ." She took a long pause. "Are you interested in a brand manager for Borrachitos?"

Ray's face lit up at her words. "Like, to grow the brand out?" he said.

She nodded.

"And possibly expand to other locations?"

She clutched his hands and nodded emphatically. "Yes! We can build out your product line, focusing on the liqueur-infused cupcakes. With my industry knowledge and your creativity, we can totally do this, Ray."

"You think so, Larimar?" he asked, his voice wavering on the last syllable.

She squeezed his hands in hers. "I know so," she said. "You have an amazing concept, and all we have to do is build it out. We can do this."

He smiled. "And there would be the added perk of spending more time with you," he said.

She flipped her hair over her shoulder. "Like, duh!" she said, and they laughed together.

"Hey, lovebirds!" Oliver called from the kitchen. "Mamá needs help getting this stuff out of the oven!" He poked his head out of the kitchen and Larimar could see he was already carrying an aluminum pan filled to the brim with lasagna.

"To be continued," Larimar said. She and Ray exchanged a glance she wished could have been a kiss, but had the same effect. Then they stood up and walked in the direction of the kitchen, following the scrumptious aromas that radiated into the rest of the apartment.

Each of them grabbed a pair of oven mitts, and one by one, they brought the cooked dishes out to the table. Besides the lasagna, pastelitos, and potato salad, there was a roasted lechón, an enormous bowl of rice with pigeon peas, and a few other Christmas dishes that Berenice had whipped up after the rum started flowing.

They dug in with aplomb, and once the meal was done, they reclined away from the table. Papi patted his belly, and Mami patted his belly too.

"Now, it's time for a little digestivo," he said, taking hold of the rum bottle once more.

"Ugh, Papi, how can you even," Larimar groaned, leaning back in her chair.

"Everything was amazing," Ray said. "Thank you so much for having me, all of you. It means a lot to me since my parents . . ." He didn't finish the sentence, and he didn't need to. Papi passed him another rum on the rocks, and Doña Bélgica leaned forward to pat his arm. He beamed at her in gratitude.

"Hey. Do you want to go for a little walk?" Larimar asked. Ray nodded, and after assuring the family they'd be right back, they lifted their coats off the coat rack and left.

Once they were on the street, Ray took Larimar's hand, and they strolled together down the lamppost-lined main street that passed by Covington Arms.

"Do you think they liked me?" he asked.

"Oh, my God. They loved you," she said. "Who wouldn't? You're so lovable."

Ray stopped in his tracks and pulled on her arm so she was facing him.

"Do you really think that?" he asked.

She nodded. "I do. I love you," she said.

"I love you too, Larimar," he said. "You're the best thing that happened to me this year. And I loved you since I saw you the very first time."

Her mouth drew an O of surprise. "At Brynne's concert?"

Ray shook his head gently. "No, not at Brynne's concert. At

the Midtown show."

"What?" she breathed, stopping dead in her tracks.

He nodded. "Yes. The very first time I saw you was in 1999, at a Midtown show in Roselle Park." Her heart stopped beating in her chest.

"What? How did you know it was me?" she whispered.

"First of all, you have the same face. Second of all, you were wearing a floor-length skirt." His mouth turned up at the corners.

Tidal waves of emotion swelled up in Larimar's chest. They meant to overtake her, and she was okay with that. She brushed away a tear that came to her eye.

"Oh, my God. This whole time you knew it was me?"

He nodded.

"Why didn't you say anything?" she asked.

"That sounds weirdly stalkerish, to say I remember seeing you twenty-two years ago. And also, it was enough for me to thank God that I found you again." He shrugged.

"Aww! That's so—" Her words were cut off when he brought his lips to hers and kissed her with all the feeling of the holiday, and the rum, and their fresh conversation about going into business together.

They ran their hands up and down each other's backs to stay warm as they kissed, and Ray pulled her tighter to him than ever before. "I love you," he said when they pulled apart.

"Let's do this," she said, and hand in hand, triumphant, they walked back to her apartment building.

EPILOGUE

One Year Later

Silicone oven mitts were for punks, and that's why Larimar insisted on baking with the cotton oven mitts Doña Belgica had crocheted for her. Until one day, when she stuck her covered hands into the oven to pull out a tray of cupcakes and got quite the surprise.

"Ray, help! My oven mitt is on fire!" she yelped, yanking her hand out of the mitt and fanning it frantically in the air. Her black diamond engagement ring sparkled under the kitchen lights.

"What? Are you serious?" Ray called from the walk-in refrigerator.

"Yes, you need to get here before the Montclair Fire Department pulls up."

"Throw it in the sink, amor!" he said, pointing to the sink.

She tossed the smoking glove into the sink and switched on the tap.

"Ow!" she said. "The flames almost got to my fingers."

In seconds, Ray was at her side with a first-aid kit. "Let me see," he said.

Larimar waved him away with her free hand. "I'm okay," she said. "Let's get on with the preparations."

The front door bells jingled, alerting them to the entrance of a patron.

Larimar walked to the front of the bakery. "Hello!" Larimar said. "What can I get for you today?"

A Black woman with short hair was waiting at the counter.

"Hi!" the woman said as she looked over the offerings behind the glass. "I'll have a half dozen of the strawberry-vodka cupcakes, and then a half dozen of the coconut arroz con dulce cupcakes." She peered over the glass to the metal table in the kitchen. "That's a beautiful cake. Is it for sale?" she asked.

In the center of the table sat a three-tiered naked cake sheathed in the lightest dusting of buttercream frosting. The top was adorned with yellow, blue, and lavender orchids.

Larimar smiled. "It's a rum-soaked vanilla cake. And I'm sorry, but this particular one is not for sale. It's for a very special wedding. But we can make one to order for you!"

The customer smiled and jotted down her details on a piece of paper.

After she left, Ray and Larimar reconvened at the metal table. "Okay, let's get this cake packed up," he said. They packed the cake in the car, as well as the cupcakes, cookies, tiny cups of flan, and rum-soaked macarons for the dessert table, surrounding the boxes with plenty of packing material. It was an almost two-hour drive to Philadelphia, and it was imperative that the cake and other desserts got there in perfect condition.

For the occasion, they did not need to take the Beetle or the

Chevy. La Isla had its own van, which was painted with their business logo: a pyramid formed by a bottle of rum atop two cupcakes with puffy frosting swirls. They had named their business La Isla in a nod to the island of their heritage and the place where their intertwining paths began before their time.

They turned their Goldfinger playlist all the way up and danced in their seats as they wound their way down the New Jersey Turnpike.

The wedding was being held at the Manayunk Brewery, which had a garden that looked out onto the colorfully painted Venice Canal. Ray pulled onto a small, winding street, and parked the van right behind the brewery. Larimar got out and knocked on the service door.

Oliver opened the door on the second knock. "You trying to break the door down? I'm not paying the brewery for a new one," he said, enfolding Larimar in a hug.

She stepped back to get a look at him. As always, his hair was gelled, but he had parted it on the side. He looked dashing in his tuxedo.

"Oliver," she said, beaming with joy, "you're one hundred percent the handsome groom. Now get out of my face before you make me cry."

Oliver laughed and edged past her. "Ha. You're next! I'm going. Let me see what I can help Ray with. Hey, man!" he called out to Ray, and started helping him unload the car.

"You guys baked all this? It's incredible," Oliver said as he took a step back to appraise the back of the van.

"How's it going with the bakeries?" he asked them.

"Great," Ray said. They exchanged a glance, and Larimar squeezed Ray's hand. "It's going great."

"And the packaged cupcakes?"

"Pretty good," Larimar said. "We're selling in twelve locations around the state now."

"Damn! Congrats, you guys," Oliver said.

"Thank you," Larimar said. She turned to Ray. "Ready?"

"Ready." Together, they lowered the pieces of the tiered table they used for weddings from the van. Inside, they began to put it together. They screwed the legs into the base, turned it over, and covered it with a white linen tablecloth.

Then they attached the tiers and began to fill them with luscious desserts. On the first tier, there were chocolate-cinnamon cupcakes, which were Oliver's favorite, and coconut cupcakes with a passionfruit center, which were Melissa's favorite.

On the second tier, they arranged the butter cookies—included in the spread with herself, her mother, and Doña Bélgica in mind—and on the third tier, the rum-soaked macarons. Larimar gave a happy sigh when they stacked the last macaron on top. It was perfect. Out of all this mess, she and Ray had made something perfect.

Melissa was every bit the blushing bride, and it gave Larimar joy to see her parents sitting with Mr. and Mrs. Kiatpaiboon at the front-most picnic table. Melissa and Oliver exchanged vows under a canopy encircled with tiny string lights. The rest of the tables were filled with family and friends, and the attached patio of the restaurant with well-meaning taggers-along.

When the ceremony was complete and Oliver had kissed the bride, Mami nudged Larimar under the ribs. "And you? When are you setting a date?"

She and Ray exchanged a glance. "We figured we would close on the house first," Larimar said. "Now that Ray's parents' house is sold and that's done, we will be setting a date soon."

"Wonderful!" Mami said. "Whoever gives me grandchildren first gets a special prize."

Ray stared at his future mother-in-law in open-mouthed shock and shot Larimar a glance with eyebrows raised that said, *Is she for real?*

"She's kidding, Ray," Larimar said.

"I am not kidding," Mami replied.

"You know what! Let's go check on the macarons," Larimar said, grabbing Ray by the hand and leading him toward the dessert table they had filled with their creations.

Author's Note

The first I ever heard about the ciguapa was from my mother, who was nicknamed ciguapa as a child because of her long, straight hair. Then in high school, I would blow dry my long, curly hair, and family members would tell me, "You look like a ciguapa!" "I look like a what?" I would respond. I became curious and began to research the legend of the ciguapa. I learned that the ciguapa was said to live in the forests of the Dominican Republic and had long, straight hair and backward-facing feet.

I began to ask family members and neighbors if they had ever seen a ciguapa. Surprisingly, some said they had, and without judgment I listened to their tales. They told me ciguapas were known for their unusual laugh and for sneaking into kitchens to eat butter and raw meat. They told me that ciguapas were usually sad and could sometimes be heard crying. There were additional stories about ciguapas being separated from their children during the colonialization of the Dominican Republic.

When I returned to research ciguapas as an adult, I learned that they are not unique to the Dominican Republic, but rather, there is a version of the ciguapa in many cultures. In Cuba, she is called the ciguaya; in Brazil, curipirá. Sometimes the characteristics are different, but there is a consensus that the ciguapa is a forest creature who is hard to see, who is sad, and who sometimes can be heard crying.

The ciguapa struck me as a strong creature who is used to living on the fringes of society but still finds a way to survive. The more I thought about it, the more I wanted to write a story for the ciguapa where she gets a happy ending, for a change. I literally had never heard a ciguapa story with a happy trajectory, and for that reason, I understood it to be missing from the ciguapa stories.

I have taken liberties here with the characteristics of the ciguapa—I have given her some, like the ability to transform on the full moon only. And of course, there are other aspects of the legend I have not included in Larimar and her family's experience. The ciguapa is often depicted as a siren-like figure whose goal is to seduce men to their downfall, and that is something I grated against. In my vision, the ciguapa is not interested in that. She is interested in having family, friends, and a healthy, happy life, even if her taste in music does put her on the fringe! ☺

I hope that readers will appreciate this version of the ciguapa story, and for those who want a more traditional version of the legend, I encourage you to do independent research. Thank you very much for reading *A Touch of Moonlight*.

ACKNOWLEDGMENTS

Thank you to my editor, Sarah Ried, for helping me make this story the best it can be.

To Maria Cardona, Anna Soler-Pont, and Pontas Agency, thank you for your guidance and support.

To my critique partner, Maribel Linares, thank you for journeying with me from Larimar's first steps.

And thank you, Sera Taíno, for reading and sharing your thoughts.

To Kanitta Keating, for your advice regarding Melissa's cooking and family.

Thank you to my husband, Joel, for your love and your support for this book. And to my children, you are the inspiration for everything I do.

And lastly, thank you to everyone who has ever taken the time to tell me their ciguapa-sighting story for sparking my imagination.

ABOUT THE AUTHOR

Yaffa S. Santos was born and raised in New Jersey. She is also the author of *A Taste of Sage*, which was named an Indie Next List Pick and Amazon Editor's Pick. Yaffa is a graduate of Sarah Lawrence College, where she studied writing and visual art. She enjoys books, coffee, and the beach, and lives in Central Florida with her family.